FAITH

A CURVY GIRL ROMANTIC SUSPENSE

F-BOMB: CURVY VIGILANTES
BOOK 9

MARY E THOMPSON

BluEyed Press

F-BOMB: CURVY VIGILANTES

Say hello to the Curvy Vigilantes, a group of plus-size women who protect their city. They have no training, but they don't need it. All they need is the desire to right wrongs and to protect the ones they love... and maybe some help from the men strong (and smart) enough to fall for these kick-ass curvy women.

F-BOMB: CURVY VIGILANTES
Forsaken (subscriber exclusive)
Fury
Framed
Feign
Fierce
Fatal
Fear
Flee
Fracture
Faith

SUBSCRIBE NOW AT MARYETHOMPSON.COM

To trusting your gut, trusting yourself, and trusting in love...
And taking a leap of faith.

1

___

Nina Rose sat in the chair she was assigned to and glared at the sleeping bitch across the room. Gwendolyn Lennox was evil. She was mean and dangerous and not worthy of the air she breathed.

Nina imagined what it would feel like the plunge a knife into the heart of the heartless bitch who took her in twelve years ago and never let her leave. If Nina had known what she was running toward all those years ago, she never would have left home.

She stood and walked across the room. Gwendolyn almost looked human as she slept. Her blonde hair stretched over the pillows. Her mouth opened slightly. Her pink lips parted with each breath she took.

She would never stop hurting people. Nina touched the black eye Gwendolyn gave her just a few hours earlier. When she decided Nina's suggestion to turn herself in was unacceptable.

Nina was going to die in Gwendolyn's house, like so many other women. Women Gwendolyn lied about and told Nina were going to live better lives. Women Gwendolyn sold into slavery and traded for favors. Women who would never be seen again because of the monster that Gwendolyn was.

Nina shook her head, fighting tears. She was so stupid. She believed all the lies Gwendolyn told her. Thought Gwendolyn was looking out for her like the sister she claimed to think of Nina as. But Gwendolyn just wanted a pet. Someone to complain to when she was in a mood and a punching bag when she was angry.

It was the last time Nina was going to be anyone's punching bag. And if there was a weapon in the room, it would be the last time Gwendolyn used anyone for a punching bag.

Instead, it was the night Nina finally decided to reclaim her life.

She was getting the hell out of there.

She walked to the door that led to the hallway. They weren't in Gwendolyn's favorite house since the police and FBI raided it, but Nina had been with Gwendolyn long enough to know all the houses. All the routines and habits and ways out.

Nina sucked in a breath and erased all the thoughts in her mind. The guards Gwendolyn hired were as ruthless as she was, and they could sniff out a lie in a second. If they didn't believe Nina's story, they'd wake Gwendolyn up and Nina would be dead.

Her life depended on her being able to convince them she was running an errand for Gwendolyn. It wasn't the first time, so Nina hoped it worked. It had to.

She opened the door quietly, spotting Fernando immediately. He gazed past Nina to the bedroom, nodding when he saw Gwendolyn sleeping.

Nina closed the door as quietly as she'd opened it and

turned to Fernando. "Is there a driver who can take me on an errand?"

Fernando glared at her. "What errand?"

Nina pointed to her eye and grimaced. "I upset her. I was going to get her some of those candies she likes so much."

Fernando glared harder. "You know better than to challenge her."

Nina nodded, letting her tears well up. It would sell the lie. "I know. And I'm sorry. I wasn't thinking. I wanted to protect her."

"What did you do?"

"I said she should think about turning herself in. Blaming Damon and Trevor and Benjamin. Tell the police she didn't know what they were doing with her company money."

Fernando's small smile was one of approval instead of dismissal. "Not a bad idea, but she'd never do it. She didn't get to where she is to play the dumb blonde."

Nina swallowed roughly, her throat sore from Gwendolyn choking her. "I know. I shouldn't have suggested it. I was worried. We were in the house when they came in. She could have been caught."

Fernando shook his head, the dark stringy ponytail he wore flopping over his shoulder. "She'll never be caught. We won't let it happen."

Nina nodded, hoping he thought it was in agreement.

"Let me see who's available. You go to that convenience store in the city, right? Close to that F-BOMB place?"

Nina nodded. It was working.

Fernando called someone and told them to get the car ready. When they questioned him, he said, "If I have to come down there, you won't be able to drive anything."

Fernando hung up and nodded to Nina. "They'll be ready."

"Thanks, Fernando," Nina said, pressing her lips into a smile. She walked away and hoped like hell she'd never see him again.

The SUV was waiting for her when she arrived. Parked under the structure, a dozen vehicles waited for whatever Gwendolyn needed them for. Decoy, transport, anything. She was the queen of her domain, and she made sure everyone knew it.

Nina didn't recognize the driver, which wasn't a bad thing. She climbed into the backseat and ignored him, watching the house disappear into the darkness as he drove away.

Fifteen minutes later, he pulled into the parking lot for the convenience store. He slid the vehicle into park and met her gaze in the rearview mirror. He jerked his head to the building.

Guess he wasn't going in. Worked for her.

Nina climbed out of the SUV and wrapped the shawl around her neck, looping it up over her face to hide as much of her appearance as possible. Gwendolyn hated when Nina let anyone see her hair. The red color was distinctive and drew attention. Attention Gwendolyn never wanted on Nina.

It took Nina way too many years to understand why.

Nina walked inside, nodding at the clerk. The man barely acknowledged her, which was just as good. If he wasn't paying attention, he wouldn't be able to tell Gwendolyn anything when Nina didn't go back out.

Nina worked her way through the store, choosing an aisle toward the back of the store so the driver wouldn't be able to see her. She got to the end and knew there was a gap.

If he looked up at the right time, he would spot her, but if she was lucky...

Nina sprinted across the half-dozen feet of space, letting out a breath when she made it to the other side and saw the driver with his nose in his phone.

The rest was easy. Get to the office in the back, the one that was never locked, and call the one man she knew would save her.

Zeke Donovan stood in the bullpen at work and listened to his boss share the rest of the rundown from the last few days. It was a fuck-ton of information. FBI Agent Lorelei Sloane had pieced together more than every other person out there.

And the fuckers who took her almost killed it all with her.

But they didn't. Lorelei was safe, and she gave them what they needed to invade the stronghold of Gwendolyn Lennox's organization.

The next step was dismantling the entire fucking thing, but that wasn't what Rose Protection Agency was doing. Their involvement was limited.

Which suited Zeke just fine.

"What's up next for us?" Austin Ward asked. Austin and his partner, Samuel MacNeil, were an odd couple that worked like ice cream and brownies. Good on their own, but better together.

"We have cases we've been working on, and a new one that just came in. Local PD might want us to protect some witnesses, especially if there are a few women who want to stick together. Most of them will go through rehab, so it might be a few months of steady work helping them out." Montgomery Rose was Zeke's oldest and closest friend. Also the man Zeke owed his life to, many times over.

Zeke knew that score was balanced, though. Zeke had saved Mont just as many times. But their scoresheet would never be even. Zeke would spend the rest of his life making up for the mistakes of his past. Working with his best friend and keeping Montgomery safe was Zeke's penance.

Mont hadn't been the same since his sister disappeared. Nina was Montgomery's favorite person in the world, and Zeke let her vanish.

He'd never forgiven himself for it. And never would.

"We're good for whatever you need. Just happy we finally know who everyone is chasing," Samuel said.

The others in the room murmured their agreement.

"When all this is done, everyone should take a few days off," Montgomery told the room. "Go to the beach or something."

Zeke snorted. "Are you taking time off?"

"He never takes time off," Berkeley said, walking into the bullpen like she owned the place. As the executive assistant, and all-around alpha male wrangler, she had every right to act the way she did.

"That's why I'm asking," Zeke said. "Come on, Mont. We all need a break. Even you."

"I'm not interested in a beach bunny or any other kind of bunny."

"Fuck, man, I didn't say that. Go skydiving or SCUBA diving or something. Get the hell out of here for a little while."

Montgomery cast a side-eye at Berkeley, who only raised one dark eyebrow at him. She was always telling him the same thing.

Zeke's phone rang, interrupting whatever Montgomery was about to say.

They all stopped, waiting for Zeke to answer the phone. In their business, when someone called, they answered. No matter what.

"Donovan," Zeke barked into the phone, locking his gaze on Montgomery's. He didn't need words to communicate with his boss.

"Zeke?" a voice whispered.

Every inch of Zeke responded to that voice. One word, and he knew exactly who it was, even if it had been twelve years since he heard her. He glanced at Montgomery. Why was she calling Zeke instead of her brother?

Zeke tore his gaze from Montgomery's. He was wrong. He had to be. It couldn't be her. And he couldn't tell his best friend it was or Mont would be crushed all over again.

They'd all lost hope, and having it back, even for a few seconds, was worse than never having it at all.

"Yeah?"

"I don't have long. I need you."

"Where are you?" Zeke was halfway to the door, moving toward the front of the building and ready to go.

"The convenience store we always hung out at when we were kids. Do you remember?"

"I'm on my way. Don't move."

"Please hurry. Park in the back."

"I'll be there in two minutes," Zeke said.

She hung up.

Zeke felt like he'd been punched. Twelve years. It had been twelve years since he heard her voice. Twelve years since the woman he loved walked out of the house and never came back. Twelve years.

His heart pounded. His palms were sweaty. Every inch of

him said he would never see her again if he didn't get there soon.

He couldn't let her disappear again. He couldn't.

"Who was that?" Montgomery asked, surprising Zeke.

"Just a client. Needs me to go get her." Zeke never kept anything from Montgomery. Brothers in every possible way. The look in his best friend's eyes said he knew there was more to the story, but he also knew if Zeke wasn't sharing, there was a reason for it.

"Are you okay to go alone?"

Zeke nodded, trying to calm his racing heart. If it really was Nina, he would bring her to Montgomery so he could see his sister. Know she was alive. Twelve years was a long time to assume she wasn't, and false hope would crush him.

Which was why Zeke said, "All good. I'll check in later. How long are you here?"

Montgomery looked at his watch and shrugged. "Another hour, at least. Are you coming back?"

"Possibly."

Montgomery tilted his head. When they picked up a client, they took them somewhere safe. That rarely meant the office. "Are you sure everything's okay?"

Zeke nodded. "I think so. I'll try to be back soon."

Montgomery nodded, even as his face betrayed his confusion.

Zeke was cutting it close and had to go. He wasn't far from the convenience store, but he didn't want to risk her leaving. He raced to his SUV and cranked it up, pulling out of the lot without bothering with a seatbelt. She was more important.

A black SUV idled in front of the store. The man behind the wheel glanced up, then returned his focus to his phone.

The rest of the parking lot was empty. The store appeared to be as well, except for the clerk behind the counter.

Zeke pulled in from the other side, where the man in the SUV and the clerk wouldn't see him. He eased his SUV to a stop next to the door that said Employees Only.

Leaving the engine running, Zeke got out. He went to the door, pulling the handle. Hope was a motherfucker, but Zeke was full of it.

The door creaked open, and there she was in the dark hallway. Standing in front of him like she'd been twelve years ago. She was older, but no less gorgeous. Her figure had filled out, giving her curves, curves, and more curves. The possessive alpha in him roared with desire, wanting to throw her over his shoulder and never let her out of his sight again.

"You came," she whispered, looking up at him. Until he saw her eyes, he had his doubts, but that gaze was seared into his brain. It was the gaze he saw in his dreams, the one he'd been chasing for most of his life. The one he never thought he'd see again.

"Holy fuck, it is you." Zeke reached for her, ignoring the flash of panic in her eyes. He couldn't wait another second to have her in his arms. He lifted her off her feet, holding her to him until she melted in his embrace and sank into him.

She sighed, then inhaled a shaky breath.

He pressed his nose to her neck and whispered, "Don't you ever fucking walk out on me again."

"Okay," she whispered.

Zeke let out a breath and stepped outside, checking that no one else was there. "We need to go."

She nodded and followed him, startling when she saw

his SUV. It was shockingly similar to the one parked in front of the building.

"It's mine. Get in. Lie down in the back so no one sees you." He opened the door for her and waited, praying she hurried up but knowing he couldn't rush her.

She took two steps forward, then threw her arms around his neck.

He inhaled deep, closing his eyes and ignoring her body odor. She was alive. Not just that, but she was back. She called him. She was going to be okay.

"Thank you for coming to get me, Zeke."

Zeke cupped her cheeks and got a closer look at her in the bright light of the parking lot. She'd lost her childish features and grown into a beautiful woman. Curves in all the right places and that same red hair that always hinted at the spark she hid from most people.

But that wasn't all that was new. She had a black eye, handprints around her throat, and more bruises on the skin exposed by her way too small dress.

Zeke's blood boiled. Someone put their fucking hands on her. Beat her and hurt her and she was so scared, she called him in the middle of the fucking night.

He had half a mind to pull around to the front of the store and put a knife in the throat of the man who was waiting for her. But one look in her eyes, that gray-green that mesmerized him when he wasn't supposed to be in love with his best friend's little sister, and he knew that wasn't the answer.

"Let's go," he whispered.

Nina nodded and crawled into his backseat. She laid down on the floor, curling herself up tight and making it impossible for her to be seen.

Zeke closed the door, then slid behind the wheel. He

watched his mirrors as he navigated the city, making more turns than necessary to confirm no one was following them. When he was confident, he breathed a little easier.

"Who was that?"

She was quiet, but he knew she understood what he was asking. "He was the driver. I don't know his name."

"Is he the one who did that to you?"

"No."

Zeke wanted to ask more. To demand she tell him everything, but the quiet answers she gave him said she wasn't ready to talk yet.

"Where are you taking me?"

"To my house. Let you shower and change, then we're going to see your brother."

"He's here?" she gasped, as though she expected something different.

Zeke glanced in the mirror, but he couldn't see her. He looked at the floor where she laid and hated he hadn't been able to provide her with more than the floor of his SUV to hide.

But she was alive.

"He never stopped looking for you."

"He didn't?" she breathed.

Zeke shook his head, then focused on the road. He drove to his home, assuming she'd want a shower and new clothes. He had something she could wear, nothing like what she was wearing, but he didn't think that dress was her choice.

He pulled into the driveway of his duplex and sighed when he saw Montgomery wasn't home yet. They didn't like the idea of having places far apart, and when the duplex was listed years ago, they jumped on the idea of having each other next door but still maintaining privacy and independence.

Something neither of them wanted for a long time after Nina vanished.

Zeke closed the garage door and let Nina out of the backseat. He helped her out, noting how fragile she seemed. He led the way around his SUV and opened the door into his house.

And was immediately met by a less than happy meow.

Nina gasped. "You have a cat?"

Zeke bent down to pick up Gene, a black and white cat with only three paws. "I have two, actually. This is Gene. He was hit by a car and lost his leg, but don't tell him because he has no idea there's anything different about him."

"He's precious," Nina whispered, petting Gene's head. She laughed, a husky, rusty sound, when Gene purred loudly.

"He's needy."

Another meow, softer and more patient, tentative followed.

Zeke turned and spotted Franklin on the kitchen counter. He nodded toward him so Nina would see the tabby. "That's Franklin. He thinks rules don't apply to him and never listens."

Nina went to Franklin and let him sniff her hand. He bumped her knuckles with his forehead, then rubbed his head under her hand, flopping on his back and exposing himself on the counter.

"Jesus, man, have some decency. She just got here," Zeke said, shaking his head at his cat.

Gene meowed, as though agreeing with Zeke.

Nina laughed again. "They're wonderful."

"They're pretty great, yeah."

The silence stretched between them. Zeke had a million questions, but he didn't think he could ask her any of them.

"So, um, the bathroom is upstairs. I'll show you where everything is and get you some clothes to change into. Montgomery lives next door, but he's not home, so when you're cleaned up, I'll find out where he is and we can go see him."

Nina nodded, patting Franklin on the head, then following Zeke up the stairs.

The cats followed along, winding between Zeke and Nina's feet and making her laugh. Zeke fought all the emotions rising up, knowing he had to keep it together until he handed her over to her brother. Zeke didn't know why she called him and not Montgomery, but it didn't matter.

She was back.

He went to his bedroom and grabbed the smallest pair of shorts he had, ones with a drawstring, and a dark tee. He didn't have underwear that would fit her, but he hoped the clothes would be enough for now. He'd buy her an entire fucking store tomorrow. Anything she needed.

She followed behind him, barely two feet away the whole time. When he showed her the bathroom off his bedroom, she sucked in a breath. "Wow."

"Take your time. I'll be downstairs. Whenever you're ready to come back down, you can, but there's no rush."

"Zeke?" she whispered.

"Yeah, Nina?"

"Thank you for getting me."

"Thank you for calling me."

Nina smiled, then turned.

Zeke left the bathroom and closed the door. He closed

the bedroom door, too. He wanted to sit in the room and wait for her, but she needed space.

And so did he.

Zeke went to his kitchen and poured himself a glass of water. He downed it, wishing it was something stronger. But until he talked to Montgomery, he had to make sure his mind was clear.

Zeke alternated between staring at the ceiling and wondering if she was okay and staring at his phone and trying to figure out what the fuck to say to Montgomery.

Hey, Mont, your sister's here. In my house. No big deal. She just called me instead of you after twelve years.

Not an option.

But Zeke was going to have to figure something out.

The shower turned off, and his heart thudded hard. She would be back downstairs soon. And he would have to take her to Montgomery.

Zeke couldn't sit still. He paced the house, listening for Nina.

But he didn't hear Nina. He heard Montgomery.

The garage next door opened, but it didn't close right away.

A door opened upstairs.

Someone knocked on the front door, then a key slid into the lock.

Zeke stood still, watching as brother and sister both moved into the room.

"Hey, Zeke. What was that call you got...?" Montgomery froze.

Nina stopped halfway down the stairs.

"Nina?"

"Hi, big brother," Nina said.

Montgomery's jaw dropped. His gaze scanned his sister. Then swung to Zeke. "What the fuck did you do to her?"

Zeke didn't have time to defend himself before Montgomery charged him. Fists first.

2

———————

"MONTY!" NINA SHRIEKED. SHE RUSHED DOWN THE STAIRS and tried to get between the two men she loved more than anything or anyone else. Ever. "Stop!"

Montgomery took a step back, his gaze flipping from her to Zeke. "Why are you here? How are you here? Why the fuck is she here?"

Zeke looked at her, but Nina didn't speak. She wasn't sure how to explain anything to either of them.

Zeke wiped his lip, blood appearing on his hand. Nina hadn't noticed the split lip, but once she saw the blood, her head spun.

She was gathered up in the next moment, her feet swept out from under her. She floated to the couch, the fresh and masculine scent of Zeke waking her up and nearly making her weep. She smelled like him, choosing the same shampoo in his shower that she'd inhaled in his SUV.

She landed on the couch softly. Zeke was right there, his face a mask of concern, before a growl permeated the air.

Zeke looked up and nodded, stepping away.

Montgomery replaced Zeke in front of her. "Did he do

this?" Monty tucked her hair behind her ear, his fingers drifting over the bruises around her neck.

"No," Nina said sharply. "No. Never. You know he'd never hurt me."

Montgomery inhaled a shaky breath and closed his eyes. "I thought you were dead."

Nina nodded. "I know."

"Where the hell have you been?"

His tone was biting, but the care beneath the fear reminded Nina that she didn't need to be afraid of her brother. "I... It's a long story."

"One you're not ready to share. Are you safe?"

Nina looked at Zeke and smiled. "Yes. I am now."

"With him." Montgomery's words were punctuated with a glare at the man who'd spent as much time at their house as Nina and Montgomery when they were young.

"I didn't think you'd be here. You were supposed to go into the military," Nina said.

"I did. But I didn't stay. I came back to look for you. I searched. Twelve years, Nina. Twelve years. Where the hell have you been?" His face crumpled, the fear and pain he felt erupting from him.

"I've been in Niagara Falls," she whispered.

"What?" Monty barked. His gaze snapped to Zeke's, then slammed against Nina again. "You've been right here. Someone had you. Wouldn't let you out."

She nodded, hoping it was enough for now. There were good times with Gwendolyn. Fewer and fewer over the years, but at first, Nina almost felt like she was lucky. She had someone who cared about her. Someone who didn't have to give up anything for her.

A dozen years brought clarity and clarity brought pain and pain brought acceptance. Nina couldn't let it continue.

"I can't..." Monty jumped to his feet and stalked away from her.

Nina stood, watching the lines of tension cross his features. His back bunched up so tight his shoulders rounded. His face looked a decade older than when he'd walked in the door. Everything about him read regret and anger.

"I have to go. I can't... I'm so happy you're here. You're home. I... Please don't leave again. Never again." Monty rushed to her and pulled her in tight for a hug. "Promise me you won't ever leave me again, Nina. I love you."

Nina smiled and nodded, her throat tight with emotion she hadn't allowed herself to feel in a very long time. "I love you, big brother."

Montgomery nodded and held her back from him. He cupped her jaw and stared into her eyes. He closed his, then he turned away from her and walked straight out the door.

Nina waited, wondering if she should go after him. A few seconds later, an engine started up and tires squealed as Montgomery left.

Nina stared after him, lost in her memories until a soft meow and an even softer touch broke through her haze.

She dropped onto the couch, smiling when Franklin jumped up next to her and crawled onto her lap. She rubbed his head, and he nuzzled against her chest.

The snick of a lock met her ears and made her jump. She knew that sound well.

Franklin jumped down as Nina bolted to her feet, panic flooding her system as she looked at Zeke walking back from the front door.

Zeke held up his hands. "I don't want anyone walking in without an invitation. Montgomery has a key. He can come back any time he wants."

Nina struggled to ease her panic. She called Zeke because she trusted him. She knew he would never hurt her. He was one of the few reasons she survived as long as she did. The hope she would see him again. Him and her brother. Seeing both of them healed a broken piece of her, but the other broken pieces were much more damaged and would take a lot more to heal.

"This is your show, Nina. Do you want me to unlock the door?"

"No," she blurted. "No. It's just..."

"You're safe here, Nina. Always safe with me. I will never hurt you."

She nodded, knowing they weren't just words. It was a promise. And Zeke Donovan didn't make promises he didn't keep.

So MANY OF Zeke's fears were confirmed by the look on her face when he locked the door. He didn't think anything of it until she stared at him, eyes wide and panicked, waiting for the inevitable attack.

She was abused. Likely assaulted. Beaten and tortured and used for whatever the bastard who held her wanted.

Zeke struggled to keep his anger at bay, wanting to go out and find the man who had her for twelve years and beat him until he couldn't breathe and would know the pain he caused.

But first, Zeke needed to know who he was going after. And make sure Nina was safe.

"Are you hungry?" Zeke asked instead of probing into the past.

Nina nodded, the motion jerky and unsure.

"If my memory is any good, your favorite food was always mac-and-cheese."

Nina's eyes welled up, her smile small and sad. "I haven't had mac-and-cheese in forever."

"Is that a yes?" Zeke asked.

Nina nodded, moving closer to him. He stood still, not wanting to scare her and not wanting to stop whatever she was doing. He needed her to trust him.

Nina didn't stop when she got close to him, just wrapped her arms around his middle and held on tight.

Zeke released the breath he'd been holding since he heard her voice on the phone and gave in to the need to hold her tight and bury his face in her hair. He inhaled deep, drawing the scent of his shampoo into his lungs and knowing he'd never want to wash with anything else ever again. The scent would forever remind him of Nina.

"Thank you for coming to get me."

"Thank you for calling me."

Nina let out a shaky breath, then eased her arms from his middle. She took a step back and smiled up at him.

"I'll start on food and you can relax and watch something if you want."

She shook her head and followed him. "I'd rather... I'd rather stay close to you if that's okay."

Zeke nodded, unable to find the words he needed to express his relief.

His kitchen was a good size for one person, but with a second, it quickly became tight. Zeke moved around the space with the comfort he'd always had in the kitchen, but the awareness that Nina was in his space. He kept his house stocked with more than enough food at all times, and had water boiling for the fusilli pasta within ten minutes.

He went through the motions automatically, shredding

three cheeses by hand and stirring the pasta until it was half-cooked. He drained the pasta, then added it to the cheese, egg, and milk mixture. With seasoning added, he scooped all of it into the glass pan and slid it into the oven.

"Thirty minutes and I'll take it out," he said, as though Nina didn't know.

She nodded, but didn't move out of his way.

"Drink? Water? Shit, wine or beer? I guess you're old enough for alcohol now."

"I don't like it. Not... I like to have a clear head."

Zeke nodded, another thing that angered him. Another clue to what she'd been through. Fuck, he was going to murder someone. How the hell could someone do those things to a person like Nina? Any person, but especially her? She was sweet and innocent. She was a kid when she disappeared.

She wasn't anymore, but she hadn't had a chance to be an adult either. She was captive. A prisoner in some sick bastard's house.

But she was out. She was safe. She was there with him. And he would never let her out of his sight again.

He led the way to the couch and grabbed the remote. Zeke turned on a comedy he remembered Nina enjoying, a show that had been off the air for a decade, but he gambled she wouldn't know that.

"I love this show. Do they ever get together in the end?" She lifted her eyes to Zeke, and he struggled to breathe.

A nod was all he could manage.

She returned her focus to the TV, unaware of the effect she had on him. Gage and Franklin jumped up next to her, making themselves comfortable with their new human. She absently rubbed both their heads at the same time.

A million questions ran through his mind as she laughed at the antics of the group of friends on the show.

Where was she all this time?

Who had her?

How did she get away?

Were they going to come after her?

What would he do if someone did?

Zeke knew the answer to the last one without thinking about it. He would kill anyone who tried to hurt Nina ever again. She was back. She was home. She was safe. And he'd never let her walk away again.

The show ended, and Zeke went back to the kitchen to check on dinner. It was almost done, so he grabbed a bag of frozen vegetables and tossed it into the microwave. He turned back to the living room and his breath stopped at the picture before him.

Nina on his couch, laughing at the TV, his cats curled up with her like she belonged to them.

Zeke had to look away before he lost it. When she was with Montgomery, he could break down. Until then, he had to keep his shit together. Take care of her, keep her safe.

The microwave beeped, and Zeke retrieved the bag of broccoli. He dumped it into a bowl and added butter, salt, and pepper, stirring it up as though it was something special.

He pushed it to the side and opened the oven. The cheese was golden brown. The smell of the food was almost as intoxicating as the woman he made it for.

Zeke couldn't remember the last time he had mac-and-cheese. Once, after she left, he cooked it, and he threw the whole thing away. It reminded him too much of her, and his guilt and pain were too heavy to let him enjoy the meal.

Since then, he hadn't considered cooking it. The memories of Nina were too strong, too painful.

He set the dish on his stovetop and closed the oven, letting the sharpness of the cheese and the memories fill him.

She was home.

"Is it done?" she asked from right behind him.

"Yeah," Zeke said, his voice cracking on the word. He cleared his throat and busied himself with searching for a serving spoon and plates for them. He dished her out a sizable portion, then gave himself an even bigger one.

She didn't move.

"Is everything okay?" he asked, his gaze going from her plate to her face.

She set her plate down and reached up for him. Her hands pressed against his cheeks softly, tentative like she thought he'd stop her.

He nuzzled against her hands, his greedy body unable to hold back any longer.

"I never thought I'd see you again, but I hoped I would. It kept me going."

Zeke closed his eyes and swallowed roughly. "I never stopped looking for you."

"I'm sorry I asked you to let me go that night. That I argued and told you I could take care of myself."

Zeke shook his head. "All that matters is you're here now. We'll get you whatever help you need. Therapy, rehab, anything. I don't care what it costs or anything. You're home."

Nina's eyes welled up. She nodded. "I'm home. With you."

Zeke couldn't take it anymore. He hauled her into his arms, holding her so tight he could feel every inch of her body against his. He struggled to keep his emotions at bay, but let them out when she sniffled against his neck.

Tears fell freely from his eyes, relief and joy blending together. "I missed you so fucking much."

"I missed you, too."

He held her until her body relaxed against his and his reaction to holding her couldn't be withheld. He pushed her away from his body, not wanting to scare her with the erection he couldn't stop. She was still Montgomery's little sister. And he was supposed to be protecting her, not imagining what was beneath the clothes he gave her to borrow.

"We'll get you some new clothes tomorrow. Whatever you want. And anything else. Food, a car? A new place? You can stay here, of course. Or with Mont. Whatever you want. Money is no object. We'll take care of you, Nina. Always."

She nodded. "I know you will. For tonight, I just want to enjoy being here with you."

Zeke drew a breath and nodded. There was nothing that sounded better than that.

Gwendolyn Lennox glared at the man who interrupted her sleep. She didn't like being woken up, but it was even worse when the man shared his news.

"What the fuck do you mean, she's gone? Where the hell is she?"

"I don't know, ma'am. She went into the convenience store, and she never came back out."

"Did you go in and look for her?"

"Yeah. Of course. But she wasn't there."

The fucking idiot acted like Gwendolyn was asking stupid questions. He needed to learn a lesson.

Gwendolyn grabbed the gun from Fernando's holster and pointed it at the fucking driver who lost Nina.

The man's face changed then. "I asked the clerk. I looked for her. She must have snuck out the back door."

"Then fucking find her. She couldn't have gone far."

"Unless she had someone pick her up," the asshole dared to say.

"And how would she have arranged that? Did she call someone?"

"No. Not that I know of."

"Then who would have picked her up? Was there another car there?"

The driver shook his head, then stopped. "Someone drove by. Slow, like they were looking for something. Went past, so I didn't think anything of it."

"Well, maybe you should have. I let Nina go there because they don't have cameras. It was supposed to keep her safe. Keep anyone from seeing her who wasn't supposed to."

"Who would be looking for her?" the driver asked, turning up his nose.

Gwendolyn raised an eyebrow. "Right now, I am. My sister is gone, and you're the one who let her get away."

"I didn't realize she was your sister. I'll go—"

Gwendolyn pulled the trigger before the man could finish his sentence. She smiled at the moment of awareness on his face before he collapsed into a puddle of his own brains.

"Huh, so he did have a fucking brain," Gwendolyn snarled, glaring at the corpse. "Get someone to clean this up. Then find Nina."

"What if she went back?" Fernando asked.

Gwendolyn glared at him. She couldn't think about Nina

going back to her family. She spent years training her, raising her, caring for her. Gwendolyn was Nina's family, not the brother who let her walk away.

"She wouldn't. But check just in case."

Fernando nodded, then left the room.

Gwendolyn looked down at the mess of a man who let her favorite pet get away. Nina didn't run. She knew better.

But she was making noise lately.

Could she have run? Gotten away?

Panic clawed at Gwendolyn's throat. Nina knew too much. She knew everything. If she left, or if she was taken by one of their enemies, everything Gwendolyn worked for would be gone.

She couldn't let that happen. No one had ever stood in her way before. She would not let anyone now.

3

———

Nina still couldn't believe she was free. She was safe. She knew it wasn't so easy, but she tried not to think about that.

By now Gwendolyn knew she was gone. Had likely already sent people looking for her. And killed the driver. Nina had a moment of regret knowing the driver was likely dead because of her, but the man chose his fate in life by working for Gwendolyn. It would have happened eventually.

Just like everyone else who trusted her.

Nina stared at the mirror and the bruises that marred her pale skin. She couldn't remember the last time she was allowed to look in a mirror, and the reflection staring back at her was only vaguely familiar. Same red hair, same muted green eyes, same woman. But different.

She tried to remember what she looked like before she left. The night she snuck out of the house. Twelve years was a long time, but it was so much more than the time. It was what she'd been through.

Nina ripped her gaze from the mirror and fought the

anger welling up inside. She didn't want to be like Gwendolyn, taking her anger out on everyone around her. Nina wanted to be a good person. Someone who helped others. And the only way she could do that was to tell Zeke and Monty the truth. The entire truth.

The sun would be up soon. Nina knew that, even though she wasn't sure what time it was. A lifetime of being awake at night, so she was available for her duties, had trained her to wait for morning. When she could sleep. As long as Gwendolyn didn't need her.

A soft knock on the bathroom door dragged Nina back to the moment. In Zeke's house. Safe.

"Do you need anything?" Zeke asked through the door.

He'd been nothing short of respectful since she called him. Not touching her unless she initiated the contact, except for his first hug. He knew more than she'd admitted so far, and she wondered what he'd seen that he could read her thoughts. She wished things had been different for all of them.

But all they could do was move forward.

Instead of answering, Nina opened the bathroom door. Zeke was right there, pressed into the gap where the door was a second ago.

He took a step back, but Nina moved into his personal space and wrapped her arms around him.

He sighed and returned the hug, holding her tight against his body. Gwendolyn's touch had been gentle and soothing when she was sad, but most of the time, it was dangerous. The way Zeke held her was reverent, like she was the most precious thing in the world and he would never do anything to hurt her.

"I'm sorry I keep hugging you. It's just so good to feel you."

He shook his head. "I don't mind a bit."

Nina had a sudden thought and pulled back. "Oh my God. Is there someone who would? I should have asked. Do you have a wife? Girlfriend? Boyfriend? I... I'm so sorry. I—"

"There's no one but you, Nina."

She was sure he didn't mean the words how she wanted to take them, but what mattered was she wasn't getting in the middle of Zeke's relationship. "You would tell me, right?"

"Yes."

"Okay." Nina moved around him, spotting the massive bed in the middle of his room. He hadn't shown her any other bedrooms. Where would she sleep?

"I'm going to sleep in the guest room across the hall," he said, as though reading her thoughts. "This door locks and has an alarm on it. The entire house is equipped. I've already set the alarm. All the windows and doors have sensors. There are motion sensors around the house. It's monitored twenty-four-seven."

"That's... Why do you need that?" Nina wondered if she made the right call by going to him. Who was he? Who had he become?

Zeke closed his eyes and sighed. "Montgomery owns Rose Protection Agency. I work for him. He has a team of twenty. We work with law enforcement, do private security, whatever anyone needs."

"Do you work for the good guys?" Nina's voice shook as she asked, hoping he knew who the good guys were. Gwendolyn made herself look good. But after the raid, Nina knew the truth was out there.

"We do. Only for people who are on the right side of the law. But that doesn't mean what we do is without risk. We have security, good security, and we have lots of training to make sure we are safe. You will be safe here."

Nina nodded, thinking of the security at Gwendolyn's. The men standing guard at all times, willing to give their lives for her.

"He won't get to you."

Nina nodded again, letting the truth stay quiet.

"I will be right across the hall, Nina. If you need anything, come get me."

"Zeke?"

"Yeah?"

"I'm sorry my brother punched you."

Zeke rubbed his reddened jaw. "I'll be okay. He still doesn't know how to throw a good punch."

Nina chuckled, feeling almost normal.

Zeke moved to the door. "Lock this behind me."

"Do you have a key?"

Zeke nodded. "Do you want it? So I can't get in unless you let me?"

She shook her head. "I like knowing you can get in here."

"Okay. I will come if you call me. Every time."

"I know you will."

Zeke moved across the room quickly, dragging her into his arms and kissing the side of her head. He released her just as fast, stalking to the bedroom door. "Lock this."

Nina nodded, following him to the door and flipping the lock once he closed the door. "Good night," she whispered.

"Good night, Nina," Zeke answered from the other side of the door.

Nina put her hand flat against the door. She exhaled and smiled. She was safe. She could sleep.

ZEKE LEANED against the wall outside his bedroom. He listened as Nina crawled into bed and settled down. He barely breathed, wanting to hear every sound.

When she stopped moving, he sank to the floor. He told himself he needed to sleep, but he couldn't walk away from her.

She was alive. She was home.

Relief coursed through him and brought tears to his eyes. Whatever happened to her was bad, but it was over. She was safe. He would never let anything happen to her again.

Zeke rested his head in his hands and settled in for a few hours. He accepted that moving away from the door wasn't going to happen. Yeah, he had a bed in the guest room, but that was another ten feet away from Nina. He couldn't do it.

Nina moved and made noises, but Zeke didn't move. He waited, listening, consoling himself that she was safe.

Gene and Franklin joined Zeke at the top of the stairs, abandoning their usual spots on the couch for the night, and settled next to Zeke. Their loud purring said they were content to stay put for the night, too, guarding Nina.

Zeke told himself Montgomery would be okay. It was a shock to see her. Zeke regretted not telling Montgomery what was going on, but it was too late for that. Mont would accept that all that mattered was having Nina back.

Hours passed, and the bedroom Zeke didn't use glowed as the sun rose. The hallway warmed up. Zeke shifted his position, stretching his legs and twisting his neck. It wasn't anywhere close to his first night on guard all night. It wouldn't be his last.

Nina stirred an hour after the sun came up, moving to the bathroom. The toilet flushed, and the water ran.

Both cats stood when they heard Nina, stretching and yawning, then sitting and facing the bedroom door as they waited for her to come out.

Zeke wasn't sure if she would leave the room or go back to sleep. He didn't move, letting her choose for herself. When the lock on the bedroom door snicked open, Zeke and his cats all looked up.

"Why are you sitting there?" she asked, smiling when Gene and Franklin greeted her with meows.

She looked healthier than the night before. The circles under her eyes were faded. A glow that wasn't there when he picked her up made her look more like the girl he remembered.

"I wanted to be close," he confessed.

She glanced at the bedroom he said he was going to sleep in and smiled. "Thank you." Franklin wound around her feet, and she bent down to pet him.

Zeke nodded and rose to his feet, scooping up Gene to keep from reaching for Nina. "Are you hungry?"

She nodded. "Yeah. Um, should we call Monty?"

"He didn't come home last night."

"What? Is he okay? What about his family?"

Zeke shook his head. "He doesn't have a family. He's single, unless you count the business."

"Oh, I thought..." She nibbled her lip. "Do you think he's okay?"

"He will be. Let's get some food, then we can go see him or go get you clothes and then see him or whatever you want to do."

"What about your job?"

"Obviously, my boss knows what's going on."

Nina nodded. "Oh, right."

Zeke fixed breakfast and filled her in on the high points of his and Montgomery's lives over the last twelve years. Military, searching for her, Montgomery started the business.

"When did he get divorced?"

"Divorced? Mont's not divorced. He's never been married."

Nina exhaled a confused sound. "Neither of you ever settled down."

Zeke wanted to tell her he couldn't imagine loving anyone else, but all he did was shake his head. "Mont's thrown himself into work. We both did, I guess. He's done very well. Saved a lot of people."

"That's what you do? Save people?"

"We keep people safe. Protect them. Whether it's a witness or an informant or someone who needs us for a short term."

"You're heroes."

Zeke grunted. "No. We're just people who know what it's like to lose the most important person in our lives."

Her soft gasp said she understood what he was saying. Tears welled up in her eyes, but she blinked them back. "I wish I hadn't left."

"You're back. That's what matters."

Nina smiled. She picked up her empty plate and carried it to the dishwasher. She grabbed Zeke's plate and mug, putting all of it in.

"What do you want to do first? Do you feel safe leaving here?"

She sucked in a breath. "I didn't even think about that. I... I don't know."

"I can order some clothes, and we can drive through and

pick them up, then go to the office. Then you don't have to walk around a public place, but we still get to Montgomery."

She nodded, her breathing steadying. "That's probably best."

Zeke pulled up the app on his phone for a big box store and showed her how to add things to the cart. When she was done, he paid for everything and tucked his phone away.

Nina freshened up in the bathroom, then sat on the bed while Zeke took a fast shower, leaving the door cracked in case she needed anything. He dressed in clean clothes, then led the way to his SUV.

"Where do you want to sit? The windows are all bullet-proof. The whole vehicle is. But if you don't want to be seen..."

"That might be best."

"Sit in the back. Behind me. When we get to the store, you can hide while the bags are put in the trunk."

"Okay."

They picked up her new clothes without incident. Zeke drove to the office while Nina searched through the bags and chose an outfit for the day.

"Should I change now or wait until we get there?"

"It's up to you."

She wrinkled her nose in the mirror. "I feel like I need to have some armor on before I face him again. I hurt him by calling you."

"He'll be okay," Zeke said, as much for himself as her.

"I'm going to change now. If that's okay."

"Of course. I won't look. Tell me when you're done." He adjusted the rearview mirror so it showed him the ceiling of the vehicle and not the woman behind him.

"Okay."

Zeke ignored the rustle of fabric and stared straight through the windshield. He hardened, swallowing the desire flowing through him at the idea of a naked Nina in his backseat.

He noticed her dress in the trash when he took a shower. The scraps of fabric she'd been in the night before were buried beneath tissues and waste from the last few days. He wanted to burn the garment, make sure she never saw it again.

Zeke turned onto the street where the office was. It was busy, morning traffic flowing through the city and slowing him down. "We're almost there," he said, hoping Nina was ready when they arrived.

"I'm dressed," she replied, the click of her seatbelt a signal he could adjust the rearview mirror again.

He told himself he was checking the position of the mirror, but he was looking at her. She wore a teal top with a light gray jacket over it. A glance back showed jeans on her legs. Slip-on shoes added to the whole look.

"You look amazing," Zeke said, his voice rough with emotion.

"Thanks. I kind of guessed at the sizes. The shoes are a little big. The jeans are good. My bra and panties are small, but they'll work for now."

"We can go back," Zeke blurted as he pulled into the parking lot for the office. "Right now. Or later. Or I can have stuff delivered."

She leaned forward and put her hand on his shoulder. "We'll figure it out later. Right now, we need to go in." She nodded to the door with the rose on it, Montgomery on the other side.

Zeke nodded once, then cut the engine and climbed out.

He opened Nina's door and positioned himself between her and any possible threats.

Montgomery met them halfway to the door and flanked Nina. Zeke and Mont's heads swiveled as they hurried her to the door and inside.

"Oh my God," Berkeley whispered. She was so much more than a business manager for the company. She'd been a sounding board and friend and knew everything about Nina. But they'd never met.

"Hello," Nina said, smiling at Berkeley.

Zeke looked at Montgomery, waiting. Nina called Zeke, but Nina was Montgomery's sister. It was his choice what to tell everyone.

"Berkeley, this is my sister, Nina. Nina, Berkeley keeps this place running. We wouldn't be here without her," Montgomery said.

Berkeley's gaze strayed to Montgomery and lingered. She opened her mouth in a small O of shock. She recovered quickly and smiled warmly at Nina. "It's so nice to meet you."

Nina breathed a laugh. "Thanks. It's good to know my brother has had someone watching out for him."

Berkeley grinned. "I'm doing my best, but he's a challenge."

Nina nodded. "But he's worth it."

"Yes, he is," Berkeley said.

Something unspoken passed between the two women, and Nina reached out and hugged Berkeley.

Berkeley was surprised by it, but returned the hug with a smile.

"Let's go to my office," Montgomery said roughly, interrupting them and moving to the secure door that led to the offices.

Zeke wasn't sure if he was invited. The look Berkeley gave him said she didn't know either, but Zeke followed anyway.

Nina looked around the space as the three of them walked through, Montgomery in front, Nina in the middle, and Zeke protecting from behind.

Zeke couldn't guess how many times they'd moved through crowds, war zones, open spaces the same way. It was ingrained in them to protect someone. The way neither of them could when Nina left.

The office was quiet, most of the guys not in yet after the late night. Zeke was grateful for it as they made their way to Montgomery's office. Zeke's was next door, as second in command at Rose Protection Agency. A position wasn't sure if he still held.

Zeke closed the door to Montgomery's office and took a seat next to Nina in the guest chairs. Montgomery sat on the other side of the desk, hands folded, staring at Nina.

Nina flashed Zeke a look, then focused on her brother. "Monty, I'm sorry. I... I didn't think you'd be in the area."

Montgomery closed his eyes. "I never thought I'd hear your voice again. See you. Be in the same room as you." He drew a breath and opened his eyes, emotion flooding them.

Zeke knew how Mont felt. It was the same way he felt. Relief, regret, love, vengeance. The emotions flickered in Mont's eyes as he stared at his sister.

"Is it really you?" Mont whispered.

Nina stood and moved around the desk. She leaned down and threw her arms around her brother's neck. "It's me, big brother. I'm back. And I'm alive."

Montgomery let out a shuddering breath and pulled her onto his lap. He held her tight, like Zeke had done the night before.

Zeke stared at them, hating himself for not giving them the moment alone. He hated himself for not stopping her all those years ago. For not following her or something. He was the reason for all the pain they were experiencing. He could have changed everything, but they were together again.

Zeke stood quietly, moving toward the door. "I'm going to clean out my office."

"Sit your ass down," Montgomery barked. "You brought her back to me. You're not going anywhere."

"It's all my fault. We all know it. I shouldn't have let her leave. And when she came back, I should have told you. All of this could have been avoided if I'd been a better friend. A better man."

"You're the best man I know," Montgomery said, easing Nina off his lap and standing. He came around the edge of the desk, Nina following him. "There's no one I want running this place with me, watching my six, more than you. And I forgave you for her leaving years ago. If I still blamed you, you would have known it."

"You were pissed last night," Zeke argued.

"I was... I was all kinds of things last night. Angry, hurt, scared, hopeful. I couldn't handle it all. But the only person to blame for all of that is the man who had her. Not you, not me, not her. Just one person. And we're going to find him and make him pay for what he did to her. Together."

Zeke nodded. "He won't get away with it."

"It's not a he," Nina whispered.

"What?" Zeke and Montgomery asked together.

Nina met their gazes with a strong one of her own. "I wasn't held by a man. I was with a woman. She's the one in charge. The one who did all of this." Nina pointed to her throat and eye, the bruises more prevalent than the night before. "I left so I could help take her down. Her name is Gwendolyn Lennox."

4

———

Nina watched the two most important people in her life as they absorbed her words. Zeke leaned against the wall, and Monty dropped to the seat next to her, his head in his hands.

She would have been more shocked if they didn't know the name. Nina was sure everyone knew Gwendolyn Lennox by now. But their reactions confirmed they were more than aware of who she was. They were intimately knowledgeable about what Gwendolyn was capable of.

"How are you alive?" Monty whispered. He lifted his gaze to hers. The pain in his was enough to send Nina to the chair next to him.

She wondered the same thing over the years, but she never let herself dwell on it. If she did, she would have lost hope, and hope was the only thing she ever had. The only thing Gwendolyn never took from her. "She liked me. I was... She called me her sister. Said we were alike, and she took care of me."

"Shitty sister," Zeke growled, his gaze locked on the handprints around Nina's throat.

Nina instinctively reached up to hide the marks. She'd done the same for years. Whenever Gwendolyn got angry with her, she would leave marks on Nina. The marks would anger Gwendolyn even more because if Nina was given to one of the customers with marks on her, the men would think it meant they were allowed to leave their own. Gwendolyn was horrible, but she didn't like her women getting beaten. Unless she was the one doing it.

"Don't cover up what she did. You need to report this. It's more evidence against her. More that can be used to keep her ass in jail when she's found." Monty's voice was harsh. His glare was worse.

Nina shivered as she removed her hand. "This is nothing compared to what she's capable of."

"We know," the men said together.

"Fuck," Monty whispered. "All this... I can't... I'm so fucking sorry." He hauled her from her seat and into his arms, burying his face in her neck.

Nina held on to her brother, never wanting to let go. She trembled against him. Over the years, she'd almost lost hope of seeing him again. Gwendolyn told her he'd left and never returned. That he moved on without her holding him back. She reinforced the decision seventeen-year-old Nina made and said Montgomery was better off without Nina in his life.

Nina hoped she could one day see her brother again, but she never hoped it would be in the same town where they always lived.

"When did you come back to Niagara Falls?" Nina asked against his chest.

Montgomery sniffed, pulling back from her and wiping his eyes. He pinched the bridge of his nose and sat on the edge of his desk. "After my four years were up, I came back. Everyone told me you were gone, but I couldn't give up. I started all of this hoping I could keep someone else from losing their sister the same way."

"And you didn't get married? Did you break up because of me?"

Monty looked past Nina to Zeke.

Nina followed his gaze and caught Zeke shrugging.

"I was never engaged," Monty said.

"What? I thought..." Nina closed her eyes. "Kids?"

"None of those, either. Why would you think that?"

"Gwendolyn told me you settled down and had a good life. Said you were better off without me."

"I'm going to kill that bitch," Zeke growled. "What did she tell you about me?"

Nina shook her head. "She never mentioned you. I... When I left, I wanted to put everything that happened behind me. We talked about my family, and I told her I couldn't have Monty give up his dreams because of me."

"I would have given up everything for you." Monty grabbed her hands and held them tightly in his. "Everything, Nina. I wanted to. The only question I had was what the Navy would say."

"You would have gotten in trouble. I heard you talking about it after Mom's funeral."

Monty shook his head. "I could have, but being your guardian would have been a special circumstance. I would have delayed enlisting, but it was possible."

"I didn't... I didn't know."

Monty shook his head slowly. "We can't go back. All we can do now is move forward and put that woman in jail forever so she never hurts anyone else."

Nina nodded, but she didn't want Gwendolyn in jail. Jail was too good for her. Gwendolyn was too connected and too powerful. She had her hands in every legal entity in the area. There was no way she would stay in jail long, or stop ruining lives.

Gwendolyn Lennox deserved to be in the ground. And Nina was going to make sure it happened.

"She needs to talk to Lorelei," Zeke said, drawing Nina's attention from her thoughts.

"Who is that?"

"She's great. Let's go. Before this place gets any busier." Montgomery stood, leading the way to the door. He opened it, letting Zeke go first.

The abruptness of their decision threw Nina off. She wasn't sure where she was going or why, but she knew they would never risk anything happening to her, and if they wanted her to meet someone, she would go with them.

Zeke drove, Montgomery in the back with Nina. Zeke looked in the mirror at her every few seconds, something that gave Nina comfort as he wound through the city streets. When he pulled up outside a house, she was more than a little confused.

"Does the woman you mentioned live here?" Nina asked.

Both men shook their heads.

"No, but I think she's here right now. Let's go in," Monty said.

Nina followed Monty out of the SUV. Zeke was already there, the two of them once more flanking her on the way to the door. Nina recognized the move from Gwendolyn and her many security people. They were always surrounding her, making sure no one could get a clear shot at the most hated woman in town.

Montgomery knocked on the door of the house and stepped back. He looked up at a camera above the door, then into the doorbell camera. He waved at both.

A minute later, the door opened. An older woman

smiled at the men. "Well, this is a surprise visit. How are you doing today?" The woman's sharp gaze zeroed in on Nina and her bruises. "Did you bring me a guest?"

Both men shook their heads and moved closer to the door.

"Frannie, this is my sister," Montgomery said.

Frannie's gasp told Nina the woman understood exactly how loaded that simple statement was.

"Oh. Let's... I think we should speak more inside."

"Is Lorelei here?" Monty asked as Frannie let them all into the house.

Frannie nodded. "Everyone is here." Frannie glanced at Nina and smiled. "Are crowds too much for you? We can speak in a quieter setting if that makes you more comfortable."

"That would be nice. Thank you," Nina said, smiling at Frannie.

Frannie nodded, then pointed to a small living room off the front hallway. Zeke and Monty went with Nina, and Frannie turned to go to the other side of the house, where female voices were loud and friendly.

Nina looked around, trying to figure out what sort of place they were in. It reminded her of B&B's she'd seen on TV. Small, cozy places in little towns where people could stay. Nina always thought they looked charming and sweet. And the one they were in was the same.

Except for the double doors in front, both with heavy-duty locks, and Frannie meeting them on the porch. That didn't happen on TV shows.

Frannie returned with a Black woman. The Black woman smiled at Nina, but her demeanor and posture were not friendly and open.

Nina took a step backward, running into someone behind her. She gasped before hands cradled her body.

"Are you okay?" Zeke asked.

Nina shook her head. "Who is that?"

The Black woman approached, her hand extended. "My name is Lorelei. I'm an FBI Agent. Frannie said you were looking for me."

"FBI? No. No. I'm not... I can't."

"Nina, you have to tell her everything. She's the one leading the investigation," Monty said.

"No. The police never did anything for anyone. Why am I going to trust her now? She's not safe. I'm not safe here. I have to go. I can't." Nina turned and buried her face in Zeke.

His arms came around her and held her tight. She trembled against him, fighting the urge to run away from the intense and dominating woman and knowing Nina wasn't safe on her own.

"Lorelei isn't going to hurt you," Zeke assured her. "She's the one who figured out Gwendolyn Lennox is behind everything. She's leading the charge toward stopping her."

Nina looked up at him. "The last time I trusted a woman, I spent twelve years in captivity."

The collective gasps around the room had Nina closing her eyes in shame. She chose to leave. She chose to go to Gwendolyn. She chose to put her faith in a woman who ended up being a worse monster than the person Nina was really running from.

Nina couldn't do it again. She couldn't sit there and let a stranger tell her she could trust her. Not when Nina knew how it worked out last time.

"Gwendolyn Lennox tried to have me killed," Lorelei said, her voice firm but soft. "She kidnapped me and tortured me to figure out what I knew about her. She didn't do it, of course, but one of her people did. He left me for dead, but I was lucky. I was found, and I was rescued, and I regained all my memories, including the ones from when I was tortured. The ones that gave me her name."

Nina shook her head as Lorelei spoke, her fear ramping up. "That was you."

Lorelei inhaled sharply. "You heard about me?"

Nina nodded, facing the woman. "Agent Sloane. Gwendolyn was furious when you survived. If she wants you dead, you're dead. She doesn't screw up, and she doesn't tolerate people who do."

"Which is likely why the man who kidnapped me had three bullets in his chest last night."

Nina sucked in a breath. She was there when Gwendolyn shot Benjamin. Three times in the chest. He fell to the ground, face down, and Gwendolyn stepped over his body. She was sending a message to anyone who dared challenge her.

Nina left hours later.

"When I was much younger," Frannie said, drawing Nina's attention, "I was friends with Gwennie. We worked at a club together. I was a dancer, and she was a server. At Club Curves."

Nina gasped. "You worked there?"

Frannie nodded. She gestured toward the couch and sat, looking up at Nina to do the same.

Nina looked at the men, then sat next to Frannie.

"Club Curves saved me. So did Gwennie. She got me the job, then she found me an apartment. She made sure I was safe. She was my best friend. We spent a lot of time together."

"Are you still in touch?" Nina asked, her throat tight with

fear. Frannie seemed sweet and thoughtful. Nothing like Gwendolyn.

Frannie shook her head. "Not in years. We were walking home one night after a shift and witnessed a murder. I wanted to call the police, but Gwen said they would never believe us. We'd been drinking, and we worked at a place that wasn't known for being on the right side of legal all the time. She told me we were bad witnesses and couldn't even be sure of what we saw. I listened to her, but my conscience got the better of me and I ended up talking to the police."

"What happened?"

"The cop I spoke to trusted me. He listened to me. He set up a lineup, but Gwennie was there when he called. She went with me, and she confused me. We couldn't agree on a person, and the case stopped."

"She did it on purpose."

Frannie nodded. "She did. But I didn't realize that until recently. I had no idea who she was. What she was capable of. It was many years after Casey Slater died before I found the man who killed her. She wasn't his last. Lots of others died because of him."

"You found him?"

"I did. His name was Damon Street."

Nina gasped.

Frannie smiled sadly. "Damon was not a good man. Another friend of mine was involved with him. Didn't know who he was or what he was capable of. He almost killed her, and she came here."

Nina looked around. "Here? What is this place?"

"It's a shelter. Shelter in the Storm. Casey Slater was one of the reasons I opened this place. After her death, I knew women needed a safe place to be when home wasn't safe.

Children, too. Many people have come through those doors. Have found solace here."

"Including me," Lorelei Sloane said. "You don't have to trust me. You don't have to tell me your story. But the two men who brought you here trust me. They knew you needed to tell me what happened. And Frannie knows it, too."

Nina looked at all of them. Her gut churned with anxiety. There was so much. Good, but mostly bad. The things she knew, had witnessed and done nothing to stop. "I didn't help any of them."

"Any of who?" Frannie asked.

"The others," Nina said. "Gwendolyn listened to me. She said I was her little sister. She would talk to me. I could have told her to stop. Or done something to make her stop. I could have—"

"Gwen would never have stopped. I'm guessing those bruises you have are from her hands." Frannie gestured to Nina's throat and face.

Nina nodded.

Frannie sighed heavily. "She wasn't violent when I knew her. Obviously, I didn't know her well. She didn't talk about herself much. Or her family. She had a brother and her father, but I never met either of them. When Lorelei first told me Gwen was behind everything, I had a hard time believing it. She was my friend. She was someone I spent time with. How was it possible I missed so much?"

Nina nodded, her throat closing. She inhaled a shaky breath. "I ran to her," she whispered. "I chose to go to her."

"She deceived you, Nina. She manipulated you into thinking she was going to be there for you. That's what happens."

"I didn't know she was so evil," Nina whispered, all her emotions and regret and fear and pain bursting from her.

Frannie gathered Nina close and held her while Nina sobbed painfully all over the woman she'd known for less than an hour. Nina couldn't stop the flood once she started, her chest heaving with pain and her lungs crying for air as she cried and hated herself for choosing to turn to a woman who would one day kill her.

When Nina's sobs turned to hiccuping breaths, Frannie pulled back slightly.

"None of this is your fault. I know you're not ready to hear that, and it'll take a long time before you are, but I want you to hear it from me. Everything Gwen has done is on her. She's to blame for her actions. Even if you tried to stop her, she would have beaten you more or sold you to someone or just killed you. You never would have made it back to your brother."

Nina couldn't accept that, but she appreciated Frannie saying it. Nina wished she'd done so many things differently over the last twelve years.

But she couldn't go back.

"Lorelei is one of the good ones. She's smart and she's capable and she's leading the charge to find and stop Gwen for good. Her partner is married to Damon's ex, the one I mentioned?"

Nina breathed a laugh. "Really?"

Frannie smiled. "She got her happily ever after. Lorelei is living with the man who found her. The other room is full of women whose lives were nearly destroyed by Gwen and Damon and the rest of them, but who found their way through that to a happiness they never expected would exist."

"Wow," Nina breathed.

"You are welcome to join us. Now or any other time." Frannie's smile was warm and kind and made Nina wonder if there was a chance at a life for her.

"Thank you."

"Will you tell me about your time with Gwendolyn Lennox?" Lorelei asked.

Nina faced the woman. She tried to build up the fear she felt when Lorelei spoke earlier, but it was gone. Hearing Frannie's story, knowing she wasn't the only one who trusted Gwendolyn and paid the price for it, told Nina she was safe.

She should have known Monty and Zeke would never put her in danger, but her instincts were rusty at best. And trusting a stranger was a mistake Nina was not willing to make again.

"I'm ready," she said, nodding at Agent Sloane. Time to stop Gwendolyn.

5

———————

ZEKE LEANED AGAINST THE WALL OF THE LIVING ROOM AND listened to Nina tell her story. His body was rigid, every muscle tense. He hated himself more with every word she spoke. Every admission of what she'd been through and witnessed. Everything he could have prevented if he'd stopped her that night.

"Gwendolyn was a friend of a friend. I went to Club Curves a few times to see Beth. We played soccer together in high school. She was a year older than me, and she tore her ACL her senior year. Went from a full ride to college to no offers at all. She didn't have money to pay for school, so she started working at Club Curves."

"Most of us who worked there had similar stories," Frannie said. "It was a place that felt safe even though it really wasn't. But we didn't know that."

"I didn't," Nina said. "Beth had been there for a while, and we'd been in touch off and on. Monty was..." Nina looked at her brother.

Montgomery leaned forward, as though he could

change what happened twelve years ago. Tension lined his body. The same tension Zeke felt.

"Monty was enlisting. Our dad came home. Said he was moving back in with me and Mom."

Zeke remembered the night. Montgomery's going away party. Everything screeched to a halt when Jeffrey Rose walked in. Abusive and mean, he'd been gone for years, but he obviously knew what was going on with his family. He saw the opportunity to rub Montgomery's face in shit and showed up to tell his son he was returning.

"Mom... Mom couldn't handle it. The only reason she was still alive was because Monty ran Dad out of the house."

"You knew about that?" Montgomery asked.

Nina looked up at her brother. "I knew about all of it. I knew you protected me and Mom. I knew you took him on when he was drunk. I knew you would never let him near us once you were old enough to throw a punch. And I knew you were the reason he left. I was so grateful. I would lie in bed at night and wonder if he would hit me, too. I saw Mom's bruises once. She tried to hide them, but I walked in when I didn't realize she was in the bathroom. She was trying to see the bruises on her back."

"What did she tell you?" Montgomery asked.

"She said she fell, but I knew she was lying. She wouldn't look at me when she said it. I didn't figure it out right away, but I never forgot the look of those bruises."

Nina rubbed her throat. The move was subtle enough that Zeke didn't think she knew she was doing it, but that made it worse. It wasn't the first time that bitch choked Nina. She'd done it before. Many times if Zeke had to guess.

"Anyway," Nina focused on Frannie again, glancing at Lorelei. "Mom took a bunch of pills that night. Killed herself so she didn't have to live with Dad. When we found her in the morning, she was long gone, and Monty was going to give up his enlistment to be there for me. I couldn't handle holding him back. He'd already stayed local for college so he could help us. But sacrificing his career? I knew I had to do something."

"You called Beth?" Frannie asked.

Nina shook her head. "Beth came to Mom's funeral. She invited me out afterward, and I met Gwendolyn that night. Gwendolyn was so nice and friendly. She said if I ever needed anything to let her know. She gave me a drink, and I quickly got drunk. I spilled the whole story to her. I told her everything. She said if I ever needed a safe place to go, I could come to Club Curves. She promised me someone would get in touch with her if I ever showed up, and that she would take care of me."

"She manipulated you," Montgomery hissed.

Nina nodded. "Yes, but I was scared. You were leaving, and Dad was coming home, and Mom was dead. I was alone. And the only person I was going to have with me was Dad. I knew what he was capable of, and I was afraid he would come after me every chance he had."

"I would never have let that happen," Montgomery growled.

Nina smiled at him. "I know, but at the time, you were leaving. The next night I overheard you saying you were going to give up your assignment and stay so I had you home my senior year of high school."

"And that's why you left." Montgomery looked defeated. As defeated as Zeke felt. The conversation she overheard was one Montgomery had with Zeke. Zeke wanted to do more, but he wasn't family. He had no legal right to step in. If he tried, if he moved Nina in with him, if he stood up to their father, he could have gone to jail. It was a part of the conversation. The one where Montgomery decided his only option was to delay his enlistment.

"I couldn't let you do it. I couldn't let you risk your future."

"And I would have gladly done it for you." Montgomery sounded lost. Broken.

Zeke felt it, too. He walked into the kitchen that night, after losing the argument with his best friend and knowing there was nothing Zeke could do to fix the situation for his friend and the girl he loved. He saw Nina at the back door, her hand on the doorknob.

"Don't," he whispered, barely making a sound.

"Please let me go, Zeke. I have to get out of here," she said back.

"I don't like you wandering alone at night." Zeke knew she did it a lot. She liked to be outside. Free. In the fresh air. She'd always been fine, but he didn't like it.

"I can take care of myself," she snapped.

Zeke hated it. He wanted to haul her against him and take care of her. Be the one she turned to. But he wasn't family. He wasn't allowed. She was too young for him. He couldn't have her. "Be back before he knows."

Nina hesitated, but she nodded.

Now, Zeke knew what that hesitation was for. She never intended to come back. He told himself something happened to her. She was taken. She couldn't return. But now he knew she never intended to.

"I went to Club Curves. Gwendolyn wasn't there, but I told someone I needed to see her. She showed up not long after I did, and she told me everything would be okay."

"She made you feel safe." Frannie's history with Gwendolyn carried weight. She knew the woman, and she understood Nina and what she went through.

Zeke wasn't sure he would ever understand. He didn't have the best childhood, but he never considered running away. He never felt unsafe in his home. Unloved, sure. But never unsafe.

"I went to her to feel safe. I needed someone who didn't have to give something up for me. To feel like I wasn't a burden."

"You were never a burden," Montgomery said.

Zeke knew the conversation was as painful for his best friend as it was for him. Probably more. They'd both lost Nina that day, but Montgomery was the only one who could have saved her if she'd stayed. Zeke let her go, and he would never forgive himself for it, but Montgomery carried his own guilt.

Nina inhaled sharply. She ignored her brother and focused on the two women.

Frannie was attentive and consoling, holding Nina's hands and offering support. Lorelei was sharp and decisive, making notes and staying silent while Nina shared her story.

"Gwendolyn took me to her house. I could tell she was rich, but I didn't know anything else. She gave me a room near hers and told me not to wander outside because I would get in trouble and go back to my dad if anyone knew I was there."

"You never called me to let me know you were okay," Montgomery said.

Nina nodded. "I thought it would be easier if I just disappeared. Gwendolyn said the same. She told me you left for the military. That you were moving on with your life. For the first six months, I thought about going back so many times, but she always convinced me you were better off without me. She said I could be her little sister, that she would take care of me."

"That bitch," Montgomery hissed.

"Just before I turned eighteen, things started to change. She had a party and asked if I wanted to meet a friend of hers. Said he was a nice man and thought I was pretty. He flirted with me, and he tried to sleep with me, but I was uncomfortable. Gwendolyn threw him out. She protected me. Kept me safe. Slowly, more things like that would come up. She was always getting rid of them, telling me she would keep me safe and apologizing for the way they acted. After the first guy, the drugs started. It was minor at first, a way to relax. By the time I turned eighteen, it was a daily thing, and the drugs were more potent. About a week after my birthday, I was so high I blacked out. I woke up the next morning... There was blood everywhere and my panties were gone. I was sore, and I knew what had happened. Gwendolyn promised retribution. Said she would never let that happen again."

Zeke closed his eyes and tried not to throw up. She was barely an adult, innocent and vulnerable. And that evil bitch prostituted her out.

"It wasn't the last time, was it?" Frannie asked.

Nina shook her head. "The drugs continued, and the blackouts became a regular. Sometimes they wouldn't even let me come down from a high before they were giving me more. Days ran together and months passed without me realizing. I started to wish I was dead. I told her I wanted to leave, but she said she was my family. That you were married and forgot all about me."

"That lying bitch," Montgomery growled.

"She was convincing. I was heartbroken. I knew I made

the wrong choice by leaving and going to her, but it was too late." Nina shuddered with her inhale.

Frannie wrapped an arm around Nina and held her close. The two women cried together.

Zeke wanted to put his fist through the wall. And then through Gwendolyn Lennox. He wanted the bitch to pay for what she did. For the pain she caused.

He knew Nina's story wasn't the only one. She was part of a collection. Women Gwendolyn auctioned off to the highest bidder, sold for a night or forever. Many would never be seen again, dead or gone, and many were like Nina and would never be the same.

"Gwendolyn would bring me to her room sometimes. She would talk to me. She still called me her sister and would tell me about things. When she was upset, she would send for me."

"She confided in you, and you know everything about her company?" Lorelei asked.

Nina looked at the agent. The distrust was still there in her eyes. She glanced at Zeke, and he nodded. Nina held his gaze for another moment, then returned to Lorelei. "I know a lot. Not everything. I know about Damon and Trevor. I know about her houses and the company. I know she's evil, and she's going to stop at nothing to keep me from talking."

"We're not going to let her get to you ever again," Zeke growled.

All eyes in the room turned to him.

Zeke stood a foot from the wall. His fists were clenched tight. His muscles corded even tighter. He was ready to fight, and he wasn't backing down. Gwendolyn Lennox would pay for what she did. No matter what it took from him to make sure she did.

"Zeke," Montgomery said.

Zeke turned to his best friend.

Montgomery looked Zeke up and down. "At ease."

Zeke shook his head. The anger was the only thing keeping him from falling apart. If he let go of it, he would collapse. He would let all the things Nina confessed inside, and it would destroy him. He could do that later, when Nina was safe with Montgomery, but now he couldn't afford it.

"Take a walk," Montgomery said.

Again, Zeke shook his head. "I'm not leaving her."

"Mr. Donovan, I need you to relax." Frannie stood and approached him. "The women and children who are my guests have been victims of violence and abuse. A man like yourself is intimidating when you're smiling, but when you're like this, you will scare them to death. I can't allow that."

Zeke looked at the woman in front of him. She wasn't afraid of him. She had no reason to be. But he knew what she was saying.

Zeke eased his hands, releasing the fists that he held so tight his fingers ached. He swallowed hard, stuffing the emotions back inside as they clawed at his throat to get out. He shook his head, fighting the tension holding him. He drew a breath and let it out slowly.

"Thank you," Frannie said.

Zeke nodded, not feeling much better but grateful she was going to allow him to stay.

Nina detailed all the houses she remembered going to with Gwendolyn while Lorelei recorded addresses and features of the homes. Nina relayed all the crimes Gwendolyn confessed to, and she corroborated a few things Gwendolyn hadn't confessed to. Things others had told Nina, or people she knew were a part of the company.

By the time Lorelei finished with all her questions, and

Nina had emptied her brain of all things Gwendolyn Lennox, everyone in the room looked worn out. Zeke wanted a drink and a shower and to beat the hell out of something. Preferably Gwendolyn Lennox.

Lorelei left the room first, letting Nina know she would be in touch with more questions and telling her to be safe.

Frannie hugged Nina tightly and whispered something Zeke couldn't hear. The smile on Nina's face said it was something good, something that made her feel better.

Zeke still had a hard time believing all of it. That she was right there under their noses for so long. That she was abused the way she was. That she got away. His guilt weighed on him. It had lightened over the years with regret and pain and time lost, but with her back, his guilt was right there again, reminding Zeke he would never be able to make amends for letting her go that night.

Frannie lingered with them, but she stepped away to let the three of them have a moment.

Montgomery pulled Nina into his arms and held her tight. The look on his face was the same as Zeke was feeling. Nina looked relieved. She was safe, and she shared information that would stop Gwendolyn Lennox from hurting anyone else.

"I have to get back to the office," Montgomery said. "Are you good to hang out there for the day with me?"

Nina glanced at Zeke. "What about Zeke?"

"I'll ride with you guys."

"No, I mean, where are you going to be all day?"

Zeke and Montgomery exchanged a glance.

"I'm going to be at the office. I can manage everything while you're gone," Zeke told Montgomery. When Mont was on assignments, Zeke took over. He wasn't sure Montgomery wanted him in charge, but on short notice, there wasn't much choice.

"You're leaving? Where are you going?" Nina asked.

Both men looked at her again. Her eyes were wide with panic.

"I'm not leaving. I'm going to be with you," Montgomery said. "I'm not leaving you again."

"You're going to be with me. I thought..." Nina glanced at Zeke.

Montgomery followed her gaze.

Zeke froze.

"I thought I would stay with Zeke. I... Is that an option?"

Montgomery glared at Zeke before swinging his gaze back to his sister. "Whatever you want."

"Are you sure?"

"You should stay with your brother," Zeke said. "He wants you to stay with him."

"And you don't want me with you," Nina said.

"No! That's not it. At all." Zeke struggled to find the right words. "I didn't protect you twelve years ago. I let you walk out that door. You should be with Montgomery, not me. Your brother is the one who should be protecting you."

"But I want you to protect me," Nina said.

"I—"

"Zeke will do it," Montgomery snapped. "He'll protect you. He won't let anything ever happen to you. He loves you just like I do."

Zeke wanted to argue, but he knew that tone. Montgomery's decision was final, and no one would change his mind.

"Thank you," Nina whispered.

The two men nodded, but Zeke knew they were going to have a conversation. One he wasn't sure he would like.

The drive back to the office was tense. Nina slumped against the side of the SUV, Montgomery sitting next to her, fully upright and alert.

Zeke parked outside their offices, as close to the door as he could get. He opened Nina's door and led the way to the office with Montgomery close behind.

They walked to Montgomery's office together. The chatter in the office around them never reached Zeke's ears. He was focused on Nina, and only Nina.

"Can I lie down on that couch?" Nina asked once they were in the office.

"Of course," Montgomery said. "We will go to Zeke's office and close the door so you have some quiet."

"You won't leave, right?" Nina asked, her gaze landing on Zeke's.

Zeke shook his head. "We'll be right next door."

Nina looked into Zeke's office, visible through the glass wall they shared. She nodded, then settled on the couch again.

Montgomery jerked his head for Zeke to follow.

Montgomery couldn't kill him until Nina was safe. And definitely not with all the witnesses around. But having the conversation about Nina staying with him was the last thing Zeke wanted to do.

Montgomery closed Zeke's office door and walked to the glass wall. He stared at Nina for a minute, then ran a hand over his head. He sank to one of the chairs in front of Zeke's desk and leaned forward. His elbows hit his knees, and his head went into his hands.

"I can't fucking believe what she's been through," Montgomery whispered.

"Yeah," Zeke said.

"I want to kill that bitch. And all the men who touched her."

"Same."

Montgomery leaned back and met Zeke's gaze. "You are my brother in every way except blood."

Zeke's throat tightened.

"I know you love her just like I do, and I know you will protect her with your life."

Zeke nodded. He'd never confessed his true feelings for Nina to Montgomery, but they weren't important.

"We do this..." Montgomery glanced around the office. "We do this to keep people safe. It's a job, but she's not just a job. She's everything. And she needs you."

"She should be with you."

Montgomery shook his head. "You and I both know how this works. She has to trust whoever is with her. She trusts you."

"She trusts you, too."

"No, I don't think she does. I think she still sees herself as a burden to me."

"She's not."

"I know, but it doesn't matter. She's alive. And you're going to keep her that way. I know you will."

Zeke nodded, all those emotions fighting to get out. "I love her. I will do anything for her. And for you."

"Then do this. Keep her safe. Don't let anyone ever touch her again."

"Done."

6

Nina woke up and looked around the room. A smile lifted her lips when she remembered she was safe. In Monty's office with him and Zeke right next door.

She sat up and looked through the glass wall to where the two men she loved were huddled together and in deep discussion. Nina didn't know how long she'd been asleep, but she felt like she couldn't get enough rest. Between the emotional toll of detailing the last twelve years of her life and the lack of restful sleep for almost that long, Nina was exhausted.

But she was safe, and that was really what mattered.

Since Monty and Zeke were working, she decided to look around Monty's office. He didn't have pictures on his desk and had very few personal items throughout the office. There was an old picture of her, maybe a school picture, on the bookshelf behind his desk. She picked it up and tried to remember the innocent girl she once was.

Teenage Nina wanted to play soccer in college. She was an excellent defender, sweeper since her freshman year.

She'd been scouted as a sophomore and knew she could have gotten a scholarship.

But she walked away from it all for her brother. And walked right into a hell she never expected.

Nina returned the picture to its spot and smiled when she caught sight of another photo. Monty and Zeke were standing on a beach, arms around each other, and smiling like they'd won the lottery. She hadn't seen either of them smile since she'd been back. Not like that. They looked happy. Free. Relaxed.

"That was the day I became a SEAL," Monty said from behind Nina.

She spun, embarrassed to be caught snooping. "Sorry."

Monty shook his head and walked closer. He stood next to her and stared at the photo. "You can look at anything. I was so happy that day. It was hard to get through that train-ing. I wanted to quit so many times, but I kept going."

"Was Zeke a SEAL, too?"

Monty nodded. "He wasn't sure what he wanted to do, but after you... He decided to join me. I knew I wanted to be a SEAL, so he signed up. Went through training after me, but he was there the day I got my trident."

"You two look happy."

Monty breathed a laugh. "We were. We felt like we were doing something. Making a difference."

Nina looked up at her brother. A ghost of that smile was on his lips, but the shadows in his eyes were different. Darker. "But you came back."

Monty looked at her. He held her gaze for a moment, then nodded. "I hated leaving when I did. It killed me to walk away knowing you were out there."

"There was nothing you could have done," Nina whispered.

"Maybe not, but it ate at me until I could come back here."

"I thought it was the best thing for you."

"I know. And maybe it was. I just wish we'd been able to talk. God, so many things... Fuck, Nina, you're here. And all you've been through..."

Nina put her hand on her brother's arm, letting his warmth and strength soak into her. "There were so many others worse off than me. I don't know why she liked me, but I was lucky. It could have been so much worse."

Monty swallowed thickly, his throat working with the effort. He drew a breath and shook his head, pinching his nose and squeezing his eyes shut. "I want to kill her for what she put you through."

"Me, too," Nina admitted.

Monty exhaled a laugh and pulled her into his arms. "At least we agree on that one."

Nina chuckled. "She's ruthless. I didn't see it for a long time, but the last few years she's gotten worse. If Zeke hadn't gotten there when he did, she would have killed me for trying to leave."

"Did you try to leave before?"

Nina shook her head and moved away from her brother. She returned to the couch and pulled the blanket over her lap. "Another girl tried once. She was nice. Didn't have anyone, but she was really sweet. Happy and positive. They picked her up in a bar, drugged her, and no one knew she was gone. She was eighteen."

"What happened to her?" Monty sat next to Nina.

Nina shrugged. "Gwendolyn. The girl's name was Annie. She fought back on everything. Told them she was going to get out of there one day. She would talk whenever they brought men in to her. Talked so much the men didn't want her. Gwendolyn told her she either had to shut up and take it or she'd be of no use. Annie snuck out that night. Tried to run away."

"Did she make it?"

Nina swallowed. She could still see Annie's face the next morning. "The guards caught her. Brought her to Gwendolyn. Gwendolyn beat her until she was barely recognizable. She lined all of us up in one room. Annie was there, her hands bound. She was bloody and bruised and naked. Gwendolyn told us that was what happened if we tried to run. If we thought we didn't belong to her. She said we were her property to do whatever she wanted to do. She shot Annie. In the chest. Made us all stand there and watch her bleed out."

"Fuck."

Nina drew a breath, closing her eyes and remembering Annie. "She was just trying to live. She wanted to be a person." Nina wiped the tears from her cheeks. "No one tried to run after that."

"How long ago was that?"

Nina shrugged. "Five years, maybe? It all kind of blends together when there's nothing to mark the passing of time, but I think it's been about that long."

"I'm so sorry, Nina. I can't..."

"Don't blame yourself. Or Zeke. The choice to leave was mine. I was so afraid of Dad, and I knew if I was gone, there would be no reason for him to come back."

"He did come back. He lived in the house for six years before he died."

"He's dead?" Nina gasped.

Monty nodded. "Drank himself to death. Passed out one night and never woke up, according to the medical examiner."

"Thank God," Nina breathed.

"Yeah. But... This place exists because of him."

"What do you mean?"

"He didn't have a will, no surprise, but since I was his only living family, without you here, everything went to me. I guess, legally, that means you own half of this place."

Nina shook her head. "This is yours. You're doing good work here, Monty. I'm so proud of you."

Monty hugged her again. "I'm so happy you're back. And anything you need, let me know. Zeke is my emergency contact, and he has access to all my accounts, so he'll get you whatever you need."

"Are you mad I want to stay with him?"

Monty shook his head slowly. "Mad? No. Curious, but you need to feel safe. I don't get to question what makes you feel safe right now."

"You know he'd never hurt me, right?"

"Yes. I would never question that."

"Except last night?" Nina asked.

Monty exhaled sharply. "Last night was... Walking in and seeing you. Seeing you in his clothes and your wet hair, those bruises. I lost my mind. I reacted."

"Did you apologize to him for it?" Nina asked.

Monty twisted his lips at her and shook his head. "No."

"Maybe you should. Make sure he knows you're not mad."

Monty rolled his eyes. "Fine." He reached back and pounded on the glass wall that separated the offices.

"Yeah?" Zeke called.

"Sorry I punched you," Monty shouted without taking his gaze from Nina.

Nina smiled, laughing at her brother.

"All good. If you put your hips into it, it might have actually hurt."

Monty pressed the back of his hand to the glass, his middle finger the only one raised.

Zeke's return laughter made Nina smile.

"It's good to see you two are still close."

"Couldn't get closer," Monty said. "He's saved my life more times than I can count." He looked out at the office, at the company he built and the people who helped him to run it. "Everyone here has. We've created a family. It's dysfunctional, but we love it."

"We wouldn't know what to do with a functional family."

Monty chuckled. "That's too true."

Nina leaned her head on his shoulder, enjoying the comfort. It was so different being back. So good.

A knock on the door lifted Nina's head. A smile lifted her lips when she saw Zeke looking uncomfortable.

"Sorry to interrupt. I wasn't sure how long you guys wanted to stay today." Zeke glanced between the two of them, waiting for someone to tell him.

"What time is it?" Nina asked.

"After four," Monty said.

"Seriously? I slept a lot longer than I realized."

"We didn't want to wake you," Zeke said.

"You didn't eat, though. You have to be starving," Monty said.

Nina shrugged. "I don't look like it, but we went without food a lot. I'm not used to eating regular meals."

"One more reason to kill her," Monty said.

"You're perfect," Zeke said at the same time.

Nina smiled at both of them. "Well, she will get what's coming to her. And I'm ready to go whenever you guys are.

I'm a high school dropout who's been presumed dead for a decade, so I have nowhere I have to be."

Zeke and Monty exchanged a pained look that made Nina regret her attempt at a joke.

"Sorry."

"We're happy you're here."

"Mont, come over for dinner. We can tell Nina more about what you've been up to without a wife and kids." Zeke raised his brows at Monty.

Monty nodded. "Sounds good. Let's head out."

Nina smiled, following her favorite people and looking forward to the night for the first time in forever.

ZEKE STOOD in his kitchen and watched Nina and Montgomery laugh. He was telling her stories about SEAL training, about life in the military, and about Rose Protection Agency.

It hit Zeke that it was all either of them had. No wives, girlfriends, kids, or anyone significant besides each other. They'd both had their share of flings and hookups over the years, but no one they wanted to keep around for longer than a few nights.

The woman Zeke was staring at was his reason. Hands down.

He could still remember the moment he fell in love with Nina. He was out of high school. Floundered for years without a path or a plan. He worked and built up some skills, but he didn't know what he wanted to do with his life.

Monty was on a break from school and invited Zeke over. Even though Montgomery lived at home with his mom and Nina, between working full time and going to school full time, they didn't see much of each other.

Zeke couldn't remember the last time he'd been there, but the night he went was Nina's birthday. She was sixteen.

Zeke was twenty-one, like Montgomery, but neither of them drank at his house after the violence Mont's father inflicted on the family. Their mom bought sparkling grape juice for Nina's birthday and baked her a cake and made mac-and-cheese for her birthday dinner.

She looked so happy. Her smile was magnetic, and the four of them laughed and talked all through dinner and cake and when they settled in the living room.

Nina sat next to Zeke on the couch, and her soft, sweet scent hit him. Her skin glowed, and he felt more than his usual stirring of desire.

Then she mentioned a boyfriend. A boy named Jeremy, who wanted to take her out on a date. She said he was nice and he was cute and she wanted to go. That weekend for her birthday.

Zeke couldn't see straight. He was so angry and so jealous that he nearly threw up. But he couldn't tell her no. He couldn't say anything. He had to stuff down his desire and keep his distance from her. She was too young, and she was his best friend's little sister.

She went on the date, and she was blissfully in love with Jeremy for a month.

Zeke went to their house every week for dinner after that. He punished himself with her presence, reminding himself she was untouchable and she deserved better than a man with no direction and no future.

Thirteen years later, Zeke couldn't say he thought any differently. Nina still deserved better than him. She was still untouchable. But she was no longer too young for him.

"Can we do anything to help with dinner?" Nina asked from the couch, laughing when Gene bumped her hand to get her attention again.

"No. All good," Zeke said, busying himself with checking on the steaks in the oven. Brussel sprouts were perfectly roasted, and the mashed potatoes were creamy and lump-free. Unlike his throat.

He wanted his best friend's little sister. And that made him an asshole. Because she was not just off-limits, but she was fragile and wounded and she needed to heal.

Zeke fixed two plates and carried them to the living room.

Nina gushed over the scent of the food, closing her eyes and inhaling deep.

Zeke excused himself, needing the solitude of the kitchen before Nina and Mont both caught the raging hard-on he was sporting. Zeke fixed his own plate, taking his time and ignoring the voices in the living room while he controlled the desire he couldn't control.

"Are you okay?" Nina asked when Zeke sat on the chair across from the couch.

"Yep. How's the food?"

"Amazing," Nina said with a groan.

Fucking hell, he was not going to survive dinner with her.

"Always good, man," Mont said.

Zeke nodded and focused on his plate. He barely tasted the food with Nina in the room. She still smelled like him, her skin soaked in his body wash. After a full day, it should have worn off, but somehow it hadn't.

Every damn thing about her was making him crazy. He thought he only had to keep it together for one night, but she wanted to stay with him. She would be in his bed again.

In his shower. On his couch and in his kitchen and in his SUV. She was invading his space, and he loved it.

And hated it.

He'd always dreamed of a life with Nina. When he dreamed of his future, it was her by his side. He'd never met another woman who made him feel the way she did.

But she wasn't there because she wanted the same thing. She was there because she needed protection.

And rule number one was don't fuck the client.

Even if Nina wasn't technically a client, the same rule applied.

"You good?" Montgomery was in the kitchen, in Zeke's space, his voice quiet.

"Yeah. What's up?"

Montgomery waved his phone. "I need to take care of something."

"You going alone?"

Montgomery shook his head. "Walker's going to meet me."

Zeke nodded. Walker St. Brown was quiet and menacing and not someone anyone wanted to fuck with. If Montgomery was going somewhere that required backup like Walker, Zeke was worried. "Everything okay?"

Montgomery nodded. "Yeah. No big deal, really. I knew Walker would be available."

Zeke returned Montgomery's smile. Walker had zero social life. Even more of a loner than Zeke was, Walker didn't pick up women or date or even talk about women. Or anyone. Walker was a mystery, but he was a reliable teammate and someone Zeke wouldn't hesitate to have at his six.

"Are you coming back tonight?"

Montgomery held Zeke's gaze for a long minute and

shook his head. "Not unless you need me to. She wants to be here with you. I'm not going to push to be a third wheel."

"Come on. It's not like that."

"I'm good. I promise." Montgomery went back to the living room and said goodbye to his sister. Nina hugged him tightly and told him to be safe. Montgomery promised he would, then waved to Zeke and let himself out the front door, locking it with his key after he left.

"Just you and me," Nina said. She patted the couch next to her, the side that wasn't occupied by cats. "Come sit."

Zeke did not want to sit next to her. He did not want to have her in his space. He did not want to be close to her and not be able to touch her.

But he couldn't say no to her.

He sat down, determined to keep a space between them, but Nina didn't get the same message. She leaned over, resting her head on his shoulder and her hand on his leg.

Zeke kept himself rigid next to her, his back straight and his body tight. He barely breathed.

Nina shifted next to him and laughed. "Relax. You're acting like I'm going to bite you."

"Just don't want to make you uncomfortable."

"You could never, Zeke. I promise. I'm good with you."

"Okay," Zeke said, but he didn't feel it.

But Nina showed him he was wrong. Her laughter eased and her body sagged and before he knew it, she was snoring softly against his side.

Zeke finally relaxed. She wouldn't be scared off by his reaction to her if she was asleep.

He kissed the side of her head and inhaled her hair. She twitched but settled again quickly.

He didn't move. He told himself he should wake her and let her go to bed, but he missed her so damn much he couldn't bring himself to do it. He sat there, watching one show roll to another and another, listening to her breathing and feeling her warmth beside him and thanking God for bringing her back to them.

When the evening news came on, Zeke knew they both needed to get to bed. He moved to turn off the TV, and she didn't wake up. The glow from the stairway lights cast a soft glow on her face. He wanted to hold her, even if it was only for a minute.

He scratched Gene and Franklin's heads, both cats waking up with a yawn, then settling down again, ignoring Zeke as they promptly fell back to sleep.

Zeke slid his arms beneath Nina's knees and neck and stood. She stirred and turned toward him, sighing as her body relaxed in his arms.

He moved around the couch, then turned sideways to carry her up the stairs. He turned off the light so it didn't wake her, then climbed one step at a time. At the top, he turned to his room and moved to the bed. He kicked the blankets back and leaned forward to set her on the mattress.

Her eyes opened when she touched the mattress. She grabbed his arm, a sharp inhale belaying her fear.

"You're safe, Nina. It's Zeke. You're in my bed."

"Don't leave me," she whispered.

Zeke warred with himself. He knew the right thing to do. He knew the smart thing to do.

"Please."

He wasn't going to do the right thing or the smart thing. He was going to do whatever Nina asked him to do. "Yes."

7

Nina moved over to let Zeke into the bed with her. She'd never shared a bed with a man, but in the darkness of night and the shadows of the truth she shared, she needed to feel him by her side. She wasn't strong enough to keep the memories at bay for another night. Not when she was already feeling the familiar terror of the night creeping in.

But when she was in Zeke's arms, all she felt was safe. Loved. Protected.

He laid on his back, as rigid as he was on the couch. Nina hated she was asking him to do things he wasn't comfortable with. She was being clingy and making it awkward between them. And he was nice enough to not call her on it.

After ten minutes of neither of them relaxing, Nina rolled out of bed.

"Where are you going?" Zeke asked.

"Bathroom," she whispered, trying to keep the pain from her voice. She needed him, and she hated that she did, but doing that was taking something from him she had no right to take.

Nina closed the bathroom door and drew a breath. Blood pounded in her ears, shame heating her cheeks. After so many years with no one, it was hard for her to rely on anyone. She told herself so many times that she was all alone and only had herself, but being free, being with Zeke, she felt like she could breathe.

But not if she made him uncomfortable.

Nina used the bathroom and washed her hands, then brushed her teeth. It was time to give Zeke some of his space back. She hadn't seen his guest room, but she would move into it so he could have his room back.

She drew a shaky breath and opened the door.

Zeke was sitting on the edge of the bed, his hands folded in front of him, forearms resting on his knees.

He looked up at her and stood when she stepped into the room. He tossed the blankets back on the bed and stood next to it.

"I'm, um, I'm going to give you your space back. I'll stay in the guest room."

"No," Zeke said, making a move toward the door.

"It's fine, Zeke. I'll go to Monty's tomorrow. I know I'm making you uncomfortable. I didn't realize it until tonight."

"Get in the bed, Nina."

Nina shook her head. "Zeke, just—"

"Get in the damn bed."

Nina looked up at him. That wasn't a look of anger. Or discomfort. It was the one and only look she recognized from a man. "Zeke?"

He slammed his eyes closed, cutting her off from the look of desire. "Please."

She nodded, even though his eyes were still closed. "Okay."

He moved to the side so she could get into bed without touching him. "Please stay."

She nodded, her throat tight. She remembered the first time a man looked at her like that. A boy really. Her high school boyfriend was not right for her, but she learned a lot from dating him. He was kind and good to her, but he was never Zeke.

The bathroom door closed behind Zeke, and Nina let out a breath. The tingles of awareness coursing through her were not new, but they were welcome for the first time in a very long time.

Nina didn't choose the life she had, but she did what she could to make the most of it. Some men she was with were nicer than others. They wanted her to enjoy their time. She knew it was mostly because it brought them more pleasure if she had an orgasm, but it allowed her to trick her mind into enjoying the experience. There were times she convinced herself it wasn't so bad.

When she forgot about the threat to her life if she left and pushed aside the lack of choice.

Sex was as much of a punishment as drugs, but once Gwendolyn trusted Nina wouldn't run, Nina had more agency in her choices. She had some repeat clients. Ones of her choosing. It was the best she could do, and the only way she could feel like her life wasn't completely out of her control.

The men who became her regulars were good to her. One asked if she was safe when she walked in with bruises. She never saw him again, but Nina appreciated the concern he had for her.

She was never grateful for her situation, but she knew it could have been so much worse than it was. And she learned to enjoy sex. She learned to make it enjoyable for her partner. And she couldn't help but wonder what kind of lover Zeke was.

Would he be commanding in bed? Maybe he was generous. She expected him to be demanding, wringing every ounce of pleasure from his partner.

Thinking about sex with Zeke had Nina wet and curious by the time the bathroom door opened and Zeke reappeared. He turned off the bathroom light and plunged them into darkness. He didn't move for a moment, then he walked toward her.

Slowly, like he was stalking her. Or afraid of her.

He laid down on the mattress next to her and tugged the sheet and comforter over both of them.

Awkwardness settled over them again, Nina shifting in the bed and wishing she'd left the bedroom while Zeke was in the bathroom. She hated making him uncomfortable.

"I don't want you to leave," Zeke whispered, his voice gravelly and rough.

"I don't want you to feel weird with me here."

"It's fine."

"That's not making me feel better."

"Let's get some sleep."

Nina stared at his profile, faintly visible in the dark room. He laid on his back, hands on his chest. Every inhale lifted his chest, every exhale lowered it. He didn't move otherwise. Didn't settle and rest.

He sat up all night the night before, guarding the door where she slept. He had to be exhausted. But he still wasn't sleeping.

Nina inched closer, wanting to feel the heat of his body next to her, the reminder he was there. She rested her hand on the mattress between them, stretching until her hand brushed his bicep.

He sucked in a breath but didn't move away from her.

She closed her eyes and let sleep come. Finally safe.

EXHAUSTION FINALLY CLAIMED Zeke an hour after Nina fell asleep. He'd been in much worse positions when he fell asleep, but he'd never had a woman in his bed.

Zeke's dream was a good one. A great one. Nina was there, her hand draped over his middle. Her gray-green eyes were full of desire, her body lush and full and ready for him.

Zeke plucked one nipple, watching her face for a reaction.

She closed her eyes and moaned softly. "More."

He was more than happy to comply. He brushed his thumb over her nipple, the peak pressing into the cotton top she wore.

She hooked a leg around his hip, rubbing herself on his erection.

"Fuck," he growled.

"Please," she begged.

Zeke yanked her shirt up, giving himself access to her breasts. He twisted both of them, loving the way her body bowed to him with the move. He buried his face between her full breasts, then licked his way up her chest, nibbling her throat, and claimed her mouth.

Hands full of breasts, mouth full of Nina's tongue, and her thighs parted and welcoming his throbbing erection was Zeke's version of heaven. He squeezed his hands, and she bit his tongue.

His eyes snapped open.

Nina was right there. Kissing him back. Writhing against

him. Her bare breasts in his hands. Her legs wrapped around him.

Zeke jumped out of bed so fast Nina almost fell.

She caught herself on the edge and looked up at him.

"Fuck," Zeke barked. He spun and went to the bathroom, locking himself in.

"Fuck, fuck, fuck. What the hell is wrong with me?" he hissed as he paced the bathroom.

It was nowhere near the first dream he had about Nina, but it was the first one that came true.

He manhandled her. Took advantage of her. He would have done more if she hadn't bit him and woke him up.

He shook his head. Did she wake him up? Or did he know it was real and want to pretend for another minute?

He was such an asshole.

An asshole with a hard-on that was not getting the message that Nina Rose was far off-limits. So far she wasn't even in the same country.

Her knock was soft, like she was afraid to interrupt him. "Zeke?"

He closed his eyes. He was acting like he was wronged, locking himself in the bathroom. He should have sent her in there. Let her know she was safe from him. Let her decide to be around him.

The thought finally calmed his erection and brought shame to his entire body. He unlocked the door and opened it, stepping back to show her he wouldn't attack her again.

"Nina, I can never apologize enough for that. I'm an asshole and I am so sorry I touched you. You can tell Mont what happened so he can kick my ass. I deserve it."

"Zeke," she said, moving closer.

Zeke backed up, holding up his hands.

She stopped.

"Don't try to make me feel better, Nina. I... There's no excuse for what I did."

"You weren't alone in that bed, Zeke."

He nodded. "I know. I know. I've never shared a bed with a woman, and I thought it was a dream. I—"

"You dream about me?" Nina asked.

Zeke stared at her, his mouth open to argue, but he couldn't lie to her. No reply was better than telling the truth.

"I would dream about you," Nina whispered. "About you showing up one day and getting me out of there. About you... and me."

"Nina."

"You don't have to say anything. I know all the men I slept with only did it because they were paying. It wasn't about me."

"All those men were garbage, and you deserved better. You deserve better than me. Better than being pawed in your sleep and treated like you don't matter."

"I wasn't asleep," she whispered.

Zeke's gaze snapped to hers, and his cock swelled with her admission. "What?"

She swallowed. "Not the whole time. At first, I was, but not the whole time. Not at the end."

Her admission hung in the air between them. Zeke didn't know what to do with it. If he acted on it, Montgomery would hate him forever. Nina was barely home. She'd been through hell. She needed therapy and time and to find normal.

"But that wasn't how it was for you." She nodded and took a step back. "So I guess that makes me the one who took advantage of you."

"Nina."

"It's been a long time since we've seen each other, Zeke.

I... God, I had such a crush on you when I was a teenager. I always wished you would notice me. There were times I would pretend I was having sex with you. That you were the one there for me. That you saw me and realized you loved me and couldn't resist me." She exhaled a long breath. "I was foolish, and it was dumb, and so was thinking you wanted me."

"Jesus, Nina, you're an idiot if you think I don't want you."

"You sure have a funny way of showing it."

"I shouldn't want you. Twelve years ago, you were too young. And now you're..."

"Damaged goods."

"No," he breathed. He took a step toward her, cupping her jaw and spearing his other hand into her hair. He tilted her head back until she met his gaze. "You're so strong. And you're so brave. And I'm so not worthy of you."

"You save people. You saved me. How could you ever think you're not worthy of anything?"

Zeke exhaled and leaned his forehead against hers. He closed his eyes and breathed her in, letting himself toy with the idea of her being his. It was the only thing he'd ever wanted. He never dared think it could be true, but his entire body ached with the hope it could be.

"Nina," he whispered.

"Zeke," she replied.

He tilted his head and brought his lips closer to hers. Her breath fanned over his cheeks. Her fingers curled against his chest. The moment hung between them, time standing still as he waited for her to choose.

She lifted onto her toes, reaching for him and bringing her lips into contact with his. Her hands went around his waist, pulling her body into contact with his from chest to hips.

She let out a sigh full of desire and peace, and he answered with a growl, licking her lips and requesting access.

She opened for him and moaned when he thrust his tongue into her mouth.

"Zeke! Nina! You here?" Montgomery's voice came from downstairs.

Zeke pulled back but didn't let go of Nina. He exhaled slowly, staring into her eyes. "Your brother's timing sucks."

Nina giggled. "Yes, it does."

"You guys up?" Montgomery called, his footsteps on the stairs.

"You go see him. I need a minute," Zeke said, pushing her toward the door.

"Why me? He's your best friend."

Zeke gestured to the erection pressing against his shorts. The very obvious erection that Montgomery definitely would not miss.

"Oh," Nina said, her gaze locked on it.

His dick twitched. "Go. Now." Zeke laughed and pushed her closer to the door. "I'm going to take a shower."

"Tease," she whispered.

Zeke chuckled and closed himself in the bathroom. He listened at the door for her and Montgomery to leave, a smile on his face.

"Monty. What are you doing here?" Nina asked as she opened the bedroom door.

Monty looked her up and down, then looked past her into the bedroom. "Did you both sleep in there?"

Nina nodded. "After yesterday... I didn't want to be alone."

Monty stared at the disheveled bed and even more disheveled Nina.

She waited for him to call her on it. She didn't lie, she just didn't tell the full truth. That if he'd shown up an hour later, she would have known what it was like for a man to truly want her.

Monty pulled her into his arms and hugged her tight. "As long as you're feeling better."

Nina nodded against his chest. "I am. Thanks for having dinner with me last night. Do you guys have to work today?"

Monty shook his head. "Nope. I thought maybe we could do something together."

"Just you and me?" Nina asked.

"I was thinking all three of us, but if you're ready to be away from Zeke, we can get out of here."

Nina laughed softly and shook her head. "No, I'm good with all three of us. But we just got up. He was about to get in the shower and I was still half-asleep when I heard your voice."

"That's why it took you so long to answer." Monty nodded as if it all made sense.

And not that she was wrapped around his best friend and ready to reclaim sex for herself. "Yep."

Monty shook his head. "You were always a pain in the ass in the morning."

"Glad some things haven't changed. Let's get food. Do you know how to cook?"

"Not as well as Zeke, but I can fix coffee and bagels."

Nina snorted. "Well, it's more than I know how to do, so I can't say too much."

"You'll learn, sis. And you'll get your life back. We will always be here for you."

"That's the best news ever," Nina said.

Nina closed the bedroom door so Zeke had privacy when he was getting dressed, and Monty led the way down the stairs.

Monty was clearly comfortable in Zeke's house, making coffee without having to search for it. When that was going, Monty grabbed eggs and bacon from the fridge and popped a bagel in the toaster.

Nina watched him move around the kitchen and knew Monty was selling his skills short. He cracked six eggs into a pan and seasoned them before putting bacon on a cookie sheet and sliding it into the oven.

"You liar. You know how to cook," Nina said.

Monty flashed her a grin. "I used to cook for us before... Don't you remember?"

Nina had forgotten a lot about her life before. Self-preservation required it. But with his reminder, she saw the breakfast-for-dinner nights Monty would lead. "I'd forgotten about that. Waffles and eggs and bacon."

"Every Saturday night," Monty said.

"We should do that again."

Monty looked at her and smiled. He nodded. "Good idea."

"What's a good idea?" Zeke asked, appearing on the stairs with wet hair, wearing a clean gray tee and dark jeans. His tattoos were on display, decorating his skin and tempting her in a way she hadn't allowed herself to be before she knew she wasn't the only one fighting it.

"Breakfast nights on Saturday night," Monty answered without turning around.

"That is a good idea," Zeke said, walking over to Nina. "Stop staring or I'll need another shower," he whispered so only she could hear.

Nina smirked at him and let herself have one more good look.

"So what's up, Mont? It's early for you to be here," Zeke said, moving away from Nina.

She chuckled to herself and decided spending the day with Zeke and Monty was going to be fun. So much fun.

8

<hr>

ZEKE'S LEG BOUNCED ALL THE WAY THROUGH BREAKFAST WITH Montgomery and Nina. Where was the line? What did he have to share with his best friend? Did he have to share?

Zeke never told Montgomery he was in love with Nina. She was seventeen when she went missing. It wasn't okay for him to want her, so he locked all those feelings up and stuffed them in a box deep inside. A box he never opened.

But the lid was off, and Zeke wasn't sure how long he could keep his feelings from his friend.

"I'm going to shower, if we have time for that?" Nina said, looking at Montgomery with a question on her face.

Montgomery chuckled and nodded. He wasn't giving her any indication of where they were going or what they were doing. Which meant Zeke didn't know either.

"We have no schedule. Take your time," Montgomery told Nina.

Nina sighed like she couldn't believe she had to put up with him, but the light in her eyes said she was happy to be there. Happy to have Mont's insufferable ass right there. "Fine, don't tell me anything."

Mont chuckled and reached for her, pulling her in for a tight hug.

Zeke wanted to leave. He was such an asshole. Mont had missed twelve years with Nina, and instead of giving them space and time alone, Zeke was always there.

Montgomery released Nina, and both men watched as she ascended the stairs. When the bedroom door closed, Montgomery let out a long sigh.

"You okay?" Zeke asked.

Montgomery turned to him and nodded. "She said she didn't want to sleep alone last night. That the day took a lot out of her."

Zeke nodded. It was the truth, but there was so much more that he should confess.

"Thank you," Mont breathed. "Thank you for being here for her. For all of this. For letting her invade your space and take over your life."

Gene's meow called out the lie, but Zeke ignored the brat and kept his gaze on Mont's. "I'd do anything for her."

Montgomery nodded. "I know. And I appreciate it."

Zeke nodded, knowing that was the best he could hope for at the moment. He wanted to tell Mont everything, to confess that he was wrapped up in Nina when Mont let himself in, but he wasn't sure how it would go. He wasn't sure Mont would be okay with it.

Because Zeke wasn't sure if he was. Nina deserved better than him. She deserved the world. A nice guy who would love her and treat her like the precious doll she was. Zeke was rough. He filled his skin with tattoos and filled his bed with women he never wanted to see again. He wasn't built for permanence.

Because he never had Nina.

He knew that was the truth, but he also knew he wasn't a

good bet. If he'd had a sister, he wouldn't want her with someone like him.

But Zeke wasn't strong enough to deny himself of a taste of Nina.

"You got any ideas for today?" Montgomery asked as they cleaned up the kitchen.

Zeke snorted. "I thought you had a plan."

Mont laughed. "Nope. Just wanted to spend time with her. Figured it might be good for her to get out of here."

"Think she's ready for that? Think it's safe?"

Montgomery shook his head, running a hand over his head. "I don't know, man. I don't want her to be afraid of everything, but is she ready? You're spending more time with her than I am. What do you think?"

Zeke thought about the stories Nina had told the day before. About being held captive. About the things Gwendolyn Lennox did to her and the others.

Zeke ached to keep her hidden. To lock her up in his bedroom and forget the outside world for a year or two. To keep her sated and safe. But that made him no better than Gwendolyn. Locking her up and throwing away the key was the same thing Nina had been through. He couldn't do it.

"I don't know if she'll ever be ready," Zeke answered honestly.

"That's what I'm afraid of." Mont sounded defeated, like he'd already failed Nina.

They both did. They stopped looking for her. They accepted the reports from the police that she was gone. They listened to the statistics. They assumed she was dead.

They were wrong, but she paid the price for their faith in the people who should have found her. No one knew where Nina went that night. They had no leads.

Which Zeke wondered now if it was intentional. Gwendolyn had cops in her pocket for years. Her and her father before her. Why had they never assumed someone was pulling the strings and keeping Nina's whereabouts a secret?

"Maybe we should just stay here," Montgomery said. His sigh was one of sadness and regret.

"No. I have an idea."

"What is it?" Montgomery asked.

"Carousel park."

A smile lifted Montgomery's lips into a smile Zeke hadn't seen in years. Childhood memories and joy flicked across Mont's face, his nod a solid agreement. "That's perfect. She always loved carousels. How did you remember that?"

"I remember everything about her," Zeke said honestly.

Montgomery looked at him, but the door opened upstairs and both men watched Nina return to the living room.

Zeke's mouth went dry when he saw her. She wore another of the outfits he bought her the day before. Jean shorts ended at mid-thigh and hugged her thick legs. Smooth, creamy skin led to bright pink socks he ached to pull off her feet inch-by-inch.

Zeke let his gaze travel back up her legs and over her shorts to a pink top that matched the socks and draped around her curves in loose, flowing fabric that did nothing to calm his raging desire.

"Cute," Mont said, reaching for her and pulling her against his side.

Zeke could only grunt. He shifted once the two of them walked past him, hoping Montgomery didn't notice the erection Zeke was sure he'd have all damn day.

Fuck.

NINA PEPPERED them with questions about where they were going while Zeke drove. He needed space between him and Nina, and told Mont to sit with her.

It didn't help. Her scent filled his SUV, blending with his own. She'd used the same shampoo as him, and every whiff of his own scent made him think of her. Of how it would smell differently on her when he pressed his nose to her neck. How it would taste when he kissed her skin.

He cleared his throat and reminded himself they were going to a family place. A place where he'd scare all the kids with his tattoos and gruff appearance, but would scare the parents if he was walking around with a hard-on pointing at their kids.

By the time they made the forty-five minute drive to Olcott, Zeke had himself under control. He parked a few blocks from the Olcott Beach Carousel Park, close to the shores of Lake Ontario.

Nina got out of the SUV and looked around. "Where are we?"

Montgomery chuckled. "His idea." He jerked his head toward Zeke. "Carousel Park."

Nina's mouth dropped open in a surprised O, and her eyes filled with tears.

"We don't have to," Zeke hurried to say. "We can go somewhere else."

Nina threw her arms around his neck and hugged him close. "Thank you," she whispered.

Zeke closed his eyes and held her. He still expected her to be gone when he opened his eyes, but she wasn't. She was real. And she was there. "You're welcome."

Montgomery smiled as he watched them.

When Zeke caught Mont, he eased back from Nina and smiled at her. "Do you want to go ride?"

"Yes," Nina said, taking a hand from each man. She tugged them to her sides, then looped her hands over each one's elbow.

The three of them walked down the sidewalk as one, taking their time as they followed families toward the park. The soft music reached them, and Nina squeezed her hands on both their elbows.

Nina gasped when she saw the building, windows thrown open, that housed the vintage carousel. She tugged both of them forward, urging them to move faster.

Zeke couldn't help his smile at her delight. She was like a kid again, enjoying something that should have been a simple pleasure. Something everyone should have been able to enjoy whenever they wanted.

Montgomery handed over a dollar to cover their rides, getting a quarter back. The three of them found their way onto the carousel. Nina debated between a black horse with a wide open mouth and a pink mane and a beige horse with a lowered head and a brown mane.

"We'll take another ride," Montgomery told her, allowing her to pick the black horse before the ride started.

Montgomery rode the horse next to Nina, and Zeke sat on a sled behind them. He stared at brother and sister, hoping they had many more good memories ahead of them.

The ride ended and Nina swung her leg to get off the horse, nearly stepping off the edge of the carousel. Zeke was right there to catch her, saving her from a twisted ankle or worse.

"Are you okay?" he asked, looking her over closely.

Nina nodded. "Always my hero."

Zeke righted her, setting her away from him with a tight

smile. He was no one's hero. He'd failed more times than he could count, especially when it came to Nina.

Zeke led the way off the carousel, his skin feeling too tight and his neck tensing with every step he took. Twelve years of failing her couldn't be erased with one save. It couldn't ever be erased. And he needed to remember that.

Montgomery and Nina raced to get back in line for another ride, and Zeke followed, knowing he wouldn't leave them alone. He and Montgomery were both checking the crowd constantly, watching for any potential threat.

Zeke doubted Gwendolyn Lennox would be dumb enough to show her face, but he knew she wasn't operating alone. She had an army. One who would do anything for her. Including take Nina out surrounded by families and kids, if that was what Gwendolyn ordered.

Their second ride around the carousel was less eventful, with Nina not losing her balance. After, they walked around the park, watching the kids and families play and laugh and enjoy the day.

"I was really hoping I'd have some nieces or nephews to meet," Nina said to Montgomery. "You never had anyone?"

Montgomery shook his head. His eyes were shaded by his glasses, hiding the truth from Nina. A truth Zeke knew as well as his own. Montgomery never forgave himself for letting Nina disappear. He never thought he was worthy of happiness when his sister didn't get to have hers.

"Never found the right one."

"You and Berkeley—"

"No," Montgomery said before Nina could finish her question. "There's nothing going on."

Nina looked up at her brother with a look that said she didn't believe him.

Zeke wondered what he missed. Berkeley was amazing,

but she was their office manager. She kept everything together and going. Montgomery never said anything about her that didn't have to do with work.

But Nina saw something that made her ask. Maybe it was because she was the only woman Nina saw Montgomery around. That had to be it.

"There's no one else. Never has been. I was in the military, then I started Rose Protection Agency, and I never slowed down to think about having a family or anything." Montgomery's words were ones Zeke had told himself for years, but there was something underneath, something Zeke felt but had never been able to name.

Nina. For Zeke, it was loving Nina. But it was there for Montgomery, too.

"Maybe one day," Nina said.

"Always the optimist," Montgomery replied.

"I have to be. I had to be. Otherwise, I never would have survived." Nina's words were a reminder of why they were there. Why they were reliving childhood memories and happier times.

"How about the beach?" Zeke asked before he could stop himself.

"Beach?" Nina asked, turning delighted eyes to him.

Zeke nodded. "There's one at the end of the street. If you're up for it."

Nina's eyes brightened even more. "Yes. I haven't been to a beach in forever."

"Let's go," Montgomery said.

Nina hurried ahead of them when she saw the sand at the bottom of the stairs. Montgomery raced to keep up with her, and Zeke realized the error of his suggestion.

They were exposed. Anyone on a boat would have a

clear shot at them. And being at the bottom of the stairs meant someone could get the high ground on them.

Zeke watched behind them as they moved closer to the sand. His anxiety and anticipation ramped up, all thoughts focused on keeping Nina safe at all costs.

Montgomery's head swung side-to-side as he followed Nina out onto the sand. But Nina was oblivious to it all. She threw her arms up, letting the warm breeze dance over her skin and lift the edges of her loose top, exposing a far-too-tantalizing strip of creamy skin that Zeke wanted to taste. She spun in a circle, laughing like she'd never been so happy in her life, and regret punched Zeke in the gut.

She should have had this all along.

Zeke stared at her and fell more in love with her every second she enjoyed something so simple as fresh air on her face. Her laughter tugged at a part of him that was so lost and forgotten he felt tears fill his eyes.

She was back. She was okay. She was beaten and broken and would never be the same, but she was alive. She was strong. So much stronger than he'd ever given her credit for. She would find her way forward.

And Zeke was honored to be there for it.

Gwendolyn Lennox snarled at the video on her phone. Nina was alive. She was happy. The bitch got away and had the fucking nerve to act like everything was fine.

Gwendolyn threw the phone across the room and watched it smash against the wall. The screen flickered, then went dark, the view of Nina disappearing.

"What do you want us to do?" Fernando asked.

Gwendolyn looked at the man she trusted as much as

any other. It was a risk to trust him, but she had no choice. Nina took more from her than the fucking agent who survived. "I don't know."

Fernando's look of surprise was quickly erased, but Gwendolyn saw it cross his face.

"You don't agree?"

Fernando shook his head. "I'm not used to you not knowing."

Gwendolyn stared at the broken phone. It had been years since she debated her actions. Since the last time she lived in the house where she was currently staying. The only house the FBI didn't raid after Nina's escape and confession.

She told them everything. The houses where they would stay. The women Gwendolyn had in her possession. The way they would move product around and who was involved that shouldn't have been, according to the law.

Two nights and two raids on the company. First the agent, then her sister. Gwendolyn's organization was crumbling around her, and it was all because of Nina Rose.

Death was too good for the sister who betrayed Gwendolyn. Especially death by one of her people. This was personal. And Gwendolyn didn't hand off personal tasks.

"She needs to die," Fernando said.

"I know," Gwendolyn snapped. "But I want to see the life fade from her eyes. After I take what matters most to her."

Fernando's grin was one of approval. But Gwendolyn didn't need approval. She'd fought her way to the top, taking what she wanted on her way up.

Being back where she started was a stark reminder of what she'd done to get to the top. Gwendolyn didn't like hiding out. She wasn't ashamed. She wouldn't hide for long. Revenge would be hers.

No one ever thought she was good enough. *Weak* and

useless were the words thrown at her as a teenager. But she proved her father wrong when she drew a knife across his throat.

After telling him his chosen heir was dead. By her hand.

Gwendolyn was not afraid to do the dirty work. It was required if she was going to prove what she could do. It was what put her on top of the family business. What allowed her to claim her rightful place.

You were never good enough.

Gwendolyn screamed, reacting to her father's voice as though he were actually there instead of a ghost who taunted her.

Fernando's gun was out and scanning the room instantly, carefully avoiding Gwendolyn. "What's wrong? What happened?"

"Nothing," Gwendolyn growled. "Put that away before you kill me."

Fernando looked around the room once more before holstering his gun. "We know where she is. Do you want us to get her?"

Gwendolyn shook her head. "No. I want her to get comfortable. To think I'm going to let her live. Keep operating as best we can."

"People are scared. The FBI is breathing down our necks."

Gwendolyn glared at him, getting in his face.

He didn't back down or flinch, which was why she let him live.

"The FBI will forget all about us soon enough. We operate as though they're not there. And if someone gets caught, they know what to do."

Fernando nodded. "Everyone knows. They won't get caught."

"Good. Bring me another phone."

Fernando nodded again. "Of course. Is there anything else you need?"

Gwendolyn looked around the room. "A new bed. And another security check."

"On it."

Fernando left, and Gwendolyn looked around the room again. She would rise again. With or without Nina by her side.

9

NINA SMILED AS SHE WALKED INTO ZEKE'S HOUSE WITH Monty and Zeke right behind her. It was the perfect day. A day for her to remember who she was. For her to feel like she wasn't so broken anymore.

Nina turned to face her protectors. "That was amazing. Thank you both for taking me there."

Monty shook his head and pointed at Zeke. "It was all him. I was clueless, but he came up with it. Said he remembered you liked carousels."

"I did. I do. Thank you." Nina's gaze slammed into Zeke's. The look in his eyes stole her breath and made her eager for her brother to get the hell out so she could figure out what that expression meant.

Zeke had been staring at her all day with different looks, but the latest one sent a shiver up her spine. A good kind of shiver. The kind of shiver that said the man giving her the look was thinking all kinds of sexy thoughts that involved her.

Nina never found those looks all that appealing. She had a purpose for Gwendolyn, and that purpose was to make men want her. Without that trap, that requirement, being desirable felt foreign and awkward to Nina. She didn't know how to appeal to a man.

But with Zeke, it wasn't so challenging.

"You guys up for dinner?" Monty asked, heading to the kitchen.

They'd stopped at a diner after the beach, then wandered around for a while and went back to the carousel for a few more rides before they headed home.

Home. Nina smiled at the word. She hadn't had that in so long. It was nice to think Zeke's house, and Monty's, could be that for her.

Temporarily, of course. Zeke would get tired of her being in his space, and Monty would want his life back, too. She would have to be on her own at some point, but not yet.

"I'm up for anything," Zeke said, surprising Nina.

She thought for sure he'd be ready to kick Monty out so they could be alone together. Maybe she read the day, and all his looks, wrong.

"Do you have anything good in here?" Monty asked, searching Zeke's freezer.

"Not much. I haven't gotten to the store in a few days."

Nina flushed with guilt. Zeke was putting his life on hold for her, to the point he didn't have food.

"I have some chicken and a few bags of vegetables. Let me go grab some stuff. I'll be right back," Monty said, already heading for the door.

"Thanks, man," Zeke said, waving as Monty left.

Nina opened her mouth to say something to Zeke, but he turned to her with one of those looks that made her mouth dry, and other parts of her not even close to dry.

"I don't know where the lines are here. I don't know how I'm supposed to act around you when he's here. What I do know is I'm barely keeping my shit together right now and I can't wait until he leaves so I can kiss you again."

Nina's smile was immediate and genuine. "I was starting to worry you wanted him as a buffer."

Zeke's head shook slowly, his gaze running over her body just as slowly. "No."

Nina breathed a husky sound, a sound she was sure she'd never made before in her life.

"I can't wait to hear what sounds you make when I get my hands on you."

Nina moaned and clenched her thighs together.

The front door opened before she could say anything. Monty held up a package of chicken and a frozen bag of mixed vegetables. "Dinner."

Nina smiled at her brother, wondering how quickly she could get him to leave.

Zeke made a noise in the back of his throat that was part laugh and part growl and all sexy. "Thanks, Mont. We wouldn't have known what to do without you."

Monty flipped Zeke off. "You're such an ass."

Zeke grinned. "Yep."

Monty chuckled, and Nina knew it wasn't the first time the two of them had done something similar.

Their friendship was on display every minute she spent with them. Living next door to each other. Working together. Being comfortable in each other's spaces, to the point where they had keys to each other's homes. They were brothers in every sense. Family.

And she was threatening that. Her presence was threatening that. The way she wanted Zeke was threatening that.

"I'll be right back," she whispered, heading toward the stairs.

Both men mumbled something as she walked up the stairs, neither paying much attention to her.

Nina made it into Zeke's bedroom and to the bathroom, closing and locking the door behind her. She'd spent years being watched every minute of the day and having the option to walk away and be alone was odd. Like she was doing something wrong.

Was she doing something wrong with Zeke? The way he touched her that morning made it seem as though he wasn't feeling pressured into it. He wanted her just as much as she wanted him. She could feel it in his touch and see it in the way he looked at her. He even said it just a few minutes earlier downstairs.

But she couldn't shake that she was a danger to more than just his safety.

If Gwendolyn found out where Nina was, she'd kill Zeke without a second thought. She'd kill Montgomery, too. She'd kill anyone in her path to get what she wanted.

Did she want Nina back? Did she care that she left?

A sharp pang had her clutching her chest. Tears flooded her eyes.

Nina wanted Gwendolyn to miss her. To want her back.

A tear rolled down her cheek, and Nina let it fall. She hated Gwendolyn. But Gwendolyn was the only person Nina had for twelve years. She was the one Gwendolyn turned to. What did it mean if she was dismissed without a thought?

Nina hated that she wondered. She hated that Gwendolyn still had power over her. Power that kept her tied to the woman who ruined her life.

Nina squeezed her eyes shut and pushed out the tears. She brought the anger to the front and reminded herself of the abuse. Nina touched her throat, the sting of her bruises making her gasp.

Gwendolyn did that. Without a care in the world for Nina. Gwendolyn would have killed her if she didn't have a reason to keep Nina around. It happened often.

There was no love there. Gwendolyn didn't know how to love. She knew how to hate, and that was the lesson Nina needed to hold on to. She would need it if she ever faced Gwendolyn again.

Because if she was ever in the same room as Gwendolyn again, they wouldn't both walk out. Nina had to make sure of that.

"You think she's okay?" Zeke asked Montgomery when Nina rushed up the stairs.

"Nina? Yeah, why?" Montgomery continued cutting up the chicken, oblivious to his sister's emotions.

"She was upset. She ran out of here like she used to when we would talk about girls when we were younger."

Montgomery snorted. "She was jealous because she wasn't getting dates and we were talking about girls we were screwing. She's not a kid anymore. Fuck." Montgomery sobered with his last thought, running a hand over his face. "I can't believe it's been twelve years."

Zeke nodded. "Yeah."

Montgomery looked at the stairs. "Should I go talk to her?"

Zeke shrugged. "I have no idea."

"I hate this. She feels like a stranger, but she's not. She's still Nina, but she's not the Nina we remember."

"There are some things that haven't changed," Zeke said.

Montgomery chuckled. "Yeah. She still loves carousels. And the beach. And food. Some of the women are so thin... Some of them were so sick when we found them, we weren't sure they would survive."

"But they are. We're taking care of them, and they're going to get the help they need. Far away from Gwendolyn Lennox."

"What are you talking about?" Nina asked, her voice shaky and scared.

Zeke and Montgomery turned to face her together. Zeke hadn't heard her come down the stairs, and judging by Mont's face, he didn't either.

Mont exchanged a look with Zeke, but Zeke didn't know what they should tell her either.

"Some of them are okay? They're alive?" Nina asked.

Zeke nodded.

"And you're protecting them?" she asked Montgomery.

Mont inhaled and moved toward her. He guided her to the couch, leaving Zeke to finish dinner.

Zeke picked up the knife and drew it through the piece of chicken as Montgomery explained what was going on to Nina.

"We agreed to help out with some of the women who were in the first house that was raided. Some went to rehab, but some were okay without it. But all the women are being watched."

"By your company?"

"Not all, but some, yes."

"Why didn't you tell me? Can I see them?" Nina's voice was small with hurt.

Zeke looked at the siblings on his couch, a sight he never dreamed he'd get to witness. Even with the pain in her voice, he knew they made the right decision to keep the truth from Nina.

"We have to keep them safe. It's our job to make sure Gwendolyn can't get to them. Or any of her people."

Nina jumped to her feet. "And you think I could be one of her spies? That I came here to get information from you to bring back to her? That I would betray my own brother, my family, for her?"

"No, I never thought that. Until you just asked that question, it was never a consideration for me."

"But now it is." Nina scoffed. "How could you Monty? How could you think that of me?"

"I don't," Montgomery said calmly. "But it's my job to keep you safe, too."

"What... what do you mean?"

"What you told Lorelei yesterday... Everything you shared was very clinical. You told her about locations and things you witnessed, but you didn't talk much about what you'd been through. About the things you had to do."

"You want to know?" she cried, turning on him.

Zeke abandoned his knife and moved toward the edge of the kitchen in case he needed to step in.

Mont shook his head, a signal for Zeke to stand down, but Zeke wasn't returning to his task until he knew things were okay.

"I only want to know what you want to tell me," Mont said to Nina.

Nina laughed mirthlessly. "You want to know about getting drugged and raped? About the times when I couldn't even clean up between men? Or maybe about the infections I got or the time I was forced into stirrups for an abortion? You want to know about all the joyful experiences I had?"

Zeke's gut twisted with every word. His hands tightened into fists. He was going to vomit.

"Fuck," Montgomery whispered.

Nina slashed her hand across her cheek to remove her tears.

Zeke wanted to go to her, to pull her into his arms and hold her until it was all a distant memory. Until Gwendolyn and every man who dared touch Nina were dead. Until Nina was healed forever.

"Is that what you wanted to know, big brother? Does that convince you that I'm not going back to her? That I'm not spying on you for her? Because she'd already be dead if she had a weapon in her bedroom. The night I left, I promised myself I'd kill her. I promised myself she wouldn't live to hurt others."

"Nina." Montgomery stood and reached for her, but she spun away from him.

"Don't. Just... don't. If you don't trust me, then I shouldn't be here." Nina moved toward the door, but Zeke was faster.

He blocked her escape, crossing his arms and scowling at her.

"Please move."

"You know I can't do that, Nina. I'm not letting you go."

"You know who you sound like, right?" she snarled.

Zeke took the blow. It was a good hit, intended to get him to move. He swallowed the pain and stared her down. "I love you, Nina Marie Rose. So does your brother. We are here to keep you safe. And that's what we're going to do. Even if we're keeping you safe from yourself."

"You two haven't changed!" She threw her hands up and tossed a glare at Zeke before throwing one at her brother. "You think you know what's best for me. You lie to me, then tell me it's for my own good. You refuse to let me do what I think is right, then say it's to keep me safe."

Zeke stepped forward, getting closer to Nina. "No. Right now, this isn't for your own good. It's for mine because the last time you walked out of a house past me, the last time every instinct of mine said not to let you go, I let you go. And I lost a dozen years with you, Nina. I've hated myself for that choice, and I still hate myself. Your confession about what you've been through only reminds me that I fucked up. That I am the reason you went through all of that. It tells me that if I move to the side and let you walk away, I'll never see this beautiful face of yours. Not alive. The thought of finding your dead body haunted me for twelve years. I've seen you in my nightmares more times than I can count. And having you here and letting you hate me is better. It will always be better. So you can hate me. You can refuse to ever speak to me again. But there's no fucking way I'm letting you out that damn door ever again. So sit your ass down and get the hell over it."

"Zeke," Nina whispered. She lifted her hand to his cheek.

He nuzzled against her. "Please don't leave."

Nina nodded. "Okay."

"Oh, thank God," Montgomery breathed from the living room.

Zeke swallowed roughly. He'd forgotten about Montgomery. All the things he said to Nina... He meant every word, but he didn't mean to say it all in front of Montgomery.

Nina let her hand fall from Zeke's jaw and took a step back. She held his gaze for another moment, then turned to join her brother in the living room again.

Zeke waited a minute, then resumed his duties in the

kitchen. The motions were repetitive and soothing with his emotions raw and exposed, like he'd peeled his skin off and had to live without the protection it provided.

Nina pleaded with Montgomery to let her see some of the women Rose Protection Agency was keeping safe. Montgomery's excuses were fading with Zeke's ability to keep himself under control. When his friend agreed to let Nina see one or two of the women, Zeke bit down on the inside of his lip until he tasted blood.

He wanted to keep her away from that world. Away from the others who'd been through what she went through. He wanted her safe.

"Hey, Mont. Watch this for a minute, will you?" Zeke called as he headed toward the garage.

"Yeah. You okay?"

"Just forgot something in the SUV. I'll be right back." Zeke left the house before either of them asked anything else.

Zeke wanted a minute. He needed it. He walked around the side of his SUV and opened the front door. He climbed in and closed the door, waiting until the interior lights faded to black once more.

Zeke pinched the bridge of his nose and let all his emotions leak out. Slowly. He couldn't lose it with Mont right on the other side of the wall, but he had to mourn for Nina. For the life that was stolen from her. The life she could have had if he'd been strong enough to say no to her.

Love made him weak back then. It made him unable to challenge her. She didn't walk all over him, he led her that way. He was young and foolish and thought giving her what she wanted was the way to get her to love him.

He learned that wasn't the case. It was never the case. Love meant being there for people no matter what. It meant being willing to sacrifice yourself for them. It meant putting them first, and knowing they would do the same for you.

Montgomery was the only person who'd ever done that for Zeke. His brother. His best friend. His boss.

And now they had Nina back. They would both do anything for her. But letting her go, knowing she wanted to, put a fear in Zeke that he couldn't shake. He had to make sure she didn't leave. She couldn't leave. He wouldn't survive if she left again.

Even if that did make him just as bad as Gwendolyn Lennox.

10

———————

Nina stared at the garage door until Zeke walked back inside. She didn't like him being out of her sight. Not seeing him for a few minutes. It made her itchy, like her skin was too tight. It made no sense.

When Zeke walked inside again, he kept his gaze down, hidden from her and Monty. Monty breezed past Zeke, returning to the living room where Nina sat. Monty didn't notice a thing, but Nina did.

She was more determined than ever to chase her brother out of the house and get Zeke alone. Something changed, and she needed to know what.

Monty kept up the conversation during dinner, sharing more stories about their past and telling Nina she missed nothing. She asked about the home they grew up in, the house where both their parents died.

"I sold it after he died," Monty said. "I couldn't stand going back there. Not after he lived there. I wasn't sure I wanted to be there after Mom died and you left, either, but all my memories of the house were bad ones. But the money, I can sell half the company to give you what you should have. I only got all of it because you were gone."

Nina shook her head as Monty spoke. "No. It's yours. I don't want anything from him."

"Sounds familiar," Zeke said with little humor in his voice.

"What do you mean?" Nina asked.

Zeke nodded at Monty, and Nina slid her gaze to her brother.

"I fought it for a long time. I didn't want his money. It felt tainted, like he was."

"What changed your mind?"

Monty smiled at Zeke and clapped his shoulder. "He did. Reminded me of one of the things we talked about all the time when we were serving."

The two men shared a moment that left Nina feeling separate. She was, and she would have been anyway, but all the moments they shared when she was gone were a reminder that she missed so much. "Are you going to tell me what it was?"

Monty smirked. "We protected sisters and mothers and wives and children when we served. We did our fair share of damage, but we believed we were doing the best thing, and every time we saved someone who'd been abused or harmed, we said we were saving another Nina. Someone else's most important person."

"Monty," Nina breathed.

Monty smiled at her, the emotion in his eyes warming her heart. "I love you, sis. I'm so damn happy you're back. And I'm sorry for making you think I would ever wonder which side you were on."

Nina grabbed his hand and squeezed tight. When they were kids, she made a game out of trying to hurt him when she squeezed his hand. She never did, but holding his hand brought back the memory and she squeezed as tight as she could.

Monty laughed. "Still think you can hurt me?"

Nina grinned and squeezed harder. "One day."

"I'll take it." Monty's tone was not talking about Nina squeezing his hand.

"I love you, big brother."

"I know. Thank you for coming back."

"I couldn't be happier that I am."

"Good." Monty pulled his hand from hers and picked up his plate. He patted her shoulder and hurried into the kitchen.

Nina watched as her brother put his dishes away and stared at the opposite wall for a minute, gathering himself and stuffing his emotions down.

Tears filled her eyes. She didn't like making him cry, but it was so damn good to know he cared. To know she wasn't as alone as she'd felt.

Nina's gaze drifted to Zeke and found him watching her. The look in his eyes was similar, but so very different. The same level of care was there, but there was more. Guilt, like he confessed to. Desire, anger, curiosity, and maybe more. More than Nina could handle at the moment.

"I'm going to head home. If you guys are okay." Monty walked back to where they sat on the couch and stood at the end, hands on his hips.

"Will we see you tomorrow?" Nina asked, getting up and wrapping her arms around his middle.

Monty hugged her tight and kissed the top of her head. "If you want to."

"Absolutely."

"Good. Then I'll see you guys in the morning."

"Not too early," Nina said with a groan.

Monty chuckled. "I'll try to remember."

Nina nodded against his chest and inhaled deeply. He didn't hate her. He hadn't forgotten her. He was still right there. Saving other people's sisters who needed help.

"Night, man," Zeke said, carrying his plate to the kitchen and putting it in the dishwasher.

"Night." Monty hugged Nina tight again, then released her and headed to the door.

Zeke followed Monty, and the two of them exchanged a few words Nina couldn't hear. She waited for Monty to leave and Zeke to close and lock the door.

The click of the lock still gave her a moment of panic, but she was able to handle it better than the first night. Especially when she looked up and saw the look on Zeke's face.

"Zeke?"

"I need to know you are okay. That you're not afraid of me. That everything you went through..."

Nina took a step toward him, but Zeke backed up.

"I... Do you trust me?"

"Yes," she breathed without hesitation. "Always, Zeke. I trust you more than anyone else on earth."

"I'm the reason you went through all of that. I could have stopped you. I should have stopped you."

"Zeke, don't," Nina said, stepping into his personal space and putting her hand over his mouth. "I can't have you blaming yourself. I was young and foolish. I made a mistake, trusted someone I shouldn't have. But I never once blamed you. From the sound of it, neither did Monty."

"I blamed myself. I still do. Jesus, Nina, what you told us..."

"I didn't want to do those things," she whispered, feeling ashamed for all of it.

"Angel, you don't have to explain yourself to me. You were captive there. And now you're captive here." Zeke took a step away from her again.

Nina swallowed roughly at the loss of him. "I was wrong to threaten that. I was wrong to say what I did. You're nothing like her."

"But I am, Nina. I will stop you from leaving. I will do whatever I have to if it means keeping you here. I don't want to, though. God, please don't make me."

Nina shook her head, the anguish on Zeke's face enough to make her heart clench. "I'm not leaving, Zeke. I over-reacted."

Zeke nodded, and Nina took a chance and moved forward again. She put her hand on his chest, and he tugged her in so tight she could barely breathe. One hand went into her hair, the other tight around her back. His lips landed on the top of her head, and he inhaled, like he was trying to pull her inside himself.

Nina held him like the lifeline he was. She couldn't make sense of how she felt with Zeke. Of the desire that slowly unfurled inside her as she breathed him in. Of the way a man who was clearly dangerous made her feel safe in a way she'd never known.

He hardened between them, and desire pulsed inside her. She kissed his chest, drawing small circles on his back. He inhaled sharply, his cock twitching against her stomach.

She licked his throat, and he growled, pulling back just enough to slam his lips down on hers. She gasped at the rough move, a flood of heat making her rub her thighs together. His tongue probed her mouth as his hand moved to cup her ass. He molded and squeezed, his fingers teasing her with his firm touch.

He pulled back with a curse, and she swayed without him there to hold her up.

"Zeke."

"Let me lock up the house. Don't lose that thought right there." He tapped her nose, then surged back at her, devouring her right where she stood and sending her brain out the window.

She pressed a hand to her lips and smiled as she watched him race through the house. He tossed the leftovers from dinner into the fridge without bothering to transfer them to a smaller container, and he dropped the rest of the dishes into the sink instead of the dishwasher.

"I thought you were a clean freak," Nina teased.

He looked at her over his shoulder, his gaze scolding her as it slid down her body. "There is something else I'm much more of a freak about than cleaning."

No one had ever bothered to speak to Nina like that. They were paying to fuck her. Romance wasn't necessary. But with Zeke, he wanted her to know he wanted her. Nina could feel it in his words and his actions.

He checked the back door, then the front door, then the garage, then flipped all the lights off downstairs.

The sudden plunge into darkness took her by surprise. She gasped without thought, fear grabbing her throat and squeezing.

"Fuck," Zeke snarled.

A light came on, momentarily blinding Nina. "I'm sorry."

"Don't you ever apologize to me," Zeke said. "Ever. I should have expected that."

Nina shook her head, willing the fear to go away. "You didn't know."

"Have you thought about therapy?" Zeke asked softly.

Nina shook her head again. "No one can possibly understand what I've been through. I don't think telling everything to some highly educated person who's never known struggle is going to make me feel better about what I've been through."

"Maybe not, but if you find the right therapist, they can be worth their weight in gold."

"Have you been to therapy?" Nina asked skeptically.

"I have." Zeke nodded. "I go still."

"Why?"

He didn't answer, just stared at her.

"Because of me?"

Zeke swallowed hard and nodded.

"It wasn't your fault."

He shrugged. "Still work to do to accept that."

"I wish I could take that guilt from you."

"I wish I could take everything from you." He exhaled, as if he hadn't meant to say the words. "I apologize. That's not fair of me."

"I know what you mean, though. There are times I wish I didn't remember."

Zeke nodded as though he understood. He probably did. "Let's turn on the light on the stairs."

Nina nodded as Zeke flipped the switch that illuminated the stairs. She stayed at the bottom while he turned off the other lights, then joined her. Nina started up the stairs, but Zeke grabbed her hand.

"I will never pressure you or force you to do anything. You're in charge here. Always. Everything is up to you."

Nina nodded, feeling self-conscious about the power he

was handing over to her. She'd never been in charge. She didn't know how to be in charge. She wasn't sure if she would like it.

"I don't…"

"You say no, I stop. No matter what. I promise you, Nina. I don't want you to ever worry about me doing anything you don't want. Whether it's making you coffee in the morning or making you come at night, you call the shots."

His dirty words had her trembling. "I want you, Zeke. I'm going to try."

He shook his head. "No, angel. You're not going to try. We're going slow. If you have any doubts, we're not even going to start anything."

"But—"

"I'm not going anywhere, Nina. I'll be here waiting for you as long as you need me to wait. As long as you want me to wait. I promise you that."

She swallowed past her dry throat at the vehemence of his words and the desire in his gaze. She wasn't sure how she got so lucky, but she was not going to fight it.

"Let's go upstairs. You first. I'm going to stare at your ass."

Nina barked a laugh at his blatant admission. She added a little sway to her walk, and he groaned.

"I'm going to enjoy when I get my hands on you, Nina."

"So am I."

Zeke growled, then caught up to her on the landing outside his bedroom door. He pressed her against the wall, letting her feel the way she affected him. He tugged on her ear with his teeth, and she felt an answering tug between her thighs.

"Zeke."

"Slow, angel."

"Please."

He slid his arm around her waist and held her tightly against his body, walking them into the bedroom and kicking the door closed behind them. He walked to the bathroom and turned the light on, then led her to the bed.

"I want you to know exactly who is here with you. I need you to know it's me." Zeke's voice was strained.

Nina cupped his jaw and pushed him to sit on the bed. She crawled on top of him, straddling him and lowering herself down until she cradled his erection between her thighs. "I want you, Zeke. I want all of you. I want to know sex isn't just an act, but it's something between people who care about each other. It can be beautiful and fun and more than a requirement."

"I wish I'd been able to teach you all those things, Nina. I wish I'd been the one to give you your first time."

Nina gasped. "You were... I was... I always wished it had been you."

"Me, too, angel. I wanted you so badly. That was part of why I let you go that night. I couldn't say no to you."

"Don't say it now, Zeke. Please. Show me what would have happened if I'd never disappeared."

ZEKE GROWLED and wrapped her tight in his arms. He knew being with her was a gift. A gift he never thought he'd ever have. He was an asshole for claiming her when she was still scared of everything, but he wasn't strong enough to say no to her.

Again.

He didn't think he ever would be. All the other women he'd ever known were easy enough to forget. One night, maybe two, and he was ready to get rid of them. He hadn't even gotten inside Nina and knew it wouldn't be enough. It would never be enough.

Nina rocked on his lap, a motion so subtle Zeke didn't think she realized she was doing it. He encouraged her movement with a hand on her hip, which had the opposite effect and stalled her.

"Keep going," he whispered against her lips. "I want to know what you like."

She shook her head. "I don't know. I... It was never up to me."

"Now it is. Your body did it for a reason. Keep going, Nina."

"Will you..."

"Anything, sweetheart. What do you need me to do?"

"Will you help me?"

"In what way?"

She shrugged. "I don't know. I don't know what feels good."

"Come here," Zeke whispered, bringing her lips back to his. He teased her mouth opened and delved inside, tasting her sweetness. He kissed her softly, then kissed her hard. He kissed her with a hand on her waist, then with his hand in her hair. He kissed her every way he could think of until her hips shifted once more.

Her body softened in his arms, her nervousness fading as her body took over. He slid one hand to her thigh, then squeezed gently when her hips faltered. He growled against her lips and filled her mouth with his tongue. His other hand cupped the back of her head, tilting it to suit his needs, and feeling her go liquid again.

She rocked and shifted, her pace speeding up as frustration and desire poured from her.

Zeke tore his lips from hers and trailed his tongue down

her throat. He sucked his way back up, nibbling on her ear. "Are you going to come for me, Nina? Are you going to let go and moan my name?"

"Yes," she whispered, her voice husky and muffled.

"What's my name, Nina?"

"Zeke."

"Yes, angel. I love hearing you whisper my name. Hearing your breath falter." He thrust up against her, and she gasped. "Oh, yeah, just like that."

"Zeke."

"Yeah, Nina?"

"Do that... More."

Zeke cupped both her hips, holding her head in place with his teeth on her ear. He dipped his tongue into her ear, and she moaned again.

He urged her to go faster, dragging her away, then slamming her body against his as he rose up and met her in the middle.

"Zeke," she exhaled, pleasure taking hold. "Oh, shit. Yes."

"Come for me, Nina. I'm right here."

"Zeke," she whimpered.

If she were any other woman, they'd both be naked and there would be no frustration. Zeke didn't hold back when he had a woman in his bed. But with Nina, with Nina... Fuck, he was holding everything back. Getting her naked would send him over the damn edge. Getting his hands on her would make him lose his mind. Getting her to come was going to send him straight to fucking hell.

But he would enjoy every damn second of the trip.

"I can't," she cried. She groaned like she was in pain, and he brought both his hands to her cheeks.

"Look at me, Nina."

She fought him but relented when he didn't give up.

"What are you feeling right now?"

"Frustrated."

"Do you want me to touch you, Nina? Do you want me to slide my fingers all over your beautiful body and make you come?"

"Zeke."

"I need you to say yes, angel. I'm not going to—"

"Yes. Please, Zeke. Yes."

Zeke inhaled her, drawing her to him for a punishing kiss that left him panting and her writhing in his lap. Her shorts were just short enough to allow him access without needing her to take them off, and he eased his hand between her thighs.

Zeke saw stars when he touched her soaked flesh. His cock demanded the same attention, but all Zeke cared about was Nina.

"Nina," he breathed into her mouth.

"Yes."

He pushed a finger inside her, and she clamped down around the digit. It wasn't enough. He needed all of her. To move and look and touch all of her.

But he didn't dare take that from her. Not yet.

He pushed her panties to the side and slicked his thumb over her clit.

She gasped, then moaned loudly.

"You're so wet, Nina. You're ready to come, aren't you?"

"Zeke."

"Yeah, Nina, say my name. I'm here with you. I'm not going anywhere. Come for me, Nina."

"Oh, yes. Zeke," she whispered. She rode his hand, forgetting all about her earlier discomfort. "Zeke."

"Yes, Nina. Let go for me. You're so fucking beautiful. So amazing. So damn strong. This is all you, Nina. All you."

"Zeke. You. For you."

"No, Nina, this is for you. I'm honored to be the one to help you get there, but this is for you. This wet pussy is all you. You taking what you need. You loving this. You coming with me. Come, Nina. Come for me."

"Zeke!" Her cry was louder than anything else, her body shaking with the power of her orgasm. She rocked against his hand, not letting up as she flooded his palm.

Zeke curled his fingers deep inside her and triggered another orgasm, one she wasn't expecting. She screamed again, soaking his hand and surprising him. His vision darkened at the edges and his balls tightened. He was right there with her, but managed to choke it back.

"Zeke," she breathed.

"I'm right here, Nina. Right here."

"I wish you'd been my first."

He kissed her shoulder and nodded. "Me, too, angel."

Hopefully, I'll be your last.

Zeke smiled at the thought. He wouldn't dare voice it, but Nina Rose was everything for him, and if he didn't know it before, getting his hands on her was all the proof he needed. Because he was right. One taste was nowhere near enough of her. And it never would be.

11

Nina hugged Zeke tight, coming down from the high he sent her on. A high she didn't know was possible. A high she'd never imagined.

She buried her face in his shoulder and tried to hide the reaction she was having. The pure joy that filled her brought tears to her eyes and a flood of emotion to the rest of her. Emotion that had her overwhelmed in the best possible way.

But she didn't want Zeke to know. He was clearly a man with lots of experience in the bedroom, and a woman crying all over him after an orgasm was a sure way to kill the mood.

"Are you okay?" he whispered against her ear, his lips so close she felt them move.

Nina nodded, not trusting her voice to answer.

"Did I hurt you?" The regret in his voice was enough to push an answer from her.

"No. Zeke, never." She pulled back to look at him, his pain and regret clear in his eyes.

"You're crying, angel. I did something."

"You made me feel cherished," she breathed. "I've never felt that good in my life. I've never had an orgasm like that."

"Are you sure that's all it is?"

Nina nodded, cupping his face and bringing his lips to hers. "Yes."

"I never want to hurt you, Nina."

"You never would." She realized his hand was still buried between her thighs, and she wiggled against him. "You feel so good."

"Almost carried me with you," he admitted, ducking his head and easing his hand from inside her.

Nina moaned at the drag of his fingers over her sensitive flesh, then stared as he brought his hand to his mouth.

Two fingers went between his lips, his tongue snaking between them.

Her body shivered at the sight of him tasting her on his fingers.

He groaned. "So good." He sucked his fingers clean, then pulled her in for a rough kiss, one that let her taste herself on his tongue.

She groaned and rubbed against his impressive cock, wanting him inside her. "Zeke."

"You should clean up, angel. Get some sleep."

"You don't want me," she said, refusing to get off his lap.

"That couldn't be further from the truth, Nina. I want you so much I'm barely keeping my shit together. But I don't trust myself right now."

"I trust you."

"And I love you for that, angel. Fuck, that means the world. But if I lose my mind and do something that hurts you, I'll never forgive myself."

"You wouldn't."

He shook his head, and she knew nothing she said could

convince him. "I almost did this morning. I was asleep and didn't realize what I was doing. I can't control myself around you. One day, if you still want me, I won't hold back with you, Nina. But not today."

"What about a blow job?" She wanted to make him feel as good as she did. To return the favor.

His dick twitching against her said he was on board with the idea. "You're not getting your mouth on me before I get my mouth on you."

"Why not?"

"Because that's how a man is supposed to treat his woman. You come first, always and in every way. Literally and figuratively."

Nina chuckled at his words. "So you're telling me you're not dying right now?"

"Fuck no. I'm about to cry because I want you so badly, but I'll be okay."

"Are you going to jerk off in the bathroom?"

"No, I'm going to hold on to all of this desire and wait for you."

"You might die."

He barked a laugh, like it surprised him. "I might."

"I'm willing, Zeke. I want you."

"I know, angel. I know. And it's a mutual feeling. But for now, we're going to go slow. Make sure you're feeling safe."

"I have always felt safe with you, Zeke."

"Good." He tapped her thighs. "Let's get ready for bed."

"Can I sleep naked?" she asked.

He groaned. "You really do want to kill me."

She giggled. "No, I just want to—"

His lips crashed down on hers before she could finish her sentence. His tongue pried her willing lips apart, plunging into her mouth and filling her with his tongue.

She moaned and sucked on his tongue. She imagined it was his cock and swirled her tongue around it, sucking hard and dragging her nails through his short hair.

His hands cupped her ass and pulled her close enough that the distance between them disappeared. He groaned and kissed her back with the same passion.

Her body responded, soaking her channel and readying for him again. She'd never known desire like that. Desire that felt all-encompassing and so fucking good.

"When I get inside you, I need it to last. Tonight I'd be done in five seconds."

"And you think waiting is going to make that better?" she teased.

"Fine, the second time I get inside you, I need it to last."

She smiled at him. "Thank you for bringing me home."

"Thank you for calling me."

Nina grinned, knowing everything would be okay with Zeke there.

He let her use the bathroom first, bringing her a clean pair of panties and nothing else.

She smiled at him, then stripped out of her dirty clothes when he left the bathroom again. She decided to splurge and take a shower, wanting to feel clean after her orgasm. Something she wasn't used to.

The water was warm, and the memories of Zeke's hands were hot. She ached to feel him again, but she understood his resistance. She was used as a blowup doll, pumped full of whatever man wanted to pay for a turn with her. She needed a health checkup and probably some meds to get rid of any lingering diseases.

Gwendolyn brought a doctor in regularly to make sure all the women were clean of anything communicable. She would get mad when someone had something because she couldn't sell them. It was a rule they needed birth control and condoms and any other protection she could come up with.

Nina was grateful for the rules after her abortion. It was painful. She didn't want the baby, but she didn't feel right cutting its life short when the baby had done nothing wrong. As with everything else, Nina didn't get a choice.

But with Zeke, she had choices. She could choose everything.

Except to leave.

She ignored the thought. It was better to be with Zeke. He said he loved her, more than once, and even though Nina knew he didn't mean it in the way she wanted him to love her, she knew he meant it.

Nina finished her shower and dried off with the thick, fluffy towel hanging next to Zeke's in the bathroom. It was all very domestic. Sharing a bed, a bathroom, sharing everything.

It was everything she'd ever dreamed it could be.

She slid the panties he chose for her up her legs and smiled. They wouldn't last the night. Neither would his resistance.

WHAT THE HELL was he thinking? Nina walked out of the bathroom and Zeke nearly exploded. "Fucking hell."

She smirked at him and walked toward him, slowly, with those hips shifting like she was on a runway instead of in his bedroom. "I'm not naked."

Zeke shook his head. "You're not naked." It wasn't enough to keep his dick in check. Or the rest of him. But it was fucking beautiful. She was beautiful.

Zeke stood when she got closer. She smiled, clearly aware of the effect she had on him. "Bathroom is all yours."

"So are you, Nina."

She shivered at his rough words, then bit her lower lip. "And you're mine?"

"You have to ask? Fuck, yes, I'm yours. I always have been, angel." He kissed her, then moved past her to go to the bathroom. He left the door open, not wanting to hide a damn thing from her anymore. He might not have been ready to admit he loved her, but he wasn't hiding that he wanted her. Or that he cared about her.

The bed rustled as she climbed in. Zeke focused on using the bathroom, a challenge with an erection that would not ease up, then brushed his teeth and stripped down to his boxer briefs. Bad idea? Definitely. But he wanted to feel her skin on his and was willing to risk it.

"Are you ready for me to turn off the light?" he asked before he left the bathroom.

"I'm good. Thank you."

Zeke enjoyed one last look of her in the light, then flipped the switch and joined her in the bed.

She curled up against his side, one hand draped over his stomach and her head on his shoulder.

Zeke kissed her hair, inhaling his scent on her. She didn't smell like sex anymore, but he wasn't surprised she wanted to clean up. After the things she confessed...

He couldn't think about any of that. Not when she was in his arms and safe.

Her breathing evened out quickly, sleep claiming her. Zeke laid there and listened to her, hoping she never left him again.

He would never let her leave him again, if he had a

choice. But his career had taught him not everyone had a choice.

NINA WOKE EARLY, when the softest glow outside was barely visible around the room darkening curtains and Zeke was still sound asleep. She wasn't sure what woke her, but after years of sleeping all day and being awake all night, she was not surprised she was awake so early.

She slipped out of bed and went to the bathroom, then crawled back in next to Zeke. He reached for her when she laid down, pulling her in close like he'd done the morning before. Nina sighed happily, loving the touch of his skin.

The room was too dark to explore his tattoos like she wanted to do, to read the script letters and to understand every mark on his skin. She wondered what had been so important to Zeke he felt the need to permanently wear it on his body.

She stared at his profile, wondering what he'd been through the last twelve years. The things he said to her had her feeling like he'd missed her as much as she'd missed him. Like he wished she'd never walked out that night as much as she had.

He groaned in his sleep, and shifted his hips, drawing her attention down to where the sheet lifted from his body, compliments of his very impressive erection.

Nina's mouth watered at the idea of tasting him. Her core flooded at the thought of him inside her. She slid her hand down his stomach until she brushed over the coarse hair that led to his boxer briefs. If she couldn't explore his body with her eyes, she would with her hand. Touching his skin and loving the dance of his muscles beneath her hand.

She dipped a finger beneath the edge of his boxer briefs, wanting to wrap her hand around him and feel his power. Even what she was doing felt like a violation of him, though. He hadn't given her permission, so she would keep her exploration in areas he'd left exposed.

Nina's fingers danced around his stomach, then drifted to his thighs. She wanted to know what all of him felt like. To touch every inch of his body and one day to taste all of him. She brought her hand back up his body and brushed over his flat nipple, getting a surge from his hips with the move.

She kissed one nipple and flicked it with her tongue, and he squeezed her tight, moaning in his sleep. She did it again, letting her hand slide lower to the edge of his boxer briefs once more.

"Nina," he exhaled.

She looked up at him, finding him watching her, his brown eyes sleepy and sexy in the dark.

"You feel good."

She teased the edge of his boxer briefs again. "Zeke?"

He exhaled a shaky breath and nodded, just once like he was unsure but couldn't bring himself to say no.

Nina didn't hesitate to slide her hand into his boxer briefs. She wrapped her fingers around him and stroked, their combined moans loud in the otherwise silent house.

"Fuck," he groaned.

"Let me taste you."

He didn't answer, and she wondered if he heard her.

He was staring at her when she looked up at him. "Please, Zeke."

"Yes," he growled.

She didn't move her hand, crawling down his body as he pushed at his boxer briefs and shoved them down his hips to free his cock. As soon as he was out, she replaced her hand with her mouth, drawing him in deep and sucking hard on him.

"Holy fuck, Nina. Fuck. Dammit, angel, this isn't going to take long. Fuck."

Nina didn't care how long he lasted. The faster he went off, the more she knew he couldn't hold back. She worked him, sucking as she pulled back and licking as she went down. She cupped his balls and tugged gently, moaning when he surged into her mouth.

"Fuck. Nina, I'm gonna come. You gotta move, angel. I'm... Fuck. Nina!"

She did not move. She refused. She wanted to taste him. To know she was the one who made him lose his damn mind as he fucked her mouth and came in thick ropes.

He twitched, whispering to her as aftershocks wracked his body. He brushed her hair back from her face and held it in one hand, cupping her jaw with the other.

She eased off him, taking a minute to swallow, then licking him clean.

He dragged her up his body, holding her on top of him as he kissed her hard. His hands were all over her, touching and molding and teasing her until she spread her thighs and rode the ridge of his remaining erection.

"You cheated," he growled.

"How did I cheat?"

"I said I was going to get my mouth on you before you got your mouth on me."

"You were too tempting," she admitted.

"Same, angel. Now climb up here."

"Zeke?"

"Panties off, ride my face, Nina. I need to taste that pretty pussy."

"Zeke," she moaned.

"Let me eat you for breakfast, Nina." His dirty words were a harsh whisper in her ear. He added a squeeze to her ass, with a finger dipped between her legs. "I want to taste you and have your scent on me all day. To know you started your day with my face between your legs and to know whenever you sit down today and your panties touch your skin, you're going to remember riding my face."

"Zeke."

He tugged her up, not waiting for her to remove her panties. The fabric rolled down her body as he yanked her up, and he pushed it farther as he moved her higher. When it didn't yield, he reached between her thighs and a rip made her gasp.

"I'll buy you more," he growled. "I can't wait."

He scooted down and moved her up.

Nina inhaled sharply at the intimate feel of him between her legs. He moved her legs to the side so she could have them flat on the mattress next to his head. His hands went to her ass, drawing her down to his face.

"So fucking perfect," he whispered. He kissed her inner thigh. "Hold on to the headboard, Nina."

"Zeke?"

He looked up at her, his face barely visible in the dark room. "Yeah, angel?"

"I've never... Um, this..."

"Fuck," he breathed. His fingers tightened on her hips, trying to move her.

"No, I..."

"I will always stop, Nina."

"Thank you."

"You're in charge here. What do you want me to do?"

"I want... I trust you, Zeke. Before... It was never about me."

"Never again, angel. This is all about you. If you're willing to let me."

"Yes," she whispered.

"If you want me to stop..."

Nina shook her head. "No, I think... Last night felt good."

"Good."

"Zeke?"

"Yeah?"

"Make me come again."

"Fuck, yes," he growled, then set his lips on her and she saw fucking stars.

"Holy. Fuck. Oh my God." She moaned as he licked her clit. His fingers teased her entrance, then pressed inside as he sucked on her clit.

Nina was positive she was going to pass out. Was this what sex was supposed to be like? Zeke was... There were no words.

He growled and urged her to get closer with his free hand.

She spread her thighs a little wider, bringing her body more into contact with his face, and he sucked hard on her clit. Nina stopped thinking and let her body take over.

She rode his face like he told her to do, without fear of embarrassment. He reached up with his free hand and cupped her breast, pinching her nipple and sending bolts of desire through her entire body.

"Zeke," she moaned.

A bite of pain had her gasping before pleasure took over, and she flew. She held the headboard and rode his face without a care in the world. One orgasm led to another, and Zeke's eagerness had her falling twice in minutes.

Her body, wrung out and exhausted, sagged against the headboard. Zeke eased out from beneath her and cradled her from behind.

"How are you?"

"Life doesn't get better than that."

He chuckled. "I agree." He soothed her skin with a warm hand on her body. "Thank you."

"Shouldn't I be thanking you?"

"No, Nina. Forever I will be grateful that you let me touch you. So fucking grateful."

"Same, Zeke. Forever."

"There might be one way life can be better."

"Not possible. What's that?"

He chuckled and kissed the back of her neck. "Let's get in the shower."

"Together?" she gasped.

"Oh, yes, angel. Together."

"Why didn't you suggest that before?"

Zeke laughed again and climbed off the bed. He held his hand out for her, holding her steady when her legs weren't strong enough to hold up her post-orgasmic body. He turned the shower on and waited for it to warm up before he stepped in, then helped her to follow him.

Nina moaned at the feel of the warm water on her back and the warm body at her front. He was right. "This is heaven."

"Can I wash your hair?" He held up the shampoo for her to approve.

She nodded, tilting her head to soak through the long locks. When it was wet, she turned away from him so he could reach her hair.

He smoothed the shampoo on her hair, then used his fingertips to scrub it in. Small circles worked the shampoo into bubbles and made her moan in pleasure. His erection bounced against her back, but he made no move to press it against her.

When he was done with the shampoo, he turned her around and worked his hands through her hair to rinse all the suds away, then grabbed the conditioner. He smoothed that through her hair, and went for the body wash.

"Thank you," she whispered.

He met her gaze. He nodded once.

"Are you okay?"

"I wish I could explain how big of a fantasy this is."

"You've fantasized about me a lot."

He breathed a laugh. "You have no idea."

"Tell me, Zeke."

He held up the loofah full of bubbles. He rubbed it under her chin. "When you were seventeen, I imagined what you'd taste like right there. If I kissed your neck."

She gasped.

He brought the soap to her breasts. "I used to stare at you when you weren't paying attention. It was wrong because you were so young, but I would dream about touching your body. What color your nipples would be. The way your skin would flush if I saw you naked. How you would respond to me."

"Zeke."

"I was never good enough for you, so I pushed all those thoughts to the side until I was alone. Until I could pretend my hand was your hand. Until I could jerk-off in the shower and pretend it was your wet mouth on me. Until I could dream about you again and wonder if I'd ever have a chance with you."

"I always thought you were so hot," she confessed. "I never thought you would notice me."

"I noticed you, Nina. I wanted you. And when you didn't come home, it killed me."

"I'm home now."

He nodded. "Yes, and I don't ever want you to leave me again." He finished soaping her body and stood in front of her, holding her gaze. "Promise me you'll never leave me again, Nina."

"I promise, Zeke."

"Good, now let me taste you again because I didn't get enough of you yet."

Before she could reply, he was on his knees with her thighs wrapped around his neck, and she was losing her mind in the best way possible.

12

———————

WHY THE FUCK DID THEY AGREE TO THIS? WHY DID Montgomery say it was okay to take Nina to see the others who were held in the house with her? Why did Zeke let it happen?

The women had been under Rose Protection Agency protection for a week. Zeke had hoped Nina would forget about them, but she pestered Montgomery for days before he made some calls and made it happen. Zeke stood in the corner of the room with Samuel and wished it had never happened.

The two women Samuel and Austin were protecting were among the lucky ones, the ones who didn't need rehab or a longer hospital stay. Not that they were okay. None of them were okay. And they were clearly not happy to see Nina.

"Are you safe here?" Nina asked one of them. Samuel introduced the woman as Star, but Zeke wasn't sure if that was actually her name.

"We were."

"Star, I'm not here to threaten you," Nina said.

"How could we possibly believe that? You were right there every time that horrible bitch said anything to us. You stood beside her and did nothing to help us."

"I was one of you," Nina whispered.

Star laughed mirthlessly, cruelly. "You were not one of us. You were her favorite. Her sister. Her pet. I never knew what was worse. If it was worse to be a prisoner of hers or to be her pet."

"I was a prisoner, too!" Nina shouted.

Star snorted. "Yeah, I see you're struggling right now." Her gaze slid to Zeke. "Screwing the protector? Tough life."

"He has nothing to do with this."

"No?" Star tilted her head and glared at Nina. "Does he know who you really are? Does he know how many men you fucked? Does he know about the ones you would scream for? The ones you waited for like they were going to save you? The ones you said were good men and nice to you?"

"Enough," Zeke said. It was taking all of his control to not rip the woman a new one.

Nina turned to him with tears in her eyes. "It's okay, Zeke. She's right. You deserve better than me."

Zeke glared at Star. "She was right there with you. She was held captive just like you. Why are you attacking her?"

Star laughed again. She flung her arm toward the woman who sat in silence on the couch, watching the exchange. "Do you see Monica? Monica, who is so scared she can barely move. Who was just starting to leave a room alone, and now she's cowering again because Nina showed up. Nina, who was a sister to the bitch who held us all captive. Who got to choose the men she fucked instead of getting whatever drugged up scum paid for us. Who escaped and ended up with you in some cushy place with new clothes and a personal protector who thinks she's some gift brought back from the dead."

"She is a gift," Zeke argued. "What you all went through was horrible. What Gwendolyn Lennox did to all of you was not okay. But none of it was Nina's fault. She knew what would happen if she left."

Star raised a brow. "Really? Because it looks to me like she's fine. Not dead. How is it everyone else who tried to run ended up in the ground and she's walking around the city free as a fucking bird? You really think you can trust her? Because from where I'm standing, she's no different from her 'sister.' She's going to turn on you. She's going to show her true colors. Just wait."

"You're wrong." Zeke knew it was anger and fear fueling Star. He also knew Nina had been through the same hell, and they were all dealing with it in their own way.

Star shrugged. "You can believe that, but I don't. I know that whore. And I know what she's capable of." She turned to Samuel. "We need to get the fuck out of here. And if you let her near either of us again, you better believe we will disappear, and when we show up again, it'll be with lawyers and a hell of a lawsuit for emotional trauma and reckless endangerment. Because that bitch is going to tell her sister where we are. And we're all going to end up dead."

"No, I won't," Nina murmured.

Star scowled at Nina. "I don't believe it. I don't believe you. Get us the hell out of here. Now. And don't tell him where we are. I don't trust him either."

Samuel nodded and held his hands out to direct Zeke and Nina toward the door. Samuel walked outside with them. Zeke opened the door for Nina to get in the SUV, then walked around to the other side, where Samuel was waiting.

"Nina is not working with Gwendolyn still," Zeke assured Samuel.

Samuel nodded. He was a man Zeke had a mountain of respect for. A former Delta, Samuel was smart and ruthless when he had to be. Zeke had never once doubted Samuel's ability to do a job or his commitment to the team. He would die for any of them, but with a wife and grown daughter, Zeke hoped it never came to that.

"You wouldn't have brought her here if you were worried. Unfortunately, we have a shitstorm brewing. She never really trusted Austin or me, and now she's going to have an even harder time. I think we might need to turn these two over to another organization."

Zeke sighed heavily. "You're probably right. I'll get in touch with Lorelei and Adam and see what the FBI can do."

"Thanks." Samuel turned to go back, but stopped before he got far. "Was she right about you and Nina?"

Zeke looked at the older man and nodded.

Samuel's brows shot up. "Does the boss know about you two?"

Zeke shook his head. "No one knows. I'm not sure how she knew."

"Probably because you were looking at Nina like you wanted to wrap her up and never let her go."

Zeke exhaled a laugh. "Guess I'm not so good at hiding my feelings."

Samuel shrugged one shoulder. "None of us are when it comes to love."

"I guess that's good to know."

"You love her?"

Zeke glanced at Nina through the window. Her head was down, her face hidden behind her curtain of hair. Zeke nodded. "Have for years."

"And you never told Mont?"

"No. She was seventeen... And there was no reason to when she was gone."

"But she's back."

Zeke nodded. "I'm not going to let anything happen to her again."

"Don't hold on too tight. That doesn't always work."

"I let go before, and we all know what happened."

"Yeah. She came back."

Zeke sucked in a breath. He looked at Samuel, then again at Nina. He was right. She did come back. But she wasn't the same. Neither was he. But they had a chance.

"You might want to find a way to tell Mont you're in love with her. All of this has really messed him up."

"What do you mean?" Zeke asked.

Samuel regarded him closely. "He's not himself right now, Zeke. I'm not sure what's going on, but he's not okay."

"Shit." Zeke hadn't noticed. He'd been so wrapped up in Nina he didn't think to check in with his best friend.

"You have your hands full. I have a feeling I'll be free soon. I'll check in on him."

"Thanks, Samuel. I... I've fucked everything up with both of them, and I need to make it right."

"One Rose at a time." Samuel clapped Zeke on the back. "Go take care of the red one."

Zeke breathed a laugh. "I'm going to try."

"Good luck."

"Thanks, man."

Samuel went back to the house, and Zeke climbed in the SUV. He turned to Nina.

"Are you okay?"

Nina shook her head without looking up. "She's right. About everything. I didn't do anything to make things better. I didn't stop Gwendolyn. I didn't help any of them."

"You couldn't. You would have gotten even worse treatment."

Nina rubbed her neck. The bruises had faded over the last week, but they were still visible. Nina wore tops that covered her neck, but the purple and blue colors told the truth.

"There was nothing rational about her. Or the situation you were in. You did the best you could."

"I should have done more."

Zeke shifted in his seat to face her and tilted her chin until she lifted her gaze to his. Tears streaked her cheeks and red rimmed her eyes. "How many times have you told me letting you walk out that night was not my fault? That everything you went through wasn't my fault? That I couldn't have stopped you and that you chose your path?"

"It's different."

"How is it different? Why is it different? If you can forgive me for deleting twelve years of your life, why are you blaming yourself for what they went through? You weren't calling the shots. You weren't sending men to them. You were trying to survive so you could come back to me."

Nina inhaled a shaky breath. "Star doesn't have someone like you waiting for her. Neither does Monica."

Zeke shook his head. "That's not on you either. I hate that they went through the same things you did, but you are not to blame. You didn't do anything wrong."

Nina swallowed roughly and nodded slightly. "Everything else she said... About the men—"

"You do not owe me any explanation."

Nina sniffed. "I... She wasn't wrong. I created fantasies in my mind about those men. About them saving me or helping me. I told myself they cared. Some of them, especially the last few years, I accepted my fate and enjoyed it."

"You had no idea if you would ever be free, angel. No clue what the future would hold. You had to find a way to survive."

"But it was wrong!"

"Why? Yes, what happened to you was wrong. What was happening to all of you was wrong. If you chose that life, if you were safe and everything was your choice, there would be nothing wrong with it. You didn't, though. That's the part that's not okay. You making the most of it, I'm not going to judge you for that. I wasn't there. I don't know what you went through. And even if I was, only you know what you had to do to survive. To cope. To hold on until you could get away or be rescued."

"Do you really believe that?" she whispered.

Zeke nodded. "I do. It kills me that another man has touched you. That you went through all the things you did. But I would never say you, or any of the women who were held there, did something wrong. I've done things I'm not proud of. I'm not perfect. But I did what I felt I had to do to survive."

"You did?"

Zeke nodded, thinking back to the worst deployment he had. The lifeless eyes of the people he killed. The stink of death. The pain of war. "You deserve better than me, Nina. So much better."

"There's no one else I want."

Zeke smiled. "Good. Let's get out of here before Star comes out of the house at us."

Nina glanced at the house and nodded.

Nina was raw, exposed, hurt. All the things Gwendolyn did came back to her as Zeke drove through the city. She wasn't sure why she thought Star and Monica would be happy to see her, but she was dead wrong. Star was furious, and Monica was terrified.

Nina was an asshole. She didn't mean to hurt them. But Star meant to hurt Nina. Nina wanted to be angry about it, but Star was right. Nina was the favorite. At times, she used it to her advantage. She got to shower more than the other girls. She got to choose her men. She got to go upstairs with Gwendolyn.

Nina never told the others about Gwendolyn's abuse. She never told anyone about it. Nina knew it wasn't okay, but she also couldn't shake that it only happened when she did something wrong. When she pushed back too hard.

Maybe Nina got comfortable. She thought she could have a normal life. She expected certain things. Things the others never got. Things Nina saw as rewards for not fighting everything.

But she was still a prisoner. She was still ordered around by Gwendolyn. Left to rot with the others when Gwendolyn didn't want her around and brought up to be praised when Gwendolyn needed someone to talk to.

She had it better than the others, but she didn't have it good. Still, to Star and the rest of them, Nina was lucky. Nina had the chance to enjoy sex. She had the opportunity to pretend she chose that life. Even if she knew the truth was a choice meant she could have changed her mind. Gwendolyn made it clear that would never happen.

Zeke took a turn, and Nina glanced in the mirror, spotting a vehicle turn behind them. She tried to tell herself it was a coincidence, but fear slithered up her spine.

"Someone's following us," she breathed.

"What?" Zeke asked.

"There's an SUV following us. Blue. Three cars back."

"Are you sure?" Zeke asked, looking in his mirror and shifting in his seat. Both hands gripped the steering wheel. Tension filled the SUV.

"Yeah. They turned with you at the last light. Last minute, like they didn't see you turn until they were right there."

Zeke put on his blinker and changed lanes.

The SUV did the same.

Zeke took the next left.

The SUV followed.

"Shit," Zeke breathed.

"They are following us," Nina said. "Oh my God. It's Gwendolyn. She found me. You have to warn Star and Monica. They could be in danger."

"I have to get you to safety first. Samuel and Austin will take care of Star and Monica."

"No, you have to call. You have to warn them. They already think I would turn them in. I wouldn't do this. I didn't. Zeke, you have to believe me."

"I do believe you, angel. I know you wouldn't do that. I know you. And Samuel and Austin will take care of whatever happens. But my priority has to be you. I have to make sure you're safe."

"Zeke, please!"

Zeke glanced over at her. He scanned her quickly, then tapped something on the screen in his car. A few seconds later, the sound of a phone ringing filled the SUV.

"Yeah."

"Picked up a tail. Watch your six."

"Copy."

The line went dead, and Zeke's attention returned to the

road. "Samuel will take care of it. He'll call for backup and make sure nothing happens to Star or Monica. I promise you."

"Thank you, Zeke. I couldn't... They've been through enough."

"So have you. You need to be safe, too."

"I know, but I have you."

Zeke took a quick turn, sending Nina against the side of the SUV. "Hold on," he growled.

Nina checked the mirror, the SUV still following them. Her pulse raced. Her throat tightened. The vehicle was closer, two cars back now. They were getting bolder, not caring that they were visible.

She did this. If something happened to Zeke, she would never forgive herself. She put him in danger. She risked his life to save her own.

She never should have called him. She should have just disappeared. Left town and never looked back.

She rubbed her chest at the thought. Being with Zeke the last week made her feel alive in a way she never knew was possible. It gave her hope for a future. Hope she could have a life.

Not to mention the way he looked at her and touched her and lit her up with both. She never dreamed of love. Not real love. She fantasized about one of her men saving her, but she knew it wasn't love. She knew it would be more of the same. She would trade one prison for another.

But with Zeke—

He jerked the wheel and turned into a parking lot.

Nina looked at the police vehicles filling the lot. The police station rose before them, a concrete monstrosity that overwhelmed the area.

She looked back just in time to see the vehicle drive

right past the parking lot and keep going. The driver didn't even look over, just stared straight ahead and kept going.

She didn't recognize him.

"He's gone," Zeke said.

Nina nodded. "I didn't recognize him. Did you?"

Zeke shook his head. "Doesn't mean anything, though. Are you okay?"

Nina shrugged and clenched her hands together. They shook, her entire body trembling with the fear coursing through her.

"You're safe now," Zeke whispered, pulling her against him, the console restricting how close she could get.

"I'm sorry."

"Nothing to be sorry for. I should have been watching more closely."

"Star? Monica?"

"We'll check with them when we get to the office. I need to make some calls and want to see your brother."

"Do you think it's safe?"

Zeke tapped his screen, calling Monty.

"Rose."

"We just left station two. We believe someone was following us."

"Where are you?"

"Police station."

"Filing a report?"

"No, nothing definitive."

"Are you coming here?"

"Hoping to. Need to do a few things. What do you think?"

"We'll be waiting. And watching."

"On the way."

Zeke hung up and put the SUV in gear.

"Watching?" Nina asked.

"We all share our locations with each other. Security reasons. He'll watch our trip and be able to tell within seconds if something goes off the rails."

"Really?"

Zeke nodded and made another turn. "Yep. There will be a wall getting us inside. You'll be safe."

"I'm always safe with you," she whispered.

Zeke put his hand on her thigh. "I will never let anyone touch you again."

Nina nodded, knowing what he wasn't saying. He would die before he let her die.

Which was part of what worried her. Gwendolyn would try. Nina wasn't free. Star and Monica and the others, they were replaceable for Gwendolyn. They were just bodies. But Nina? Nina knew things the rest of them didn't know. Nina was a risk.

And that meant Zeke was in danger.

And willing to die for her.

She could not let that happen.

13

———

Nina thought Zeke and Monty were going too far with the protection at the office, but she couldn't shake the fear she felt and was grateful for the wall of men surrounding her. Even though she would never admit it to them.

Inside, she was ushered past the front desk and into the security of the office beyond. Zeke and Monty kept her between them and led her to Monty's office.

Nina went to the couch and hugged her knees to her chest while Zeke detailed the whole thing to Monty.

"So you're not positive they were following you?" Monty asked.

Zeke glanced at Nina and shook his head. "No. It appeared as though they were. They followed every turn I made, even at the last minute, turning quickly like they weren't prepared for the turns. If I was betting, I'd say they were following us, but I can't guarantee it."

"Fuck. And that means they know where Nina's staying."

"Hard to imagine they don't."

"What about Monica and Star?" Nina asked.

"Samuel and Austin are taking care of them. Getting

them out of the house and over to the FBI for protection." Monty spared Nina a glance before returning his focus to Zeke. "They didn't see anything."

"That's good. Hopefully it means they're safe," Zeke said.

Nina got the feeling the men were thinking something but keeping it to themselves. Or between themselves because the looks they both gave her said the same thing. She just wasn't sure what that was. "Why are you looking at me like that?" she snapped.

"Like what?" Monty asked.

"Like there's something else." Nina stared down her brother until he sighed.

"We've been worried about you. We've talked about moving you to a safe house or getting protection around the clock."

"I have protection. I have you two."

Monty shook his head.

Zeke moved toward the door. "I'll let you two talk."

Nina opened her mouth to argue, but she realized they already had this conversation. Sometime when she wasn't around. Sometime when they agreed what was best for her without her input.

Zeke closed the door behind himself and walked into the bullpen, sitting at a desk next to a Black man whose name Nina didn't remember.

"You're not safe, Nina," Monty said. "You said she lied to you about me, but it's obvious she knew where I was this whole time. Probably Zeke, too."

"She didn't know anything about Zeke."

"She knows everything. She knows so fucking much, Nina. And she knows you do, too."

"I know." Nina picked at her nail, wishing she could go back and never walk out that night. Even her father couldn't have been as bad as Gwendolyn. But Nina didn't know that when she was seventeen and vulnerable and scared and made that decision.

Monty sat on the couch next to Nina, pulling her close.

She dropped her feet to the floor and leaned against her brother. "I never wanted you guys in danger."

"We're used to it. We expected it. But now that we have proof that she's watching you, we can't leave you so exposed."

"I can't go back into hiding. I can't... I need to be free." Tears flooded her eyes and tightened her throat. It wasn't the same, but it felt the same. Stuck indoors, watched constantly, not allowed to go anywhere alone. Nope.

"And you will be once we find her and bring her in. But all the places you told the FBI about were empty. She's smart. She cleaned out everything. Nothing was left behind, not even DNA that could be linked to her."

"She's always a step ahead," Nina whispered.

"Yeah. But that means we need to do everything in our power to keep you safe."

"I just want to live my life," Nina said. "I just want to be free."

"You will be. I promise you, Nina. I will do everything to make sure you're free. But first, I need you safe."

A knock on the door had Nina and Monty looking up. Monty waved for Zeke to come in.

"I was going to grab some food. Are you guys hungry?" Zeke asked from the door to the office.

Nina sat up and nodded.

Monty stood. "Why don't you ask Berkeley to order for the office? Put it on the company card."

"Call her and see," Zeke said, nodding toward the phone.

"No, just go ask her," Monty said quickly. "She gets annoyed when she feels like she's not a part of things."

Zeke rolled his eyes and nodded. "True." Zeke left, heading toward the front where the office manager's desk was on the other side of the security door.

"Should I know something about you and Berkeley?" Nina asked.

"What? No. Hell no," Monty said without meeting her gaze.

"Are you sure? Because you're acting like there's something to know."

"Nothing. She works for me. That's it." Monty's tone said not to push the topic, but Nina knew her brother. It didn't matter that it had been twelve years, she knew Monty when he liked someone. And he had a thing for his assistant, no matter what he said.

Nina let Monty have the lie and let him return the conversation to her imprisonment. "I know you hate it, but I don't think I can do my job if I'm worried you're not going to be around next time I come home."

Before Nina could argue again, Zeke returned with visitors. Agent Lorelei Sloane and a white man Nina was sure she'd seen before but didn't know where.

Zeke knocked again, letting himself in without waiting for an answer from Monty. "Found these two up front. Berkeley's ordering lunch to be delivered. The agents wanted to talk to all of us."

Monty approached them, his hand extended. "Good to see you both again. What can we do for you?"

Agent Sloane approached Nina. "Nina, this is my partner, Adam Johnson."

Nina sucked in a breath. "Raina."

"You know my wife?"

"You're the ones Frannie mentioned?"

"Uh, I'm not sure, but we know Frannie."

Nina shook her head. "Frannie said Damon's ex was married to the man who saved her, but I didn't realize it was you. Gwendolyn was furious with Damon for chasing Raina down. He was putting the company at risk with his actions, and she was ready to kill him herself. When he chased you two all over, Gwendolyn was tracking him. She said…"

Nina rolled her lips in and looked at the four of them. They stared at her, hanging on every word she spoke.

"What did she say?" Adam asked.

Nina closed her eyes. Telling them wasn't part of her plan. She didn't want to say what Gwendolyn said, but she'd gone too far. "Gwendolyn said she didn't understand what everyone saw in Raina London. She wanted her as one of her own girls because she figured Raina had a magical pussy if both you and Damon were willing to travel all over the east coast for her."

The collective intake of breath was shocked and angry. Lorelei scowled. Monty closed his eyes. Zeke pinched the bridge of his nose. Adam just stared back at Nina, his bright blue eyes kind.

"I'm pretty partial to my wife's magical pussy, but I'm not very good at sharing so your former captor is going to have to go fuck herself," Adam said.

A shocked laugh popped out of Nina. She clapped a hand over her mouth, and Adam winked at her.

"Raina will love hearing that, but it's also going to terrify her that Gwendolyn knows who she is," Adam said, rubbing a hand over his chin.

"If it helps, I think she was jealous. Gwendolyn didn't like anyone else having more power than her, and Damon wouldn't listen to anything she said because he was too busy chasing Raina. Gwendolyn would scream about him more than she would about Raina. Said he had a job to do and he was messing it up because of Raina."

"Sounds familiar," Lorelei said with a smirk.

"It's that magical pussy of hers. I couldn't help but fall in love with her while we were running for our lives," Adam told Lorelei with a huge grin.

"She's going to love hearing that you're telling everyone about her magical pussy," Lorelei said.

"If you got it, flaunt it," Adam countered.

"Did you two come here for a reason?" Monty asked, sounding frustrated and uncomfortable.

"Sorry, yeah," Lorelei said, containing her laughter. "We wanted to see if Nina has any other ideas about where Gwendolyn Lennox could be. We've searched all the properties you mentioned, and all the places we had on our list, which wasn't many more, and we're out of ideas."

Nina shook her head as Lorelei spoke. She tried to think back over the last twelve years. The first house that was raided was Gwendolyn's favorite. Most of their time was spent there. After that one, the place Nina escaped from was next, then the other four she told Lorelei about before. "There are places she would keep the girls. Different houses around the city. But I don't know where any of those are. You could ask Star or Monica or any of the others."

Lorelei and Adam exchanged a look, then turned those looks on Zeke and Montgomery. "That's why they requested to be moved? Because she knows about them?" Lorelei asked.

"It's my fault," Nina said before her brother could fall on his sword for her. "I overheard them talking and forced them to take me."

"Forced how?" Adam asked, his hand going to his hip.

"Whoa, no," Monty and Zeke said at the same time. They both held their hands up and stepped in front of Nina.

"She did not force anything," Monty said. "She's my little sister. I couldn't say no to her. I take responsibility for it. But she did not threaten us or force us or do anything else to get her way. Do either of you have a sister?"

Nina stared at the four people in a standoff in front of her. Zeke and Monty were protecting her from FBI Agents because she said something wrong. Because she didn't know what her words said to them until they reacted the way they did.

She was about to say something when Adam sighed and removed his hand from his gun.

"Yeah, I have a sister. And I get it. I'd do anything for her," Adam said.

"Poor choice of words," Lorelei provided, peering between the men to Nina.

Nina nodded. "I'm sorry. I wanted to see them. I... I thought we were friends. They didn't agree."

"I'm sorry," Lorelei said. "And for the record, none of the locations they've given us have turned up anything, either."

"So now what?" Monty asked.

"Now we try a different plan," Adam said, looking at Nina.

"What plan?" Zeke asked.

"We offer something Gwendolyn can't resist," Lorelei said.

"What can't she resist?" Monty asked.

"Getting me back," Nina said.

All four of them turned to her, but only Zeke spoke.

"Fuck no."

ZEKE SAW RED. Fucking blood red with black slashes through it. Angry, evil, claw-like slashes he felt in his chest at the thought of Nina being anywhere near that monster. His chest was tight, his fists already curled, ready to attack.

"What he said," Montgomery growled. "Not happening."

"Look, we know—" Adam started.

"You know? You know. You know what she's been through. You know what she had to do to survive there. You know about the drugs and the rapes and the beatings and you still think this is a good idea?" Montgomery shouted.

Everyone in the room fell silent.

Zeke was happy Montgomery said it because he felt all of it. Every word, every thought, every piece of that truth. Nina already risked her life. She already walked away and ended up in the clutches of that demon. There was no fucking way he was ever going to let it happen again.

"It's my choice," Nina whispered.

"You can't possibly be considering this," Montgomery said, turning his ire on his sister. "No. It's not happening, Nina. I'm not going to let you."

"You're not in charge of me, Monty. I love you, but I need to make my own decisions. I need to be able to choose what I do." Nina stood and faced him, her hands in tight little balls of fury that would do nothing if she swung at Montgomery. Or anyone. She couldn't defend herself. She would be gone, disappear again, and this time, she wouldn't call him to come get her. She'd be in the morgue. If she was ever found.

"Why this?" Montgomery asked. "Why would you risk it? Why would you even consider going anywhere near her again? You know she'll kill you."

"She's going to anyway," Nina said.

"No. No, we're not going to let that happen. We're going

to keep you safe." Montgomery wiped the tears from his cheeks.

"As long as she's out there, I'm not safe. I'll never be safe. She knows I talked. She knows I'm a risk. She's not the kind of person who offers forgiveness. She shoots first and asks questions later."

"And you want to go back to her?"

"No!" Nina laughed mirthlessly. "Hell, no. I want to stop her. I want her dead. I want her to end this hell she's put so many people through. His wife, her, all the others Frannie told me about. So many more no one knows about. Women who've been sold off, who were killed, who will never have a life to go back to. Why would I want someone like that running around free and I'm trapped in a house and hiding for the rest of my life, hoping and praying she doesn't find out where I am? You don't know what she's capable of, Monty. No idea. She's evil. She will kill anyone she thinks will cross her. Why would I not do everything possible to stop her?"

Zeke heard the words, but it was Nina. It was the woman he loved. It was the most important person in the world to him. If it was someone else, anyone else, he might agree it was the right thing. He might understand.

But it was Nina.

Montgomery was silent after her outburst, and Zeke's gut sank.

"You can't possibly be considering this," Zeke growled at his best friend. "We already agreed!"

Montgomery looked at Zeke. It was all right there. All in his eyes. The truth and the guilt and the acknowledgement that he was going to say yes.

"No! Fuck no! I'm not letting it happen. I can't." Zeke turned to Nina and grasped her hands, forcing her to look at him. "Don't do this. Don't go to her. Don't leave me again. Just stay. We'll leave. We'll go on the run. I'll protect you forever. I'll never let her get to you, and when they find her, we can come back."

Nina shook her head as Zeke spoke. "I can't do that, Zeke. What if they never find her? What if she hurts someone else? What if someone dies because of me? I can do something. I can help. I can draw her out. She'll be stopped. She'll be done. People will be safe."

Zeke shook his head, unable to believe his ears. They were all looking at him, all dismissing his thoughts. All acting like this was no big deal. No concern, no worries. She would be fine.

She wouldn't be fine. Zeke knew how these things went. He knew even if she survived, she wouldn't be okay. Not with the devil staring at her. Gwendolyn Lennox was not going to play fair. She wouldn't follow the rules.

And Nina was not going to be the same if they went through with the plan.

Zeke looked around the room and had to walk away. They weren't going to listen to him. He had no authority. He wasn't the boss. He wasn't her brother. He was just the man who wanted to love her forever. He didn't count.

They all called after him as he walked away, but Zeke didn't stop. He didn't care what they had to say. He was not going to change his mind. He was not going to approve the whole thing. He just couldn't. He couldn't.

He slammed his way into the bathroom, stopping short when he almost hit Samuel with the door.

"Whoa. You good?" Samuel asked.

"No," Zeke growled, ignoring his friend and pacing the bathroom in front of the stalls. He punched a door, enjoying the slam of it hitting the wall and bouncing back. He punched another one. Then another.

"What's going on?" Samuel asked in that way of his. The way that said he'd been around and seen some shit and probably knew exactly what to say to make you feel better.

Zeke didn't want to feel better. He wanted to stew in his anger and be pissed off at the world. Because he was terrified. She was going to walk away from him again, and he couldn't stop her again.

"Want me to guess?"

"No," Zeke blurted. "Fuck no." Samuel came up with the worst guesses. Weird ass shit that no one wanted to hear.

"You finally worked up the nerve to tell Mont you're in love with him and he wants to run away together?" Samuel asked.

Zeke laughed at the absurdity of it. "I think that would be easier."

Samuel's brows went up at that comment. "Okay, that's not what I thought you'd say."

Zeke shook his head slowly. "They want to use Nina as bait and draw out Gwendolyn Lennox."

Samuel stared at Zeke, waiting for the rest. When Zeke didn't continue, Samuel narrowed his eyes. "Are you surprised by that? I mean, that's an easy option. And with a case like this one, it sounds like a really good option. I know she's the boss's sister and all, but..."

Zeke glared at Samuel, not liking the look Samuel was giving him. "What?"

"You want a vote but can't get one unless you admit you love her." Samuel was too on the nose for Zeke.

"She wants to. She said she'll do it. And she convinced Mont that it's a good idea."

Samuel whistled low and long. "She's one tough cookie, isn't she? I can understand why you fell for her."

"I fell for her before. When she was too young and I wasn't allowed to be in love with her."

Samuel shrugged. "She's still strong. Sounds like she was pretty strong to walk away when she did, back then and now, even if it was bad. Only problem is now you're involved with her and haven't told Mont and can't think like you need to because you're too in love with her to see what makes sense."

Zeke scrubbed a hand down his face, relieved to finally talk to someone about Nina. "Yeah."

"The hard part is you loving her doesn't change anything."

"The fuck it doesn't."

Samuel shook his head. "It doesn't. And if it was any of the rest of us, you would be saying that. Yeah, you love her. Yeah, you're sleeping together. Maybe she loves you. But there's still a threat out there. A very real one that's coming for her. She's in the crosshairs every day. She will be until this is over."

"So she should just stand out in the open and pretend there isn't a mark on her?"

"No, but she has to handle it. And if she wants to, you telling her no is not going to win you any favors."

"Fuck favors. I need her alive."

"Even if she never speaks to you again?"

Zeke felt that same slice of fear as before. Like he was gutted with one swipe of the monster's claws. "Fuck."

"It's not easy. None of this is easy. But you trying to control everything and standing in her way of doing what she thinks is right isn't going to make things easier. All it's going to do is drive you apart."

"But she'll be alive."

"You don't know that. I wish I could agree, but if there's one thing we've learned about Gwendolyn Lennox, it's that she's evil. She's not stopping until she gets what she wants. And right now, it seems she wants your woman. So you have to decide if you're willing to trust Nina or if you're going to be the big bad hero and lock her up in your basement and not let her out until you've scorched the earth to protect her."

Zeke didn't like those options. Why wasn't there another one?

"Think about it." Samuel clapped Zeke on the shoulder and left the bathroom.

The sound outside the door reached Zeke for a moment before silence returned.

Zeke sank to the floor, put his face in his hands, and tried to decide which outcome he could live with.

14

NINA NIBBLED ON HER NAIL AND LISTENED TO THE PLAN Lorelei and Adam had in mind. Clearly, they weren't just coming up with this. They'd been thinking about it for a while.

"Do you really think she'll show up?" Nina asked.

Lorelei shrugged. "We don't know. She's smart, so it's possible she won't. But even if she sends someone else, it'll be another person we can take into custody and get information out of. We don't think she'd send anyone in her place unless they were someone she trusted."

"She doesn't trust anyone," Nina said.

"Except you and Frannie. You two are the only ones we think she ever trusted," Adam said.

"That's why you want us together. At a coffee shop. In broad daylight, where she can come and capture us," Nina said. She was liking the plan less and less. Yeah, she wanted to take down Gwendolyn. Yeah, she knew others would get hurt. But she was just starting to figure out what life could look like. Giving it all up was not appealing.

But it was necessary.

Nina made her choice. She knew it was the right thing. She just hoped she would walk away and be back in Zeke's arms. If he'd still have her.

"You don't have to do this, Nina," Monty said. He hadn't left her side, a solid wall of strength beside her.

Nina looked up at her brother. She missed so much with him. She wasn't ready to miss more. "They're not going to let anything happen to me."

"They better not," Monty growled. "I want to be there."

Lorelei and Adam both shook their heads. "You know that's not a good idea. We have every reason to believe she knows who you are."

"I don't think I can watch from far away."

"We will figure it out," Lorelei said before Adam could argue again. "We know this is not an easy thing to do. But we believe it's the best option."

"So you'll capture this bitch and put her away forever?" Zeke asked from the door.

Nina's head snapped up so fast her neck cracked. He came back. She didn't know what it meant, but she was relieved he was standing there.

"Yes," Lorelei said. "No one wants that more than me."

"I wouldn't be so sure about that," Zeke said.

"Zeke?" Nina whispered.

He looked at her. The emotions she was feeling were reflected in his gaze. One side of his mouth lifted in a small smile. "When is this happening?"

"Tomorrow for breakfast," Adam said.

"Not wasting any time, are you?" Zeke's question was rhetorical, but Lorelei and Adam both nodded.

"She's too dangerous to give her time to come up with another plan," Lorelei said.

Nina sucked in a breath. She was scared. In less than

twenty-four hours, she would see Gwendolyn again. Anything could happen. It might be her last moments alive. Frannie could be hurt. When Gwendolyn was involved, it was bound to be a disaster.

But so was leaving her to continue her operation. So Nina was going to do what she had to do.

"Are we done here? I think Nina needs some time to relax," Zeke said.

Lorelei and Adam both rose. They shook hands with Nina, then Monty. "We will meet here in the morning and run down the plan one more time."

Monty nodded. "See you then."

Lorelei and Adam shook hands with Zeke, then made their way to the front of the building and out the door. Before the door swung closed, Berkeley came through, carrying two bags of food in each hand.

"Lunch is here," Nina said, knowing her brother and Zeke would go help Berkeley and Nina would have a minute to herself.

Both men left the office, and Nina watched as they approached Berkeley. Monty took two of the bags from her, and another man took the other two. Zeke followed Berkeley out of the office, laughing at something she said.

Nina was absolutely not at all jealous of the pretty, curvy, confident assistant who'd known Zeke for years and was completely appropriate for him to date.

Monty came back into the office carrying two sandwiches. He handed one to Nina, then went behind his desk and unwrapped the other one.

Nina unwrapped her sandwich and took a deep breath. She knew Monty didn't want her to put herself at risk. "Thank you for letting me do this."

Monty sighed. He stared at her long enough that Nina

fidgeted in her seat. "I hate it. I want to send you away with Zeke and find that bitch and make sure she can't ever get close to you again. But instead, I'm letting you walk into a meeting with her. One that she doesn't know about and is likely going to be a disaster."

"I have to do it, Monty. I can't let her hurt anyone else."

"What if she hurts you?"

"Then she'll be caught."

Monty swallowed roughly and leaned back in his chair. "I'm not sure I can handle that."

"I know. But I can't handle knowing she's out there and other people could be hurt."

Monty shook his head. "I'm not going to argue with you anymore. I know you're doing this. Just... be careful, okay?"

Nina nodded. "Yeah."

ZEKE WANTED to go back in and pretend like nothing was wrong, but he couldn't. It might be the last night he had with Nina, but it was also the last night for Montgomery. Zeke was not going to intrude on the siblings' time together. He would have Nina overnight, and that had to be enough.

"What did the FBI want?" Berkeley asked when they walked back up front. She had two more bags of food on her desk, chips and drinks and more sandwiches. She grabbed one and handed it to Zeke, leaving one sandwich and a bag of chips on the desk.

"What are you doing?" Zeke asked, eyeing the food.

"Eating my lunch." Berkeley looked at him like he was crazy. "What am I supposed to be doing?"

"Come back and eat with everyone else."

Berkeley shook her head. "I don't think that's a good idea."

Zeke tossed her food into the bag and grabbed the second one. "Let's go."

Berkeley scowled but followed him to the back where everyone else was going through the bags of food and looking for a sandwich.

Zeke added the other two bags to the mix and pulled Berkeley's food out before the rest of them could steal her lunch. "Here."

She grabbed the sandwich and eyed him.

"Don't run back out there. Sit and talk. We haven't seen much of you lately. It's like you're hiding from us back here," Zeke said.

"Yeah, Berk. What gives?" Austin asked. Austin flirted with Berkeley as much as anyone else, but she told Zeke she knew Austin was a good man, even though he and Samuel got into it sometimes about Samuel's daughter.

"It's been busy," Berkeley said, smiling at Austin. "It's a full-time job keeping all of you in line."

The men chorused boos at her and laughed when she winked.

"That's mean, Berk. We are perfect gentlemen," Samuel said.

"You are. Valerie trained you right," Berkeley teased.

Samuel chuckled while the others razzed him. "She did. I'm not going to argue with that one. The rest of you are just jealous that I have a good woman to go home to at the end of the day and you're all playing with yourselves."

Berkeley laughed. The other men cursed at Samuel. Zeke just sat back and listened. He wasn't really either at the moment. He had a good woman to go home to, but she wasn't his woman. Not entirely. What would happen when

Gwendolyn Lennox was no longer a threat? Where would Nina go? Would Nina go?

Zeke hoped she wouldn't. He wanted her with him for good. But Samuel was right earlier when he told Zeke he had to let her make her own choices. Would she choose him?

The question rattled around in his mind the rest of the day. Montgomery and Nina spent time together in his office, probably planning out the next day. Zeke struggled to focus on his work and answered questions when any of the guys needed something, telling them to leave Mont alone so he could spend time with Nina.

Zeke hated that he was planning for her to not come back, but he preferred to think he was being considerate. Giving her time with her brother. They hadn't had a lot together with Nina staying at Zeke's house. He was trying to be thoughtful.

"Are you ready to head out?" Mont asked from the door.

"Yeah, whenever." Zeke stood, closing his laptop and locking his desk. He avoided meeting his best friend's gaze. A part of Zeke felt guilty for talking to Samuel about Nina, but another part of him knew it was easier to talk to Samuel than Montgomery.

Their whole lives, Montgomery and Zeke agreed they weren't meant for permanent relationships. That women were lucky to have dodged a bullet where they were concerned. It never bothered Zeke because he felt that way. He wasn't a good fit for any other woman because he always compared them to Nina. Nina was his model, his angel, his fantasy woman. He never wanted another woman.

But it didn't mean Montgomery would change his mind about Zeke and what any woman deserved when she set her sights on him.

Mont wasn't any different, but he was a good man. If he decided there was a woman who suited him, Zeke had no doubt Mont would change his entire life for her. But he wasn't sure Mont would see the same in Zeke. If he would be okay with Zeke getting involved with Nina. Especially after all she'd been through.

"Listen, I know you don't like this. I don't either, but we both know she's stubborn and telling her not to do something is only going to make her want to do it more."

Zeke nodded. "I get it." He tried to walk past Montgomery, but Mont put a hand on his shoulder and waited until Zeke looked up at him.

Montgomery's eyes narrowed, studying Zeke in a way he didn't like at all.

Zeke resisted the urge to shuffle his feet and get the hell out, knowing that would only make Mont more suspicious. More curious. He stared down his best friend, waiting for the judgement that would come.

"I know you're mad at me for agreeing."

Zeke shook his head, but Mont pushed on.

"I am, too. Fuck, I hate all of this. If it was any other witness, I wouldn't think twice about letting them, if they wanted to. But it's Nina. I mean, fuck, it's my baby sister."

Zeke knew he couldn't say anything that would make it better. He accepted Nina's choice, but he didn't like it. He wanted to tell her no, but Samuel was right. More than Mont, Samuel's words kept rolling around in Zeke's head.

"I know you're feeling the same way I am. I'm sorry. We both love her. We are going to make sure she's safe."

Zeke nodded sharply.

"Are you going to come in the morning?"

Zeke exhaled. He'd hoped Montgomery wasn't going to ask him that. He didn't want to be there, but he had to be there. He had to make sure she was safe. "Whatever you want me to do."

"I think we'd both feel better if you were there. The FBI wants us to stay out of sight because they think Gwendolyn knows who we are, but I said there's no way in hell we're sitting it out. We'll be in a van or some shit, watching the whole thing."

"Okay," Zeke said, a thread holding him together.

"Let's get the hell out of here. Dinner? I can pick something up and bring it over if you're okay with me invading you two again."

"You're always welcome," Zeke said automatically. It was true. He never wanted Montgomery to feel like he couldn't join them, or just Zeke once Nina moved out and built her own life. Not that Zeke was ready to think about that.

"Thanks. When you're ready to head out, we'll go."

"I'm ready."

Montgomery nodded, looking closely at Zeke again, but he didn't say anything before he turned and went back to his office to get Nina.

Zeke couldn't stand there and pretend he was okay, so he walked to the door, waiting for them and taking the front as they walked outside and got Nina in the SUV. Montgomery waved and jogged to his vehicle, and Zeke got in his SUV with Nina.

She was quiet as Zeke pulled out of the lot and headed toward home. He wasn't any more talkative than she was, and the silence between them grew more and more awkward.

"I'm sorry I upset you," she whispered when they were halfway to his house. "I never wanted to do that."

Zeke drew a breath. He couldn't have a rational conversation about her putting herself in danger, especially when he was driving, but it seemed she was ready to talk. "It's fine."

"Really? Because you don't seem like it's fine."

"What do you want me to say? That I'm pissed off? That I hate that you're going to do this? That I am honestly considering locking you up so you can't go?"

She chuckled softly. "I know you'd never do that."

Zeke shook his head. "Maybe not, but it's tempting. I feel like I'm being torn in half. I understand now why that was a medieval torture method. It's fucking painful when it's not real."

She put her hand on his arm, and he jumped. She quickly moved her hand back to her lap. "I'm sorry."

Zeke sighed and reached for her hand. She let him take it and wind his fingers through hers. "I can't lose you again, Nina. I won't survive. She's going to kill you if she gets the chance. And the FBI can't stop that. You get that, right?"

Nina didn't reply, so Zeke looked at her. She was staring out the window and nibbling her bottom lip.

"I'm not trying to scare you, angel. I'm trying to be honest with you. What you agreed to is not safe. Their priority is bringing her in. But if they bring her in after she shoots you in the face, you're just a casualty. They still get what they want."

"Is that how you would do it?" she whispered.

Zeke shook his head and knew the truth. "Yeah. I hate it, but yeah. We've lost witnesses that way. A perfectly planned op can go sideways in a heartbeat. An innocent person can die. A criminal gets away. The whole thing goes to hell. It happens all the time."

"I still can't say no."

Zeke exhaled heavily and shook his head. He pulled into his driveway and straight into the garage before he replied.

"Why not? Why is it so important that you're the one who takes her down?"

"That's not what matters. I don't care who gets the credit for it. I'm not doing this so I can say I stopped her. But she needs to be stopped. No matter what, she needs to be stopped. And if that means I have to die in the process, I'm willing to do that."

"Why? Why would you sacrifice yourself? You just came back. You've been gone for so long, and you're finally back, and you're willing to die?" Zeke's voice cracked with emotion. He gripped her hand tighter and fought against the panic rising inside of him.

"Zeke," she breathed.

He pulled back, removing his hand from hers and wiping at his eyes to erase the tears building. He didn't say anything before he got out of the SUV and made his way around to her side. He opened her door, then led the way to the house.

Two meows sounded when they walked inside. Gene wrapped himself around Zeke's legs, and Franklin jumped off the counter and made a beeline for Nina.

Zeke picked up Gene and nuzzled the cat against his chin. He pressed his cheek against the top of Gene's head and cradled the cat.

Nina crouched down to pet Franklin, chuckling when the greedy cat jumped up on her knees and made himself at home on her lap. He stretched his front paws to her shoulder and bumped her chin with the top of his head.

Zeke watched his cat love up on his woman and knew nothing would ever be the same again. Even a week with her changed his life. She loved his cats like she'd known them forever. And they loved her like she was their person, too.

"I want more time with you," Zeke whispered. "I'm not ready for you to be gone."

"I'm not ready for that either," Nina said. "I know you're scared. I am, too. Can we... For tonight, can we not think about it? Can we just enjoy the night and not worry about tomorrow? Not worry about Gwendolyn or anyone else? Please?"

Zeke nodded slowly. He wouldn't be able to turn his mind off, but he could try to at least act normal for Nina's sake.

She smiled at him, the anxiety in her eyes saying she wasn't any more sure about tomorrow than he was.

For now, that was going to have to be enough to convince him that she would be safe. Because nothing else would make him feel better about the day to come.

15

———

Every moment felt like a goodbye for Nina. The way her brother hugged her a little longer than usual, the way Zeke kissed her before they got out of bed, the way they lingered in the shower and sipped coffee and took the long way to the Rose Protection Agency office. It was all a little slower than usual, a little softer, a little harder.

The bright sunshine outside was an unfair distraction for the day. She wanted gloomy and dark. Something that matched her mood and gave her an excuse to feel sad.

"Are you ready?" Lorelei asked as Nina pulled her shirt down to cover the microphone clipped to her bra.

Nina shook her head. "Is anyone ever ready for something like this?"

Lorelei pressed her lips into a sad smile. "I don't think so. But we're going to be watching every second and we will make sure you're safe."

Nina looked into the eyes of the agent. "Do you really mean that?"

Lorelei didn't hesitate to meet Nina's gaze. "Yes. I know what that woman, and her employees, are capable of. I know hurt first and ignore the questions later is their MO. And I know they won't hesitate to kill you, no matter what the consequences are."

"How are you going to prevent that?"

"You're not going in there alone. We worked with the owner and have agents posing as employees. We have cameras and security you've never heard of and we will know exactly what we're dealing with before they walk in the door."

"What does that mean?"

"It means we will know if Gwendolyn and her people are carrying guns or knives or any other weapons. We will know how close someone needs to get to you to hurt you. And we will make sure that doesn't happen."

Nina exhaled slowly, trying to trust the agent she wasn't sure she trusted.

"I know you don't know me. I know trusting a stranger isn't easy. I wish we'd had time to get to know each other, but every single person involved in this operation is doing it to stop her. If I could be there without causing suspicion, I would be."

Nina snorted. "You don't think me and Frannie having coffee is suspicious?"

Lorelei grinned wryly. "I'm sure Gwendolyn will know it's a trap. But we're hoping it's a big enough one that she can't resist."

"How are you letting her know we're there?" Nina had been wondering that the whole time. Did they assume Nina was being followed? Or Frannie? Or did they have a leak in the department?

"We know she's watching both of you. Your brother and Zeke are aware of it. We wanted you in protection yesterday, when we found out you were followed, but they insisted on giving you one more night with them."

"What?" Nina gasped. "What does that mean?"

"It means after this, we don't know what's going to happen, but we're going to do whatever we have to do to keep you safe."

"Even if I refuse?" Nina hated the idea of being captive, even if it was for her own good. She told Monty and Zeke that the day before. Why didn't they tell Lorelei?

"No," Lorelei said. "We can't force you. But we hope you'll consider it."

"I won't. I was her prisoner for long enough. I'm not going to be anyone else's."

"Understood," Lorelei said, not fighting but also not happy. "Frannie should be here soon, and we can go."

"Isn't she getting wired up?"

"Her husband did that already. Marcus wanted to make sure Frannie was okay and got her set up at home."

Nina drew a breath. Why didn't Zeke do that? Or Monty? They both disappeared when Lorelei said it was time to get her set up.

"There's Frannie," Lorelei said, stopping Nina's runaway thoughts.

Nina stood and watched Frannie make her way through the office with her hand securely in the police captain's. Nina hadn't met Marcus Patrick, but she'd heard enough about him from Gwendolyn to know he was a good man. Gwendolyn didn't hate people unless they were good.

Frannie walked into Monty's office and dropped Marcus's hand, abandoning him to approach Nina. Frannie pulled Nina into a warm hug and held her tight. "I'm so glad you're going to be there with me for this."

"Why?" Nina blurted.

Frannie breathed a laugh and released Nina. "Because you're strong and smart and together, we are going to make sure Gwennie comes in safely."

"Do you still care about her? Think she can change? That she's good?"

Frannie shook her head. "I don't know. I struggle to match the woman I knew years ago with the monster you and Lorelei know. Gwennie had me fooled for a long time. She was never evil to me, but I know that wasn't the case for most of the people who knew her."

Nina snorted. "Definitely not."

"As for her changing? I don't know. I've seen too many women abused over and over again by the same man after he promises not to hurt her for me to think people change easily. I think we have to have a reason, a damn good reason, to want to be better. I think maybe I want to believe people can change, but I also think some people are beyond the point where they can or are willing to try."

"She's never going to change. She's a murderer. Even if she stopped hurting people, she needs to pay for what she's already done."

"Yes, she does. And I think the best thing for that is prison. She deserves that."

"Not death?" Nina asked. It was what she thought Gwendolyn deserved. A slow, agonizing death that gave her a taste of what all of her victims went through.

"Death is too easy," Frannie said. "It's an escape. People think death is the answer, but death is just death. It means she never answers for what she did. She doesn't have to sit there and listen to people like you tell their story. It's freedom from persecution. I don't think anyone deserves to get out of it easy."

Nina sucked in a breath and wondered if Frannie hated

Gwendolyn even more than Nina did. "I can't let her hurt anyone else."

"I agree."

"Shall we go?" Lorelei asked.

Frannie nodded and took Nina's hand. They turned to the door, and Frannie smiled at her husband. "Nina, this is Captain Marcus Patrick, my husband."

"I know who you are," Nina said. "Gwendolyn hates you."

Marcus smiled, a delighted glint in his eyes. "I think that makes me very happy."

Nina chuckled. "It should. She said you've ruined too many of her plans." Nina looked at Frannie and Marcus. "Probably for far longer than she ever told me about."

Frannie nodded. "I met Marcus when Gwennie and I were still close. She told me to stay away from him, but I didn't listen."

"She probably would have gotten you involved in her business."

Frannie nodded. "Probably." She stopped and reached into her bag.

For a second, Nina panicked. Was it all over? Was Frannie going to kill her right there? With her cop husband and all the protectors around them? With the FBI standing there?

When Frannie pulled out a black scrap of fabric, Nina tried to calm her racing heart. "I know this is a weird thing, but I wanted to give this to you. It's a mask. It's something we all have. The first time I faced Damon, I wore mine. It made me feel strong. Like I could do anything." She handed over the simple black mask with an elastic loop to hold it in place. "I know it would be strange to wear it now, but I hope you'll accept it. We all feel as though you're one of us, and we are all with you today and always."

"All?" Nina asked, studying the mask and feeling oddly touched by the gesture.

"The Curvy Vigilantes. We've all fought against Gwendolyn and her organization. Tried to stop them. From Frannie at the beginning of all of this years ago to you today. All of us want the same thing, and we've all worked to move closer to ending this," Lorelei answered for Frannie.

"You're one?" Nina asked Lorelei.

Lorelei pulled out a black mask that looked just like Nina's and slid it on. "Proudly."

Nina put the mask on, feeling silly but not caring at the moment. She looked up and saw Frannie wearing one, too.

Frannie reached for Nina's and Lorelei's hands, grasping both tightly. Lorelei offered her other hand to Nina, giving Nina the option to grab hold or not.

Nina slid her hand into Lorelei's and drew a breath. Curvy Vigilantes. She wasn't alone. She didn't need to know the others to feel their power. They were connected. The beginning and the end.

And it would end. Gwendolyn would stop her reign. Nina would make sure of it.

"Thank you," Nina said.

"Thank you," Frannie replied.

"Time to go," Lorelei informed them.

NINA SAT across from Frannie at the coffee shop and tried to feel normal. She'd never once in her entire life sat at a coffee shop. Ever. When she was a teenager, they didn't really have the money for her to go out with friends and do things like get coffee. And when she was with Gwendolyn, she couldn't be seen in public.

"Just relax," Frannie whispered. "We're okay."

Nina tried to smile, not feeling less anxious just because she was being told to relax. They were at a table with four chairs toward the back of the coffeeshop. Nina wanted to sit in a booth, but Frannie said no. If someone sat next to one of them, they would be pinned and unable to get away if necessary.

Yeah, *relax* was not happening.

"Tell me about your brother. You two seem close," Frannie said.

Nina knew it was a way to distract her. Get her talking and stay on a safe subject. Monty and Zeke and God knew how many more people were listening, but Nina could sing Monty's praises for days. "He's amazing. I mean, he's a pain, but he's amazing. He was always someone I could count on, even when we were little."

"With your dad?"

Nina nodded. "Mon... my brother always protected me. From everything. Never wanted anything bad to happen to me."

Frannie smiled at Nina's slip. No names. It was harder than Nina expected.

"It's nice to have someone like that in your life."

"Did you?"

Frannie smiled. "I had a friend like that. And now my husband."

Nina knew Frannie was talking about Gwendolyn. It was hard for Nina to think of Gwendolyn as a person who had friends. She left the house less often than Nina, and Nina never left.

The front door to the coffeeshop opened, and a man

walked in. He was turned away from them, but there was something about him that had Nina on edge.

The man walked to the counter and ordered. Nina stared at him the whole time.

"Do you recognize him?" Frannie asked in a quiet voice.

Nina tried to shake her head, but then he turned. A smile lit his face, and he approached.

"Nina! Is that you? Good to see you out and about. Who's your friend?"

Nina gawked at him. Robert was one of her regulars. One of the men she thought were there for her. Who would protect her if she'd ever needed him to. Seeing him in the daylight, in a random coffeeshop, was shocking, to say the least.

"Never mind," Robert said, pulling out the chair next to Nina. "I already know who Frannie is. It's so nice to meet you."

Frannie didn't blink, just smiled. "It's always good to meet friends of Gwennie's. How is she doing? Is she joining you?"

Nina struggled to keep up. Robert was there instead of Gwendolyn? No. It wasn't possible. Was it?

"She's great. Really sorry she couldn't be here. The two of you together, though. What are the odds?" Robert laughed loudly, leaning back in his chair.

The flash of something shiny caught Nina's gaze. The heel of a gun. She gasped, and Robert followed her gaze.

"Whoops. Should keep that hidden. Wouldn't want to make anyone nervous."

"What are you doing here?" Nina asked.

"I was told you'd be here. I jumped at the chance to see my girl. How could I not?" He tucked a stray piece of hair behind Nina's ear.

How many times had he done the same thing before? How many times had she thought it was a sweet and thoughtful gesture?

His fingers lingered on her jaw. "Have you missed me?"

Nina couldn't breathe. The barista brought Robert's coffee and breakfast sandwich to the table.

He looked up at her and smiled brightly, thanking her for delivering his order, then sipped his coffee. He groaned in pleasure, a sound Nina knew well from their many times together.

"This coffee doesn't taste nearly as good as you do, Nina."

"What are you doing here?" she asked again.

Robert smiled. She used to think that look was charming and kind. Not anymore. It was a sneer. A judgement. He scanned her body and lifted his gaze to hers. "I was sure I had to be mistaken when I showed up for our weekly appointment and was told you were gone." He leaned closer, kissing her neck. "Do you really think you can disappear on me?"

Nina shivered at the threat in his voice. "I don't belong to you."

"Yes, you do." He took another sip of his coffee, then picked up his sandwich. "I paid for you. I paid more than if I'd just bought you, but I paid for you. I even paid to make sure you were clean when I arrived, so you're welcome for that, too. I paid to keep others away from you. I needed to know I wasn't going to get something from you."

"You know all of that was illegal, right?" Frannie asked.

Robert looked at Frannie, the condescending smile one you'd give a child who spoke out of turn. "I guess being married to a cop has given that moral compass of yours a good straightening, hasn't it? It wasn't so true years ago when you walked away from a dying Casey Slater."

Frannie gasped.

Nina swallowed. "What do you want, Robert?"

"Well, first, my name's not Robert. Did you really think I was going to use my real name with you? No. But I did use my real dick when I fucked you. Every week. For years, Nina. It was so good. You could have come to me when you ran away, but you had to go to your brother's friend. I mean, I get it, the man is a specimen, but Gwendolyn is pissed. She thought she could trust you. All those years together. She took care of you. Do you remember when she used to brush your hair at night? When you two would have dinner together? All the things you used to do. She missed that."

"That was a long time ago."

Robert pounded the table, making all the mugs and plates jump. "I was talking, Nina. You don't get to interrupt. You're the whore who takes my dick when I tell you to. You don't get an opinion."

"She's not a whore," Frannie growled. "And she's never going to touch you again."

Robert shook his head slowly. "You never should have left, Nina. And if you're smart, you'll go back home. Let Gwendolyn take care of you again. She misses you."

"I'm never going back to her," Nina whispered. She'd lived in fear for most of her life. First her father, then Gwendolyn, but sitting next to Robert and hearing the venom in his voice told her Zeke was right. The FBI wasn't going to stop Robert or Gwendolyn or anyone. They wanted someone in custody, and they were willing to sacrifice Nina and anyone else they had to in order to get what they needed.

"Shame," Robert said. "A real shame."

He grabbed Nina so fast she couldn't react in time to stop him. His lips came down on hers hard. Punishing. His tongue tried to press into her mouth, but she fought him. He yanked her hair, making her gasp, and he pushed his tongue into her mouth. His other hand went to her thigh, trying to pull them apart so he could get access to her.

"FBI, hands up!"

Robert pulled back just enough to look into her eyes, tugging her hair to control her. "We could have had a few more years together, Nina. Until you let those crazy ideas about us out and I would have had to put an end to you."

Nina gasped.

"Enjoy your last few days."

Robert was yanked away from her, his hold on her hair jerking her forward.

Nina put her hand to her mouth, wincing at the cut from his bite, and watched as Robert was forced face down on the counter. Handcuffs were slapped on him, then he was dragged from the coffeeshop and into a black SUV waiting outside.

Nina was still shaking, the whole thing taking a minute or two.

"I'm so sorry," Frannie whispered. "I thought I was ready for this, but I never thought... Are you okay?"

Nina shook her head. Tears leaked down her cheeks. She felt dirty and violated and ashamed. She needed to hide. To get away from everyone and take a shower and try to forget about the last twelve years of her life.

"All those thoughts you're having right now, don't listen to them," Frannie said. "They're wrong. You were tricked, and you were threatened, and you did nothing wrong, Nina. Do you hear me? You did nothing wrong."

Nina shook her head again. "How can you say that? How

can you even think it might be true? I told myself he was good to me. That if the situation were different, he might have been someone I could care about. But he was lying to me the whole time. I had no idea."

"He was good at it. He manipulated you just like she did."

"I let it happen. I wanted to believe it all. I wanted someone who cared."

"You have people who care. And they'd never do anything like that to you." Frannie nodded to Zeke and Monty, both arguing with the agents at the door.

Zeke looked up and his gaze connected with Nina's. She expected disgust or disapproval, but all she saw was the same look he'd given her since she opened the door and saw him waiting for her outside the convenience store.

Zeke deserved better, but with everything so raw, Nina wasn't strong enough to walk away from him. All she wanted was to be in his arms and feel safe for one more night.

16

ZEKE DIDN'T CARE WHO HE HAD TO FIGHT, HE WAS GETTING inside the fucking coffeeshop and getting Nina in his arms. Now.

"For fuck's sake, we were in the damn van with Agent Sloane and Agent Johnson," Montgomery growled at the man guarding the door.

"I have orders not to let anyone in or out—"

"Let them in. Now," Adam Johnson snapped. "They have made all of this possible. Let all of us inside." Adam flashed his badge at the dude who refused to let them all in and gave the man a heated glare that Zeke would not have wanted to be on the other end of when he was younger.

But it worked, and Zeke was grateful as fuck for it when he and Montgomery were able to rush past the other people crowding the coffeeshop and get to Nina.

Montgomery reached her first, pulling her against his chest and kissing the top of her head. Zeke twitched with the need to hold her. He wasn't her brother, or her lover, or anyone who mattered, but after listening to the conversation, he needed to touch her. To feel for himself that she was uninjured.

Montgomery cupped her face and looked at her closely. "Are you okay?"

Nina laughed mirthlessly and shook her head. "No. Not even a little."

Montgomery pulled her in again, his shoulders tight with the tension of the day. Nina held on to her brother, Zeke standing to the side like a third wheel who couldn't take a hint. He didn't fucking care.

Montgomery eased back from her again. "What can we do?"

Nina shook her head. "Nothing. I just... I trusted him, and it hurts to know I was wrong. That nothing was what I thought it was."

"None of that is on you," Montgomery declared. "Not one second."

Nina jerked her head behind her. "That's what Frannie said."

"She's right," Zeke interjected. "You were lied to for years. How could you have known that? But you're safe now. You're with us."

Nina looked straight at him, but there was something different in her gaze. A question maybe? Something that said she wasn't so sure about them anymore.

Fuck that.

"Come here," he said roughly, reaching for Nina.

She went to him, her lower lip wobbling before she clamped it between her teeth and stepped into his embrace.

"You are so damn strong," Zeke whispered. "So strong, angel."

Nina relaxed against him with his words, letting him

hold her as she finally crumbled. Sobs shook her body and echoed around all of them.

Zeke scooped her up and carried her to a booth. He shoved the table to one side and sat on the bench.

Nina hung on him, her strength barely enough to keep her in place.

Zeke held her, both arms wrapped tightly around her. He whispered to her as she cried, reminding her how strong she was and hating that she had to relive the worst parts of her hell.

When Nina told him about the men she felt connected to, Zeke was jealous. He wanted that with her. He wanted her to trust him, to count on him. Hearing that it was all a lie, that she was manipulated into those relationships, had his heart cracking.

Nina deserved the world. She deserved love and care and passion. She deserved to be with someone who would always put her first.

Zeke wanted to be that person for her, but he wouldn't force her into it. He would make sure she knew he was there and always would be.

Montgomery kicked Zeke's boot. Zeke looked up, his heart skipping when he saw the look on Mont's face. "What do you need?"

Mont's quiet question was directed at Zeke, not Nina. Zeke shook his head, trying not to be upset that Mont was asking.

"I can take her," Mont whispered.

Zeke shook his head again. There was no fucking way he was letting her go. She was his. Until she decided she didn't want to be, she belonged to Zeke. He would forever belong to her.

Mont nodded. He turned to the rest of the coffeeshop,

blocking them from all the others who were there. Arms crossed, feet planted wide, Mont was protecting Nina.

"I'm sorry," Nina whispered to Zeke. "I shouldn't be crying to you."

"Why the fuck not?" Zeke asked.

"You didn't sign up for this."

"I'm here for all of it, angel. Every bad moment, every good moment, every threat, every celebration. I want all of it. I'm not going anywhere."

Nina looked at him, her watery gaze searching his for the truth. He let her look, not caring what she saw in his eyes. He wasn't leaving her. "Thank you."

"Always, Nina. I will always be here for you. No matter what."

She nodded. "I know. I always knew."

"That will never change. You understand me?"

She sucked in a breath and nodded. "Zeke."

"We need to speak to her," Lorelei said to Montgomery. She glanced around him and caught Zeke's gaze. "I know how bad this part sucks."

"Not stopping you, though," Montgomery told the agent.

Lorelei shook her head. "You know I can't."

"We're not leaving her," Montgomery declared.

"Wouldn't ask you to," Lorelei told him.

Montgomery looked back at Zeke and Nina.

Zeke raised an eyebrow at Nina, and she nodded. She moved to sit next to Zeke on the bench, next to the wall. She grabbed his hand and held on tight.

Zeke pulled the table back into place so Lorelei could sit across from him and Nina. Montgomery stood at the end of the booth, arms crossed and maintaining their privacy.

"First, he's in custody. He is not talking, but we are not letting him go," Lorelei said.

Nina nodded. "Thank you."

Lorelei looked at Zeke, then Montgomery, then back to Nina. "Are you comfortable discussing what he said with them here?"

Zeke squeezed her hand, praying she agreed. He couldn't walk away.

"Yes," Nina said. "They know everything."

"Okay. Can you confirm the things he said? He was a regular client of yours who paid to be with you."

"I was never given any money. All of that was handled by Gwendolyn or whoever she had taking care of it. But our relationship was not completely consensual."

"Meaning?"

"Meaning we didn't meet at a bar and hookup. He was brought to me and I was told he paid good money for me and if I didn't show him a good time, there would be consequences."

Zeke ached to carry her away. To stop all of it and just leave. Love her until she forgot about all the others, until the past was a dream and not so real her pain radiated off of her with each word.

"But eventually it became more?" Lorelei asked.

Nina sighed. "Gwendolyn liked me. Let me be more selective. Decided I could have regulars who would only see me. He was one who asked for that. That's what I was told."

"And you agreed?"

"He was still paying. We didn't go out on dates. We didn't have wine and romance and relax and watch TV. We weren't a regular couple, and I knew that. There were others. Do you want me to say I was involved with all of them? That I liked them? I trusted him. I believed he cared. I wanted to believe he wasn't just fucking me because he was paying for it even though I knew he was. I wanted to think someone gave a shit about me." Nina tensed, her entire body curling in on itself. She gripped Zeke's hand tighter, but he knew it wasn't conscious.

"That's enough," Zeke growled at Lorelei. He liked her, but he was not going to sit there and let her make Nina feel worse than she already did.

"I have zero sympathy for Gwendolyn Lennox or anyone who was working for her by choice. That piece of shit we just took out of here was no better than her. He lied and manipulated Nina, likely to get information for Gwendolyn. To find out if she was loyal. He's a piece of garbage who will never see the light of day again because of the things he confessed to." Lorelei's anger was clear.

"Why would he do that?" Nina whispered.

Lorelei shook her head. "We're trying to figure that out. He knew we were watching. Gwendolyn did, too. We don't believe it was an accident that he showed up here. She sent him. What we don't know is what her end game is."

"She doesn't let people talk. When they're in custody, they're dead," Nina said.

"We know," Lorelei agreed. "We have agents with him. He won't be alone."

"That doesn't mean he's not going to die."

Lorelei nodded. "We're expecting something. We don't know what, but we know it's likely. No matter what, we're not going to let him get away with what he did to you."

"Thank you," Nina whispered.

Lorelei reached across the table, offering her hand to Nina. Nina put her free hand into Lorelei's. "I'm sorry we asked you to do this. I know this was not easy. But your help was invaluable. Even if we don't get more out of him, we know she's watching. We just have to figure out how and find her."

"I hope you do."

Lorelei nodded. "I'm not giving up until we do."

"Good."

Lorelei thanked all of them, then said they were free to go if they wanted to get out of there. She promised to keep them updated if they learned anything from Robert, and asked again if they wanted to be in protective custody.

"No," Nina said. "Zeke and Monty are the best protection I could have."

Lorelei nodded. "Be safe. All of you."

As soon as they got to Zeke's house, Nina went to shower. She felt dirty after talking to Robert, or whatever his name was, and she needed to escape. To separate herself from Zeke and Monty.

Zeke watched her as she made her way up the stairs, his gaze on her back burning a hole in her. She turned back when she made it to his bedroom door, and she smiled at him.

He nodded once, but the look on his face said he wanted to be there with her.

She wanted the same.

A meow at her feet drew her gaze to where Gene wound himself through her legs. He nudged her leg, then went into the bedroom.

"Did he send you up here to guard me?" Nina asked the cat.

Gene jumped up on the bed and meowed at her.

Nina chuckled. "I guess he did. Well, let's go then."

She took off her clothes, tossing everything in the laundry basket before turning the shower on and getting in.

A meow had her eyes flipping open as she tipped her head back. Gene was on the toilet, watching her intently.

"I'll be out in a minute. You probably don't want to be soaked."

He jumped down and pawed at the door.

Nina raised an eyebrow. "It's wet in here."

He cried again.

"Suit yourself." She opened the door, waiting for the cat to yell at her.

Nope. The crazy thing stepped into the shower and sat down at the far edge, mostly outside the spray but still in the shower.

Nina chuckled. "You're an odd cat."

He meowed once, then licked his paw and stared at her.

It was a little unnerving, but strangely comforting. She tipped her head back again, letting the water flow through her hair. It cascaded over her body and rinsed away the day. She let the tears come, cleansing herself from Robert and what happened. She washed her hair and her body and inhaled the now-familiar scent of Zeke.

She didn't want to put on any of the clothes he bought her. She needed to be surrounded by him, to breathe his scent. She didn't think he'd mind, so she pulled on a pair of panties he'd bought her, then searched through his drawers until she found a sweatshirt and a pair of lounge pants. She towel-dried her hair and ran a brush through it, then scratched a very content Gene behind the ears.

"Are you ready to go back downstairs?"

Gene chirped at her and went to the door.

"Smart cat."

Nina opened the door, then stopped when she heard a female voice.

"She's strong. And brave. She's changing lives, but it's going to take a toll."

Nina wondered who Berkeley was talking about. Was it rude to interrupt or worse to listen?

"Nina has always been strong," Zeke said with conviction.

"Yeah, she has been," Monty agreed. "I just wish she didn't have to be so strong."

Nina inhaled a breath. She was used to negativity and dislike. Not encouragement.

"Are you sticking around for lunch?" Zeke asked.

"I should go," Berkeley said, her voice changing.

Nina started down the stairs, not hiding her steps in hopes it would delay Berkeley's departure.

She made it to the bottom and saw it worked. "Berkeley. I didn't know you were here."

"I just brought some lunch. Lorelei came by the office, and I ran out to grab stuff for everyone. I don't know what you really like, but I got a bunch of stuff from the Italian place we order from sometimes. I know what these two like and added extra."

"You're going to join us, right?" Nina asked.

Berkeley shook her head. "I should really get back to the office. Lots to do."

Nina went to Monty and poked her brother in the side. "Tell her to stay. She needs to eat lunch anyway."

"You should stay," Monty growled.

Berkeley stared at him for a long moment, the tension in the room climbing with each tick of the clock on the kitchen wall. Berkeley finally pressed her lips into a smile and nodded. "Okay. I will."

Nina hugged Berkeley, the impulse to make the other

woman comfortable overwhelming her. "I'm so happy to hear that. I think we will be friends."

"I hope so," Berkeley said. "I've heard so much about you over the years. It's an honor to get to know you."

"Oh, I haven't done anything worthy of that. But I'm excited to get to know you, too."

Berkeley smiled and led the way to the bags of food she brought over. She told Nina what everything was and handed over containers to Monty and Zeke without breaking her explanation.

"Whoa, what did you give them?" Nina asked.

"They always order the same thing. I have more of both, though, so you can choose what you want and they have leftovers if you don't want the same thing."

"What do you like?"

Berkeley's gaze strayed to Monty before she forced it away. "I like everything. My hips tell you that."

Nina chuckled and shook her head. "Mine say the same. Size does matter. Bigger is always better."

Monty choked on air. Zeke stared open-mouthed at her. Berkeley just laughed.

"I like you."

"I like you, too," Nina told her.

Berkeley smiled and helped herself to some lunch.

The four of them sat in the living room. Zeke took the seat next to Nina on the couch, with Monty on her other side and Berkeley on the chair across the room.

Nina and Berkeley kept up most of the conversation. Berkeley was funny and friendly and kind. She was the kind of person Nina wanted her brother to end up with. Someone who would keep Monty on his toes but also take care of him.

"How did you all meet?" Nina asked.

"She applied for the job," Monty growled, not offering more information.

Berkeley forced a smile. "I saw a posting for a business manager and applied."

"How long have you been at Rose Protection Agency?"

"Three years."

"Wow. That's a long time. Dating? There are some cute men working there."

Again, Berkeley's gaze slid to Monty, but she tore it away and shook her head. "Not at work. I don't think that would go over well."

"Outside of work?"

"What's with the inquisition?" Monty asked, jumping up.

"Whoa. What's with you? I can't get to know her?" Nina replied.

"I didn't say that. I just don't get why you have to ask her about dating. It's her business if she's dating." Monty stalked to the kitchen, his back to all of them.

Nina watched her brother, then swung her gaze back to Berkeley. "I apologize. I didn't realize asking you about dating wasn't okay. I'm... I really am sorry."

Berkeley smiled kindly. "It's okay. I didn't mind. But I'm not dating anyone right now."

"I won't bother you about that again. I really didn't mean to make you uncomfortable."

"Then maybe you should stop," Monty barked.

Nina opened her mouth to say something but closed it. She didn't know what she did wrong, but she knew better than to keep pushing. She learned that lesson with Gwendolyn and didn't need a refresher from her brother.

"It's okay," Berkeley said, rising. "Um, I should go. I have some things to finish before the end of the day."

"Thanks for bringing lunch, Berk," Zeke said. He stood, the loss of his leg against Nina's as much of a shock as Monty's attitude.

"Yes, thank you," Nina added, frozen to the couch. She smiled at Berkeley but didn't make a move to hug her or walk her to the door.

Monty didn't say a thing.

Zeke and Berkeley spoke quietly, their words too soft for Nina to hear. She watched as Zeke gave Berkeley a quick hug, looking away when he caught her watching them.

Nina focused on her hands in front of her, her cheeks burning with understanding. Berkeley and Zeke were not just coworkers, but no one wanted to tell her that. Berkeley probably hated Nina. Not only had Nina moved in with the guy she was interested in or dating or something, but Nina was falling for him and risking his life and getting way too close to him and more-or-less forcing him to pause whatever was going on Berkeley.

The door closed, and the lock flipped. Nina tried to find the words to apologize to Zeke, but before she could say anything, he spoke.

"What the fuck is wrong with you?" Zeke growled.

Nina turned to answer, ready to apologize, but Zeke wasn't talking to her. He was in Monty's face.

"Let it go, Zeke," Monty snarled.

"She brought us lunch. She was being nice. And instead of saying thank you, you're attacking Nina for getting to know Berk, and snapping at Berkeley. What the hell?"

"It's nothing," Monty said.

"It's not nothing. What the hell is with you lately? Ever since—" Zeke stopped mid-sentence.

Nina wanted to ask when, but she knew when both men looked at her. Ever since she came back. Ever since they found out she left. Ever since she blew up their lives. Nothing was the same.

"I need to go." Monty moved toward the door.

"Don't do this, Mont."

Monty stopped, looking past Zeke to Nina. "I'll see you tomorrow, okay?"

Nina swallowed the lump in her throat and nodded. Monty slid a look to Zeke, then walked out the door, closing it softly behind him.

"I never should have come back," Nina whispered.

17

____

ZEKE TURNED SLOWLY, HOPING HE HEARD HER WRONG. "WHAT did you say?"

She shook her head, her long hair tumbling over her shoulders and reminding him of a long ago moment when she refused to do something Montgomery told her to do. She looked the same. Small, vulnerable, innocent. "I am messing up everything for both of you. I'm in the way and I'm screwing up your lives. I shouldn't have called you. I should have just run."

Zeke stalked across the house to her, doing his best to stuff down the anger coursing through him like a toxin he couldn't fight off. "Don't you dare say that. You being here is a gift. It's something Mont and I have dreamed about for twelve years."

"He's all angry and whatever, and I'm in your way of things with Berkeley."

"Whoa, what? We'll talk about Mont in a second, but Berkeley? There's nothing going on with Berk and me. Never has been, never will be."

"But you were whispering, and you hugged her. You seem close."

Zeke scrubbed a hand over his face and tried to measure what she thought she saw with what it meant she thought about him. He took a careful step back. "Berkeley is a good friend. She's someone we've relied on for years to help coordinate things at work. She's kind and she's funny and I care about her. But she's like the sister I never had, not a woman I want to fuck."

Nina flinched at his harsh word, but he didn't fucking care. She needed to understand what he was saying.

"I always thought I was the sister you never had," Nina said.

Zeke shook his head slowly. "No. I haven't thought of you as a sister ever. You were the woman I wanted in my bed. The woman I wished was mine. The woman I thought about when I jerked off. You were never a sister to me. Not even close, Nina."

"Oh," she whispered.

"As for you thinking I would have something going on with Berkeley and sharing a bed with you, tasting you, getting you on your knees... I don't even know what to say about that. That's not who I am. I don't fuck around on women. I have never been involved with more than one woman at a time."

"I didn't mean..."

"Yeah, you did. You thought that little of me. You asked me before and you still thought it." Zeke shook his head and went to the kitchen, needing the space from her.

"Zeke."

"It's okay. You don't know me. Not really. Not anymore. We may as well be strangers."

"I do know you, Zeke. I just... I've never been allowed to be jealous before."

"You have no reason to be jealous now. Not with me. You're the only woman I see, Nina. You're the only one I want in my bed. The only one I've been dreaming about fucking every night since I can remember."

"Zeke." She took a step closer, pausing until he met her gaze. She moved toward him slowly.

His heart beat faster with each step she took. He wanted to carry her to his bed and show her exactly how he felt. He wanted her to forget every other man who fucked her and only feel him for the rest of her life. But possessing her wasn't for her. It was for him.

"I want you, Zeke."

He shook his head. "I don't want your pity or guilt or whatever this is. I'm not that guy either."

"Why are you making this so hard?"

Zeke sighed. "I'm not making anything hard, Nina. I'm trying to be honest with you. I'm trying to tell you who I am. I'm not involved with Berkeley. And if I was, I would have told you the first time you asked if there was someone else and I would not be involved with you. Mont was a dick earlier, and I was making sure she was okay. Because he can be that way with her. Especially when she talks about dating. I don't get it, but tonight was worse than usual. I was asking her if she was okay."

"I think my brother's in love with her."

Zeke shook his head. "That's not it. He counts on her for everything. He's not going to mess that up by getting involved with her."

"I don't think people control who they love. But what do I know? I've been an unpaid prostitute my entire adult life."

Zeke inhaled sharply. He closed his eyes and tried not to picture Nina and Robert together.

He failed.

A hand on his arm had his eyes opening. Nina was right there in front of him, looking up at him. "I'm sorry I thought you and Berkeley were involved. You looked... intimate. Close. Like there was more going on than I knew, and after the way Monty was acting, I realized how little I know about either of you and your lives since I've been gone. I... I've carried a lot of regrets. I didn't think coming back was going to be easy, but I didn't mean to blow up your lives."

"You didn't, angel. Having you here is the best thing to ever happen." Zeke pulled her into his arms and held her close, absorbing the shudder that raced through her.

"I wish I'd never left," she whispered.

"Me, too. But you're here now."

She nodded.

"As for Mont, I think he carried a lot more guilt than I realized. He blamed himself for not protecting you. He built Rose Protection Agency so others had someone there for them, like you didn't."

"I thought I did."

Zeke nodded. "I get it. But we didn't know that. You just didn't come home. We thought something happened, and twelve years is a long time to wonder and worry, and he's struggling."

"Do you think I should do something? Is there something that would help?"

Zeke shook his head. "Just don't give up on him. And stop saying you wish you'd never come back. It doesn't matter what it does, we want you here."

Nina nodded.

"What do you want to do with the rest of the day?"

"Don't you have to work?"

Zeke shook his head. "I'm not leaving you. Things are being handled at work. It'll be fine."

"But you would normally be there?"

Zeke nodded. "Mont and I are both pretty much always at work. Neither of us had anything to go home for."

A meow argued with his statement.

Zeke chuckled and looked down at Gene. "Did you enjoy your shower, you weird thing?"

"He does that to you, too?" Nina asked.

Zeke leaned down and scooped up Gene. He held the cat like a baby and rubbed his belly. "Yeah. I don't know why. He seems to like the water."

"I always thought cats hated water."

Zeke nodded. "Not this one. Franklin will howl like he's being murdered if you get water on him."

Nina looked around, spotting Franklin on the back of the couch. She walked over and rubbed his head, getting a nuzzle for her efforts. "I think this is a pretty perfect day. Cats and you."

His heart squeezed. He wanted the same. Forever. "I'll make popcorn. You find something to watch."

"Is he dead?" Gwendolyn asked Fernando when he walked into the room she was using as an office. It sucked, but she had no choice.

Fernando nodded. "Yes. Did exactly what he was supposed to do."

"Good. I can't risk someone else telling the FBI anything."

"Do you think she'll take the bait?" Fernando asked.

Gwendolyn knew it was a risk to send 'Robert' to see Nina. When she heard Nina and Frannie were at the coffeeshop, Gwendolyn wanted to go herself. It was obviously a trap, but it was a damn good one. "I wouldn't have taken the risk and sent him if I thought she wouldn't."

Fernando nodded. "Do we need to do anything?"

Gwendolyn grinned. "Get her room ready. She won't get away again."

NINA COULD BARELY STAY on her side of the couch by the time Zeke made dinner and they started season three of a show she'd never heard of but was absolutely in love with. But no matter how good the show was, she was entirely focused on Zeke. Every touch on her thigh, every glance he thought she didn't see, every shift of his body to draw him closer to her.

She wasn't lying when she said she wanted him. Resisting him was a challenge for her, and having him right there, his scent wrapping around her and his heat burning into her, she was failing at keeping her mind on the movie instead of how good he felt with his tongue on her body and his dick in her mouth.

"Do you need anything?" Zeke asked, grabbing his glass and standing.

"You."

Zeke stopped for half a second, then continued to the kitchen. He refilled his glass, then returned to the couch. His hand went to her thigh again, keeping her close. "I've never been in a relationship."

Nina looked over at him. He was staring at the TV, but what he was telling her was important.

"I dated a few girls in high school and before the military, but I was always waiting." He cut himself off.

"What were you waiting for?" she whispered.

"You."

He met her gaze, and her breath stopped.

"I wanted you, Nina. I was so gone for you, I couldn't bring myself to get involved with anyone else. Not seriously. A night or two, and I would stop calling. I always felt like I was cheating on you, even though you had no idea. When you left... I never shook that feeling."

"Zeke."

"I need you to understand that when you say you want me, it's a fantasy I've had for most of my life. But I don't know what Montgomery is going to say. I never told him. All he knows is I've never been able to commit to a woman. He's going to tell you to stay away from me."

"I won't listen."

Zeke squeezed her thigh. "You might, but either way, I want you to hear all of this from me. I want you to know why I've never committed to anyone else. It's always been you. But I can't promise I'll always do the right thing. I can't tell you I know what the right thing is. What I do know is I will do whatever it takes to keep you safe, whether you want me the same way or not. You are important to me, Nina. You are the most important person to me. Sitting in that van today and listening to all of that..."

Nina swallowed and waited for Zeke to reject her. For him to tell her it was too much and no matter what he felt for her before, it all changed after that.

"Listening to all of that made me want to rush in there and tear that fucker to pieces with my bare hands."

"What? He was telling the truth. He was telling you who I was."

Zeke tucked her hair behind her ear, his fingers lingering on her neck. "No, angel. He was telling me who you had to be. He wasn't telling me who you are. When we're in life and death situations, we can't be rational. It's instinct."

"Have you been in those situations?"

Zeke nodded. "Mont and I saw some bad shit. Did some bad shit. I know we had to, to protect our country and to save lives, but it wasn't easy. What we do now isn't always easy either. We are protecting people from others who want them dead. Our hands are not clean."

"You're helping people. You're heroes."

"It doesn't feel like it."

"You are," Nina insisted. "You have no idea how good of a man you are. How happy it makes me to know you haven't changed. That you're still someone who will protect others the way you always did for me when we were younger."

"I'll always protect you, Nina. If you ever need me, I will always come for you."

"I need you now, Zeke. I want you to love me. I want to feel you inside me and erase all the others. To take back what they stole from me."

He inhaled deeply, holding his breath as he leaned his forehead against hers. "Are you sure you're ready for that, angel?"

"With you? Yes, Zeke. Please."

"You know I can't say no to you."

"Then don't. Love me, Zeke. Make love to me. Show me how good it can be."

He nodded and stood, reaching for her hand.

She let him help her up and laughed when he tugged her into his arms.

He hugged her tight, his hands wrapping around her

and covering her back. He buried his nose in her hair and held her for a long moment.

When he pulled back, he didn't hurry to drag her upstairs. He took his time, walking around the house and making sure everything was locked, lights and TV were off, and the cats were good for the night. He met her at the bottom of the stairs and kissed her again, his warm lips soft against hers instead of demanding.

Tears welled up in her eyes. This was what her first time should have been like. A man who cared. A man who cherished her.

Zeke took her hand and turned her to go up the stairs first, staying close enough to keep her hand in his. When they made it to his room, he turned the light on inside the room, then turned the stairwell light off. He closed the bedroom door and walked to the bathroom to turn that light on, always making sure they weren't in the darkness.

He pulled the bathroom door mostly closed, then turned off the bedroom light. Nina stood next to the bed and watched him. She wanted to get her hands on him, to feel his warmth and strength. She was nervous, more nervous than she thought she'd be. She wanted him, but it was different from all her other experiences.

Would he enjoy himself? Would he still want her afterward?

He stopped in front of her, tilting her chin slowly until she met his gaze. "You say stop or no or anything, and I stop. You understand me?"

"Yes. I will do the same."

He chuckled. "Oh, angel, I'm never going to say no to you. And I'll never want you to stop."

The truth of his words scraped over all her vulnerable parts, healing pieces of her she never wanted to admit were so raw. She swallowed roughly, something he noticed with his hand on her jaw.

"What is it?"

She tried to smile. "I don't want to disappoint you."

"You never could." He moved closer to her. "Can I kiss you, Nina?"

She nodded, and he leaned down, giving her more than enough time to stop him.

His lips landed on hers in a gentle touch, feather-light, like he wasn't sure she was really on board. His erection nestled against her stomach, and her breath faltered with her inhale.

His kisses were soft and sweet, barely more than the kiss she would give her brother but so much more intimate. So much more everything because it was Zeke.

He parted his lips and brushed his tongue over her lips. When she opened for him, he sighed and brought her body against his. His hands cradled her back, not rushing them to anything else.

Nina didn't know how to handle his delicate touches and his slow pace. She'd never had time. She'd never been allowed to savor a man. Never wanted to. But that was what it felt like. Zeke was savoring their time. He was enjoying every second of it.

And so was she.

He lifted the back of her shirt, his warm hand touching her bare skin as a moan escaped her throat. He inhaled past her cheek, the rush of cold air a contrast to the heat of the rest of him. He tilted his head and deepened the kiss, twirling his tongue around hers without retreating.

His hands moved higher, then a groan had him pulling back. "No bra?"

She shook her head. "I wanted to be comfortable."

"It was tempting to see you in my sweatshirt and pants all day, but to know your bare breasts were brushing against the fabric makes me crazy, Nina."

"Is it okay?"

"Also-fucking-lutely, angel. Anything I have is yours." He brought his hands around to her front as he spoke, teasing the underside of her breasts. "Can I take it off?"

She nodded, moving to help him take the sweatshirt off.

He groaned and cupped both breasts, bringing them together and ducking to take both nipples into his mouth at the same time.

She whimpered at the feel of him. It didn't matter that she'd been naked with him already, or that he'd touched her all over, it was different. It was sensual and teasing and made her feel worthy.

He kissed down her stomach and dropped to his knees. He wrapped both arms around her and hugged her to him, his head against her belly. "Thank you for coming back to me, Nina."

"Thank you for answering my call. And coming to get me."

Zeke kissed her stomach, then swirled his tongue in her bellybutton.

She gasped at the way the simple move made her tremble. Everything Zeke did seemed to have that effect on her.

"Can I take off your pants?" he whispered against her bellybutton.

"Yes."

He hooked his fingers in the waistband and grabbed her panties with the lounge pants. "Panties, too?"

"Yes."

He eased both down her legs, letting them fall to the floor at her feet. She stepped out of them, and he tossed both to the side, leaving her completely naked in the middle of his bedroom. "You're so beautiful, Nina. God, I'm so lucky to be here with you. Thank you."

"I'm the lucky one," she replied.

He kissed her thigh and shook his head. "No, angel, I am. I've waited for this day for longer than I care to think about. And if today isn't the day I make love to you, that's okay. I can keep waiting."

"I want you to, Zeke. Please."

"I'm going to enjoy every second of tonight, Nina. We don't need to rush."

"I want you."

"I'm right here, angel. Lay on the bed and spread these legs for me. It's been too long since I had my mouth on you."

She hurried to the bed and did as he asked. He crawled over to her, his gaze on her body and sending heat all over her. Moisture pooled between her thighs and dripped from her body before he made it to her.

He slid a finger into her, catching the wetness. "You're ready for me, huh?"

"Yes," she whispered.

"Oh, this is going to be so much fun." His mouth was on her as soon as his whispered words stopped.

Nina gasped and shook with the power of his tongue against her clit. Her hips rose to meet his face, and he growled in approval. His finger pumped into her, a second one quickly joining the first, and Nina stopped thinking about what came after. Tonight was all about Zeke.

18

————

Watching Nina orgasm was the second best thing in the world. The best was knowing he was the one to bring her there. To have his name fall from her lips, to taste her on his tongue, to hear her beg for more.

He was more than happy to do exactly what she wanted. Her first orgasm rolled through her with a shiver and a tightening, but he knew the second one would open her up in a new way. He pressed a third finger into her channel and lashed at her clit with his tongue, just the way she liked it.

For years he wondered what would do it for her. Friction, suction, hard and fast or slow and deep. Finding out exactly how to take her from dripping wet to gushing and beyond was a perverse joy Zeke couldn't get enough of. She was what he couldn't get enough of.

"Zeke," she whispered, her hand reaching for him.

He kept his tongue on her clit and his fingers inside her and took her hand with his free one. He brought her fingers to her clit, letting her feel the way he licked her. Giving her access to her body to add to the pleasure he gave her.

"So good. Zeke. So good."

Zeke groaned in agreement and licked her fingers. He alternated between her fingers and her clit until she shuddered and tightened around his fingers. He sucked hard on her clit, trapping her fingers in his mouth until she came with a shout.

"Oh, God, yes. Zeke. Yes. Oh, shit, so good."

His dick pulsed with desire, but he wasn't ready for that yet. He knew there was more from her. He was crazy for it. For her. He nipped at her fingers and flicked her clit with the tip of his tongue, curling his fingers inside her.

She was already at the edge and didn't fight it, falling quickly and freely into another orgasm. Her shout was louder. Her tremors were harder. He had to grit his teeth to stop himself from going with her, pumping his fingers into her as she bucked his face away. He chased her, licking her again and sending her into another orgasm before the last one finished.

"Oh, shit. Zeke. Zeke. No more. I can't. Oh my God. I need you."

Zeke withdrew immediately. He looked over the hills of her body at the flush of her skin, the rosy pink of her nipples, the freckles scattered all over her. He memorized all of it, praying he didn't have to relive it only from memory going forward.

"Come here. Please, Zeke. I want you. Please."

He rose, leaning over her and kissing her hard, plunging his tongue between her eager lips and letting her taste herself on him. She groaned and wrapped her legs around his hips, pulling his body on top of hers and whimpering.

"What do you want, angel?" he whispered against her ear.

"You, Zeke. I want you inside me. I want you to make love to me."

"You say stop, I stop, angel. No matter what, you're in charge here. Okay?"

"Don't stop, Zeke. Love me."

"Always, angel. Always." He choked back the declaration and extracted himself from her arms. He tore his clothes off, not caring where they fell as long as he was inside her as soon as possible. He grabbed a condom from the drawer beside his bed and offered it to her.

She'd moved to rest her head on a pillow, her eyes locked on him as he stripped. She took the condom and licked her lips, leaning toward him and taking his dick into her mouth.

"Fuck. Nina."

She moaned around his cock, dragging her tongue up the underside of him.

He jerked, her mouth feeling too fucking good. "Sorry, angel. Fuck."

She groaned and deep-throated him once more, making a noise in her throat when he hit the back, and he swore.

"This is going to be over too soon if you keep doing that," he growled.

She released him, kissing the tip of his leaking cock, then rolled the condom down his length. She laid back, pulling him with her and guiding him between her legs.

He stared at her, spread out on his bed, her red hair scattered all over his pillow, her wetness soaking his sheets. Never in his life did he hope he would live the moment. He dreamed of it, he prayed for it, but he never let himself hope it could be real.

But it was. She was real. And she was there, watching him with a sweet smile and a flush all over her body.

He cupped her jaw, caressing her cheek with his fingers. She turned her head and kissed the center of his palm. She nuzzled against his hand and wrapped her thigh around his hip.

"I want you, Zeke. I want to feel you inside me. I want to only remember you."

Zeke couldn't reply. If he did, he would tell her he was in love with her. It was too soon, too much. But he could show her. He could do what she asked and love her with his body.

He lined himself up with her entrance, letting her feel his erection.

She inhaled a shaky breath and sighed happily. She grabbed his hand, holding it against her cheek, and shifted her hips to bring him inside her body.

Zeke told himself to hold back. He told himself to go slow. It all went to shit when he sank an inch into her warmth. He surged forward, sliding deep until his entire cock disappeared into her.

She moaned and licked his hand. "So good, Zeke."

"Fuck, Nina." He stilled inside her. Her body rippled around him, holding him in place. His throat tingled. The base of his spine pulsed. Every cell in his body screamed at him to go. Faster, harder, deeper, more.

He wanted it. He wanted her. But he didn't listen to his body. He couldn't. He needed the night to last. To give her every ounce of pleasure possible. To show her how he loved her.

"Zeke," she whispered, bringing his attention back to her face. She smiled sweetly, pleasure drooping her eyes. She licked her lips and glanced down his body. "Please."

"What do you want, Nina? Tell me what feels good."

"You feel good, Zeke. All of you."

He shifted, and she moaned.

"Yeah, that. All of it."

"Are you going to come on me? Are you going to let me feel you come with me inside you?"

"Yes," she whispered.

He retreated slowly, letting her feel every inch of him leaving her, then pressed back inside just as slowly, watching her body stretch to take him in. "You're so fucking perfect, angel. Like you were made for me."

"Yes," she breathed.

He brushed his thumb over her swollen clit, and she gasped, her core tightening. "Is that good, angel?"

"Yes."

He did it again, and she surged to meet his stroke.

"Fuck, Zeke. So good. So good."

"Yes, angel. So good. Perfect. I love feeling you all around me."

She moaned in answer, words finally failing her as he worked her toward another orgasm.

Zeke kept talking, wanting her to hear his voice and remember he was the one there with her. "You feel so good, Nina. I love the way your body ripples with your pleasure. The flush of your skin when you get close. I love watching my dick disappear into you. My thumb on your clit as you come." He pressed harder and waited her out as she came with a shiver and a gasp.

"Yes."

"You're so beautiful."

"Come for me, Zeke."

"Come with me, Nina."

"I'll try."

He withdrew, then slammed into her, knowing he hit the right spot when she clenched the sheets in both fists.

"Oh, fuck."

"Yes, beautiful. Fuck. So good."

"Zeke," she begged.

Zeke lifted her hips and supported them on his legs. He spread her thighs wider, her pretty little clit poking out and begging for his touch. He licked his thumb, then brought the wet digit to her clit and rubbed it fast and hard.

"Oh, God. Zeke. Yes. Oh, shit, yes. Zeke!"

Sweat trickled down his back and beaded on his forehead. He didn't let her get away from him, his dick and thumb working her together and sending them both to bliss. She pulsed around him, her core tightening with each stroke inside, making it harder for him to withdraw.

He ached to close his eyes and lose himself to the feeling, but it was Nina. It was the woman he pictured more times than he could remember. He wasn't going to miss one second of the reality of her coming apart on his dick. He pounded into her, letting all the feelings inside him build. He gritted his teeth and swirled his thumb around her clit and slammed his body to hers, his balls bouncing against her ass. Everything ached from holding back.

Her cries blended with the wet sounds of their bodies clashing until she got louder, begging for a second before she let go.

"Zeke! Oh, fuck. Zeke. Good. So good. Fucking... yes. Zeke!"

He was lost in watching her and forgot about his own orgasm until it erupted inside him, his vision going black around the edges as he burst. He pressed hard on her clit, triggering another orgasm from her as he slammed deep into her, his body jerking uncontrollably with the force.

"Nina. Fuck. Love. Good. Damn, angel. Yes." He grunted and swore and nearly blacked out.

Then he collapsed onto her, all his weight pressing her

into the mattress for a second before he rolled them, bringing her on top of him so she wasn't trapped.

She panted for breath, her body as soaked as his. Her limbs hung next to him, her body dead weight on top.

Zeke ran his fingers up and down her back, soothing her as much as himself. Nina. His Nina. She was in his bed, fully sated. She cried his name and took his cock and made his dream a reality.

"Is all sex like that?" she whispered.

Zeke chuckled. "No, angel. It's never been like this for me. That was…"

"Transcendent."

He kissed the top of her head. "Yeah."

She was quiet for a minute, and he let her have her silence. He wondered what she was thinking, but what mattered more was she didn't run from him the second they were done. She laid there, her head on his chest, listening to his heartbeat.

"I should use the bathroom," she whispered.

He nodded and helped her up, smiling when her legs were shaky. He gripped the condom and pulled it off, following her to the bathroom to throw it away. He moved to leave when she sat down, but she grabbed his hand.

"Can I shower?"

Zeke remembered her saying she wasn't allowed to before. He wanted to smell like her as long as possible, but it was different for her. "Of course."

"Will you join me?"

"Fuck yes."

"Will you bring another condom?"

His cock twitched at the question. "Yes."

Nina smiled.

She still didn't realize he would do anything she asked. Anything.

AFTER THEIR SHOWER, and round two, which was somehow even better than round one, Nina slid between the covers with Zeke. Neither of them bothered with clothes. Nina hoped it was because Zeke wanted her again during the night and didn't want to fight to get to her. That was her thought.

He pulled her close and kissed the top of her head. His heartbeat was steady, solid, just like the rest of him.

Nina had never felt so safe in her life. Yeah, she knew Gwendolyn was out there. She knew everything was far from over. But Zeke had shown her at every turn that he was the man she remembered. The man she built up in her memory and dreamed of saving her. Yeah, he had changed, but he was still the same where it mattered.

"What are you thinking about?" he asked her.

She smiled and kissed his chest. "How lucky I am to know you."

He squeezed her tight. "I feel the same, Nina."

She ran her hands over his body, his tattoos nearly invisible in the dark room. After a week of wondering, she had to ask, "Will you tell me about your tattoos?"

He sucked in a breath. "I'll tell you anything. What do you want to know?"

"Which one was your first?"

His arm flexed under her hand. He sat up and turned on the lamp next to the bed. He sat against the headboard and dragged her up with him, holding her in his arms again. "This one." He pointed to the rose tattoo on his forearm. "A year after you disappeared, Mont and I went and got them. He has the same one. We were on leave and wanted to mark the day. Sounds weird, but the first year was hard. Harder than the rest, I think. We started to lose hope after a year, but we still had it when we got these."

Nina ran her fingers over the tattoo, a rose on its side, similar to the logo for Rose Protection Agency. "Is it the rose on the door to the office?"

Zeke chuckled. "It is. When we got them, it was a reminder of you. A rose for Nina Rose. We knew we would never forget you, but we wanted to carry you with us. To always have a piece of you." He stopped, his voice dropping to a whisper. "There was no news about you. No one knew anything. We wanted to believe you would be found, but we marked the day and vowed to carry on for you. When Mont started the agency, it was another way for us to heal from losing you. We talked about you a lot, about how things would have been different if you'd had someone. Using the same rose felt like the right thing to do. Everything we've done... both of us... we've always hoped you would come back."

Tears slid down Nina's cheeks. "I'm sorry I caused so much pain for you both."

Zeke tugged her against him and brushed his fingers through her hair. "You're back. You're safe. We love you, and we're going to keep you safe from now on. She will never get close to you again. I promise you, Nina Rose."

"Thank you." She laid against his chest and held tight to him. "Tell me more, Zeke. What do the rest mean?"

"This one was a joke. Mont picked it out one day. Said I was too serious and needed something to make people laugh." Zeke pointed to a mermaid on the back of his forearm.

"She is pretty hot."

Zeke snorted. "She always reminded me of you."

Nina gasped. "That's a compliment."

Zeke stared at her for a long moment.

Nina wanted to know what he was thinking, ached to hear him voice the thoughts running through his head, but he just smiled, then pointed to another tattoo.

"The bird is for freedom. The words *La Vida Loca*... We said that a lot when we were overseas. Those two I got after my first deployment."

"How long were you deployed?"

"Six months the first time. We left just after the first year. When we got back, I got those two."

"What are all the other roses?" Nina asked, realizing he had more than one rose.

"One for every year," Zeke whispered.

"Zeke."

He kissed her, soft and sweet and heartbreaking. "A dozen roses for you, Nina. I never forgot you. You've always been a part of me." He pointed to the one on his chest, right over his heart. "I carried you in my heart, Nina. With me forever, angel."

She kissed the rose, then kissed him. She climbed on top of him, his erection growing as she kissed him. Tears fell between their lips, and Nina let herself feel his love. She let herself be loved. She let herself heal, just a little, as he rolled a condom on and pushed inside her again. She let him soothe her body and soul and heart with his.

And when she fell asleep listening to his heartbeat, she pushed away the fear that she was being selfish and putting him at risk. She would protect Zeke with her life, just like he vowed to do for her.

ZEKE REACHED for Nina during the night, sliding into her and loving her again. He woke to her rolling a condom down his length, followed by her riding him until they both let go and came with blended shouts of pleasure.

His entire room smelled of them. Of their love, sex, and orgasms that left them wrung out and needing more. He loved that she didn't race to the shower after the first time. That she let his scent linger on her skin. He needed to change the sheets, but he hated to lose the smell of her on them.

"Shower?" she asked after their bodies cooled and their breathing slowed.

"You wet and naked is always going to get a yes from me," he said, nipping her earlobe and loving the way she giggled and moaned.

"You're spoiling me with all this sex."

"Making up for lost time."

"Oh, so you don't promise this forever?"

"I never said that. Twelve years without you is a lot of sex to make up for. I figure by the time I'm dead, I'll have gotten halfway to feeling like I've had you enough."

"I hope you're planning to be around for a while."

"Definitely."

She kissed him, then walked shamelessly naked to the bathroom.

He followed, bringing a new condom into the shower with him and bringing them both to new heights. Again.

Montgomery called when they were having breakfast and said he needed to talk to them. Zeke was on edge, knowing Mont was not going to bring good news. He wanted to keep it at bay, but he knew if Mont was calling, it couldn't be delayed.

"We're up," Zeke said, meeting Nina's eyes. "Let yourself in."

"Be there in a minute," Mont said.

Zeke hung up and looked at Nina. "He needs to talk to us."

"That can't be good."

Zeke shook his head. "I don't know. He didn't tell me."

They both turned to the door as Montgomery let himself in. He locked the door behind him and faced them, a look on his face that said it was definitely bad news.

"Just tell us," Nina said, bracing herself against the counter.

Zeke wanted to hold her, to support her, to make sure she knew she wasn't alone, but he stayed put.

"Robert... the man who you knew as Robert, he's dead." Montgomery kept his gaze on Nina.

Zeke stared at her, too. He wasn't sure what he was waiting for, but he expected something. Sorrow? Anger? He didn't know.

"I'm not surprised," Nina said after a minute. "And I'm not all that disappointed."

"Nina," Mont said.

Nina held up a hand to stop him from getting to her. "No. Don't tell me I should feel bad. He lied to me, and he was just as bad as her. He wasn't a victim. He wasn't innocent. If she sent him, he was more involved than I ever knew. She doesn't send people unless she intends for them to not return. He served his purpose. He got in my head, in Frannie's head. He doesn't get my sympathy."

"Are you sure you're okay?" Mont asked.

Nina shook her head. "No. I'm not okay. I'm not going to

be okay until all of this is over. But that has nothing to do with Robert. And you being here isn't the end of what you need to tell us, so spit it out."

Zeke stepped forward, realizing Nina was right. That wasn't enough for Montgomery to call and say he needed to talk. Something else was going on.

Montgomery looked at Zeke. "We've been summoned. They need our help. All three of us. Now."

19

———

ZEKE DID NOT BELONG IN THE ROOM WHERE DECISIONS WERE made. He wasn't in charge, he didn't have any advanced education, he was just Montgomery's best friend and Nina's protector. His opinion wasn't important.

So he stood against the wall and kept his mouth shut tight. No one asked him questions. They talked. They all talked. Where was Gwendolyn? How were they going to find her? Everything they'd tried had failed, for years, and they needed a new idea.

"She's a step ahead of us," Adam growled. "How in the fuck is she always ahead of us?"

"We closed all the loops in the department," Marcus said.

When the news broke about local cops being involved, doing anything from killing witnesses in custody to handing over confidential information to getting rid of evidence, the local cops were vilified in the news and in public. As police captain, Marcus took the brunt of that. He got rid of cops, did investigations into all of them, and hand selected the few he brought into the secret task force Zeke and the others had been asked to join.

It wasn't the first time Rose Protection Agency had been involved with the investigation, but it was the first time Zeke and Montgomery were specifically called. And the first time they were all together.

The group included law enforcement, civilians, and the women who called themselves the Curvy Vigilantes. As soon as Zeke, Montgomery, and Nina walked into Dawn Patterson's mansion, Nina was wrapped up by Frannie and the other women. Nina sat on a couch across the huge living room, where Zeke could watch her, between Frannie and Raina London.

The whole thing was insane to Zeke. It violated every law he knew about how investigations could work, but the knowledge in the room trumped any laws, apparently. Each person had a unique interest in finding Gwendolyn Lennox. Personal, in most cases.

"How is she finding out what we're doing? Could she have bugs somewhere?" Braden Wright asked. The firefighter's girlfriend was framed for murder and nearly ended up a victim herself. "In our phones or something?"

Lorelei shook her head. "We don't think so. My phone and Adam's have top level security and are checked constantly for any spyware or unapproved software and hardware. I imagined the police is the same."

Marcus nodded. "Especially ours." He jerked his chin toward the other cops in the room. Pryce Murphy and Drake Foster both nodded in agreement.

"Everyone else could be a risk, but we're not all together before every operation." Lorelei looked as defeated as the others.

"How did she know about the raid on her house?" Adam asked, turning to Nina.

Nina shook her head and swallowed roughly, taking in all the attention on her. "She didn't. Not as far as I know. We were in the house when it started."

"You were?" Marcus blurted.

Nina looked at him and nodded. "Her primary guard came in and told her we had to go."

"And she took you with her?" Pryce asked.

"I was her favorite. She would call me her sister. Said she wanted to keep me safe," Nina told him. The flush rising on her cheeks said she knew what the others were thinking.

Marcus and Adam clearing their throats said they knew what the others were thinking, too.

"Nina is on our side," Adam said definitively. "She's done nothing but help us since she got away from Gwendolyn. We all have full trust in her, so any of those thoughts need to go away right now."

"Thank you," Nina whispered, straining for a smile at Adam as Raina took Nina's hand.

Zeke stared at Nina, willing her to look up at him. When she finally did, he winked at her and smiled, hoping it would help her relax and remember she belonged in that room, stopping the woman who destroyed the last twelve years of her life.

Nina smiled back and marginally relaxed.

"Did anything Robert say remind you of something? Anything you didn't think to tell us before?" Lorelei asked.

Nina thought for a minute, then shook her head. "No. I..." She paused to control herself before continuing. "I've told you everything I've thought of. I want her gone as much as everyone else."

"More," Frannie said, wrapping her arm around Nina's

shoulders. "Nina has been through the worst hell of all of us because of Gwennie. She spent twelve years with her. Nina came to us right away to tell her story. She's been trying to help since day one."

Nina smiled up at Frannie, but it wasn't a confident smile. It was one that said the attention made her anxious.

Zeke wanted to say something, to take the attention from Nina, but he had nothing to add. He caught Mont's eye and tried to convey his thoughts, thankful when Montgomery stepped forward.

"We still don't have a plan. Gwendolyn is out there. She's scared. She's trapped. She has to have a place to hide. Somewhere we don't know about. What would you do if this was any other suspect?" Montgomery asked.

Lorelei and Adam exchanged a look. They were the ones in charge of the investigation and the team.

"We'd ask the public for help," Adam said. "We would put her face everywhere and offer a reward for any information leading to her capture."

"Then why don't we do that?" Montgomery asked.

"We don't know what she looks like. Any photos we have are from years ago, and they're not clear. We can't go to the public unless we can tell them who we're looking for," Lorelei said.

"I know what she looks like," Nina whispered. "I can describe every detail of her. And the others who are probably with her."

All heads turned to Nina as she spoke, as if they just realized what she was saying. Zeke wondered why none of them thought to ask her to describe Gwendolyn before, but he was so damn proud of Nina for offering.

"Do you have a sketch artist I can work with? Someone you trust?" Nina asked.

Marcus and Adam smiled at each other.

"Yeah, we know someone," Marcus said.

Adam left the room, his phone already to his ear.

The others looked at Marcus in question.

"His cousin is an owner at F-BOMB, and their office manager is an artist. Kyra was a witness to a bank robbery a few years back and drew the sketch of the crew and was instrumental in capturing all of them," Marcus explained.

Adam walked back into the room and pocketed his phone. "They'll be here in ten minutes."

"Sounds like we have time for coffee. Anyone need a cup?" Dawn asked. She stood and led the way to the serving table set up on one side of the room, most people following her.

Zeke headed for Nina, catching her elbow before she was able to trail after the others.

She turned quickly, gasping in shock.

"Sorry. I didn't mean to scare you," Zeke said.

She shook her head. "It's okay. I guess I'm just on edge."

Zeke pulled her into his arms, closing out the world around them and protecting her from everyone else. "You are so fucking brave."

She held onto him, her body trembling. "No, I'm not. I'm hiding."

"You're helping find the woman who tried to break you. You're fighting back."

Nina exhaled. "It doesn't feel like I'm doing enough. I know her. I've been with her for years. I should know where she is."

"If you knew everything, this would be a totally different situation."

"I thought I knew. I should know."

Zeke pulled back and tucked a strand of Nina's red hair

behind her ear. "You are amazing. She lied to you, manipulated you, and hid a lot from you. She didn't trust anyone."

Nina swallowed. "It's like that Stockholm Syndrome. There are moments when I struggle with the woman they all know and hate so much. She was good to me sometimes. She treated me like a sister at first. Gave me a place to live. I thought when I turned eighteen I could leave. That was my plan. Figure out what I wanted my life to look like and go out on my own. Back then, she really was like a sister. We would talk about my future, about the dreams I had and the things I wanted to do with my life."

"And she used all of that against you."

Nina sniffed. She swallowed. Her lips lifted into a sad smile. "She did. God, I was so stupid."

"No, you weren't. You'd never met anyone like her. You didn't understand how she operated."

Nina shrugged. "My dad was like that."

"No," Zeke breathed. "Your dad was an asshole. He was horrible. He was cruel and mean, but Gwendolyn is a whole other level. She makes your dad look halfway decent by comparison, and we both know he wasn't."

"Yeah," Nina whispered.

"Come here," Zeke said, drawing her back into his arms. He ached to kiss her, to whisk her away and never come back. To hide out and let the others figure it all out.

He hated the thought, but the worse thought was having someone hurt Nina. Letting Gwendolyn get her hands on Nina again. It wasn't in his DNA to run and hide, not when he could help, but everything inside him needed Nina to be okay. Needed her to be safe.

She'd already chosen to meet with Gwendolyn, and even though Gwendolyn didn't show up, standing in the way of Nina doing anything else to help wouldn't go over well.

He had no choice but to accept that she was the same as him. She needed to run toward the fight, too. Which meant if he wanted her safe, he could never leave her side.

NINA DREW strength from Zeke and absorbed it in. She wanted to stay there forever, to pull from him until she felt like she could do anything, but someone rang the bell and the tentative levity of the moment ended.

Dawn and Adam left the room to answer the door. Everyone else stayed put, watching the hallway and listening for the voices to draw closer again. Dawn and Adam returned with a man and woman. The man and Adam talked together, easy laughter flowing between them. The woman was a little more tentative but spoke with Dawn and seemed comfortable enough. The woman carried a sketchbook and had a searching gaze that stopped when she found Nina.

Frannie walked her over and reached for Nina's hand, bringing her to Dawn and the woman. "Nina, this is Kyra O'Keefe. Kyra, this is Nina Rose."

"Nice to meet you," Kyra said warmly, offering her hand.

Nina shook it and smiled, feeling more at ease than she expected. "You, too. Thank you for coming so quickly."

"Liam said you guys needed some help." She nodded to the man who was talking to Adam. Both men approached.

"Nina, this is my cousin, Liam. Liam, this is Nina Rose." Adam nodded heavily at Liam, passing on a message Nina was pretty sure meant Liam knew who she was.

"Nice to meet you, Nina. We've done some work with your brother's agency. We were all happy to hear you were home and safe." Liam smiled, his friendly demeanor further relaxing Nina.

"Thank you." Nina wasn't sure how to take that she was borderline infamous, but she figured it was a good thing so many people who spent their lives protecting and helping others were out there.

"Kyra, where do you want to go?" Frannie asked.

Kyra looked at Nina. "Wherever you're comfortable. I just need a place to sit, maybe somewhere to put my sketchbook, but that's not required."

Nina looked back at Dawn. Nina didn't know the massive home well enough to know what their options were.

"You are welcome wherever you feel comfortable," Dawn said. "This room is busy, but the dining room is a little quieter. I have a library you can use, another sitting room that's smaller. If you'd like more privacy, you can go upstairs to a bedroom." Dawn clasped her hands together in front of her.

"Oh, I don't want to invade your private space," Nina said. She looked around the room and jumped when someone on the other side of the room laughed loudly. "Um, maybe somewhere quieter."

"Let's go to the library," Dawn said.

Nina followed Dawn, Frannie, and Kyra, but Zeke lingered behind. "Are you coming?"

"Do you want me to?" Zeke asked.

Monty appeared next to Zeke. "What's going on?"

"Sketch artist," Zeke answered.

Nina stopped and looked between Kyra, Dawn, and Frannie and Zeke and Monty. She turned to the women. "Can they come with me?"

"Of course," the women said at the same time.

Nina looked at the men, feeling better knowing they would be there with her. Always with her.

Frannie stood outside the library to let the others move inside. The space was cozy and large, but it would work. Kyra sat in an armchair near the window, with Nina in a chair opposite. Frannie took a seat closer to the door, but still close. Monty sat next to Nina, and Zeke stood just inside the door.

"Are we okay? Does anyone need anything?" Dawn asked, a gracious hostess.

Kyra nodded and looked at Nina.

Nina shook her head. "We're good."

"Okay, I'm going to let you do your thing. If you need something, one of these men can come get me." Dawn squeezed Zeke's arm and nodded to Monty.

"Yes, ma'am," they both said.

Dawn chuckled and left the room, leaving the door open since Zeke was standing in front of it.

"Nina, I'm going to ask you to close your eyes and describe what you remember. Liam said it's a female?" Kyra asked as she flipped open her sketchbook.

"Gwendolyn Lennox," Nina said.

Kyra gasped. "Oh. Um, I didn't realize that. Okay. Is she the only one?"

Nina shook her head. "There is a man who is with her all the time. There are others, but only one I know for sure is with her. But the others could help lead to her, I guess."

"Let's do anyone you remember clearly, and we'll let Marcus and Adam decide what they want to use. Is that okay?" Kyra asked.

"Yeah, that sounds good. Thank you."

"You're so welcome. I know this isn't easy. So first, close your eyes."

Nina did, her other senses firing. She immediately opened her eyes.

"What's wrong?" Monty asked.

Nina looked around the room. "Sorry. It's…"

"She doesn't like the dark," Zeke answered for her. "Is closing your eyes hard, too?"

Nina nodded.

"You can try with your eyes open," Kyra said. "Usually it's better to close your eyes and block out everything else."

"Hold her hand," Zeke said.

Monty looked up at him, then reached for Nina.

She put her hand in her brother's and drew a breath. She closed her eyes again and took a deep breath. "I'm safe," she whispered.

"Yes, you are. Zeke and I are right here. He's at the door, and no one's going to get in." Monty's words were soothing.

Nina nodded. "Gwendolyn is a little taller than me. Dark blonde hair. It's a little wavy at the ends, but straighter on top. The longest parts go to the tops of her breasts with the shortest closer to her collarbones. She wears suits, sometimes without a shirt underneath. She likes that she has power. Short nails, no polish."

Nina swallowed at a long ago memory. The night before Nina turned eighteen, Gwendolyn surprised her with a night of pampering. Massages and mani/pedis. A facial. The technician who painted Nina's nails gave her a fun, flirty pink polish. Nina talked Gwendolyn into the same color, said they should match.

Gwendolyn agreed, but the next day, her nails were clean and free of any color. When Nina asked why, Gwendolyn scolded Nina and said she couldn't risk anything that stood out and that she wasn't a child.

Those were the first harsh words Gwendolyn ever spoke

to Nina, and the first time Nina realized the perfect life she thought she ran to wasn't so perfect.

"Did you think of something else?" Kyra asked.

"No." Nina shook her head and refocused to the last time she saw Gwendolyn. "She has brown eyes, pouty lips. She has a sharp chin, thin I guess. No jewelry, nothing flashy."

"That's all good, Nina. I'm going to ask you some questions to help narrow down everything and get a good picture of her. Is that okay?"

Nina nodded. "Yeah."

Kyra was gentle with her questioning, giving Nina time to think about an answer. When she asked Nina to look at what she'd drawn so far, Nina gasped.

"My God that's her." Nina shook in her seat, the cold, dead eyes of Gwendolyn seeming to stare back at her. Nina pulled her legs up onto the seat and hugged herself, panic and fear winding around her body.

"Move," Zeke growled, stomping into the room. He picked Nina up and held her against his chest, returning to the chair with her in his lap. "You're safe, angel. I got you. She's not here. She can't touch you. Never again. You're okay."

Nina nodded and listened to Zeke's voice, the calming tone soothing her and bringing her heartbeat back down to something normal.

"Are you okay, angel?" Zeke asked.

Nina nodded. "Thank you."

"Always. Are you done?"

Nina shook her head.

"Nina," Monty said.

"No. I can't let them get away with it. I can't. I have to

help. I have to do this and make sure they don't hurt anyone else ever again."

"I'm so proud of you, angel," Zeke whispered against her hair. "So fucking proud."

Nina inhaled, her body shaky. It was the right thing. It was the only thing. She would stop Gwendolyn.

Kyra went through the same exercise with Nina for Fernando and the others Nina could remember. They were less painful, but Zeke didn't move, holding her in his arms the entire time.

Nina felt her brother watching them, but she couldn't bring herself to care what Monty thought about Zeke holding her. She needed him, his strength, and she wasn't giving that up for anyone, including her brother.

When Kyra was finished with the six drawings, she thanked Nina and left the room. Frannie was right behind her, talking quietly as they left.

"Are you okay?" Zeke whispered.

Nina nodded. "I'm better now. Thank you."

"You're welcome."

Monty got up first, reaching a hand to Nina and helping her off Zeke's lap. He shot Zeke a look, but Zeke didn't seem to notice it.

Nina asked her brother to stay with her when they went back to the other room. Zeke stayed close, but Nina knew coming between the two most important men in her world was not what she wanted.

"We'll get these sketches onto the news by tomorrow," Marcus said. "This is great work. Thank you, Nina."

"It was all Kyra," Nina said.

Kyra shook her head. "Not even a little. I just drew what you told me. Thank you for being willing to do this."

Nina nodded, knowing everyone in the city knew what

Gwendolyn was capable of, what she'd done. At least some of it.

"Thanks, Kyra. We really appreciate your help," Adam said. "We know this will help."

"Happy to do whatever I can. It looks like we're heading back to work. See you all soon." Kyra waved and followed Liam to the door and out.

"Now, we get the public involved, and we put an end to all of this," Adam said.

Nina closed her eyes and said a prayer he was right.

20

——————

ZEKE STARED AT THE TV FOR THE FOURTH STRAIGHT DAY, studying the drawings of the people Nina described. Four days with zero credible tips. People were calling in, but nothing led to Gwendolyn. She and her people were still out there. Watching. Waiting. Hiding.

It drove Zeke crazy. Knowing they were out there and knowing they could strike at any time but not knowing where they were.

He wanted to go after Gwendolyn. Every night when Zeke held Nina, their bodies cooling after loving her, he felt her shaking and knew it was fear. She was jumpy and on edge.

They needed Gwendolyn and her people arrested. Peace. Safety.

"Still nothing?" Nina asked, coming downstairs from her shower.

Zeke nodded and turned away from the repetitive news. "She can't hide forever."

Nina didn't reply. She didn't agree. She knew Gwendolyn

better than anyone else, and that part scared Zeke because it went both ways.

Gwendolyn knew where Nina was. Her stand-in, Robert, said as much. Nina might not have confirmed that they were sleeping together, but Robert still knew. Which meant either it was a good guess or Gwendolyn had a way to see into his house.

Zeke had taken to sweeping his house for bugs multiple times every day, securing windows and doors and keeping blinds and curtains closed around the clock. He didn't want to risk anyone seeing inside his house.

He didn't know if it mattered.

"Maybe she left town," Nina said.

"Do you think she would do that?"

Nina shrugged. "If it was her best option, yeah."

"Would she start over?"

Nina nodded. "I'm sure she would. She has contacts all over."

"Does Lorelei know this?"

"Yeah. We talked about it. She asked where else Gwendolyn would go, and I told her with the connections she had, she could be anywhere. Lorelei was putting out something to all of the FBI with the drawing of Gwendolyn."

"That's good."

Nina nodded and rubbed her hands up and down her arms. She stared at the TV, but the story had long changed.

"What do you want to do today?" Zeke asked.

"You don't have to babysit me, you know."

Zeke walked over to her, pulling her into his arms and holding her close. "I'm not. I'm spending time with you. And if you were a client, we would be doing the same thing."

"But I'm not a client. I'm not paying you."

"No, but Mont's maintaining my salary. I'm good."

"That's not fair. Don't you have to work?"

Zeke released her and stepped back. He studied the lines in her face. "What's going on?"

She shook her head and hugged herself again.

"Talk to me, Nina. Why are you all worked up?"

"I just want this to be over. I want to forget about her and all of them. I want to move on."

"And you will," Zeke said. "I know you will. We're going to keep you safe, and the FBI is going to find her."

"What if they don't?" Nina whispered. "What if she finds somewhere to go and just never comes back?"

"Then we move on."

Nina chewed her lip, clearly not satisfied with the answer.

"Listen," Zeke said, grabbing her hand and pulling her to the couch, "she's going to be found. She'll slip up. At some point in time, it will all be over."

"It took years for Damon to be caught, even though Frannie saw him murder someone."

Zeke nodded. "And Gwendolyn manipulated that situation. She made sure the police couldn't count on Frannie's statement. If Frannie had been able to tell the truth, it would have been different."

"Would it, though?"

"Yes."

"How do you know?"

"Because I have to believe in the good of people. We all have darkness in us, but I think we all have light, too. We want good things. The darkness comes out when we believe someone else is unfairly getting what we believe to be ours. That's not the way life should be, but it's reality."

"After everything I've been through, I'm not sure I can find the good as easily as you do."

"Then we find it together."

Nina's smile was soft and tentative, like she was debating whether to believe Zeke or not. When she leaned against him, resting her head on his shoulder, he sighed.

"Good is holding you in my arms. It's sliding into you at night. It's listening to you laugh and hearing you shout my name. It's showers together and lunches and dinner with Mont. It's putting away the people who want to hurt others and knowing my team is always there to have my back."

"I don't have any of that."

Zeke kissed the top of her head. "Yes, you do, angel. You have me and Mont and Frannie and the Curvy Vigilantes. You might not feel like it right now, but you are loved by so many people."

"Thank you."

Zeke held her for a few more minutes, loving the quiet of the morning and the softness of her next to him. He closed his eyes and let his imagination run to the future, Nina laughing at something he said, a baby in her arms, another running around the living room. The vision was so vivid he almost expected it to be real when he opened his eyes again.

"I don't think I could have handled all of this without you," Nina said. "I can never repay you for everything you've done for me."

"If there's ever a psycho who wants to kill me, I'll let you protect me. How about that?" Zeke teased.

Nina laughed and nodded. "Okay. Sounds good."

He kissed her slowly, taking his time sweeping his tongue through her mouth. When she moaned softly and leaned against him, Zeke was done. He was gone. He was so in love with her, he wasn't sure he'd survive when she left.

If she left.

He had to keep telling himself she could want the same thing, but the little voice in the back of his mind said there was no way. She was with him because she was scared. One day, she would feel safe on her own. And when that day came, he would just be her brother's best friend again.

But until that day, Zeke was going to love her with every piece of himself and not think about what would happen when his happiness was taken from him.

NEARLY EVERY WEEK, Monty asked Nina if she wanted to move in with him. And every week, her answer grew more and more certain that she was in the right place at Zeke's.

She was happy. For years, she didn't think that was possible. She didn't dare to dream it could be. But Zeke was perfect. He was kind and attentive and loving and a dream in bed. The level of pleasure he gave her was mind-blowing. The kind of thing she thought was fictional until she experienced it for herself.

A month after the drawings went out to the public, Nina was starting to wonder if Gwendolyn really did leave the area. Packed up and bolted, saving herself from the FBI.

It was hard to believe, but with each passing day and no sign of her, Nina hoped it was true. She hoped she was safe, that Monty and Zeke and Monica and Star and all the others were safe. That they could move on with their lives and not ever think about Gwendolyn Lennox again.

It was a weird feeling for Nina. She wanted Gwendolyn dead. The night she left, she thought about how good it would feel to watch her die. To be the one who did it.

The darkness that feeling brought out scared Nina. It was the darkness Gwendolyn lived in. The darkness she thrived in. Nina never wanted to be like that, but Gwendolyn brought it out in her.

Being with Zeke made that darkness recede. It was like drowning and coming up for air and filling her lungs with it and knowing she was alive again. She was cared for and safe.

And it tore her up.

So many others didn't have what Nina had. They didn't have a man like Zeke to love them at night, or to tell them they were strong. They didn't have a brother out there doing everything possible to bring down Gwendolyn.

Many of them didn't have their lives at all.

Nina still thought about Monica and Star, but she didn't ask Monty about them or any of the others. They didn't trust Nina, and she had to accept that.

"What are you thinking about?" Zeke asked, coming up behind her and wrapping his arms around her waist. He kissed her neck and nibbled on her ear.

She sighed happily. Her body tingled with awareness, knowing they would end the night in bed, naked and sweaty, like they had every night for the last month. "I'm so lucky to have you."

He growled and squeezed her tighter. "I'm the lucky one."

She spun in his arms and wrapped her arms around his neck. "How are you still single?"

He chuckled. "I didn't know I was."

She grinned. "How were you single? The women in this city were so dumb to let you get away."

"None of them were you."

She grinned at his words. She knew he didn't mean them the way she hoped, but she enjoyed them. When there was some kind of proof that Gwendolyn was gone, Nina wouldn't have to live with him anymore. She could give him his life back. Let him go back to the way things were before.

She should probably do that anyway, but she was selfish. She didn't deserve the kind of happiness Zeke gave her, but she wanted to hold on to it for a little longer.

He cupped her ass and pulled her tight against his body, his erection already thick between them. "Are you going to let me fuck you again tonight?"

"Yes," she whispered, already halfway to orgasm with the ridge of his cock pressed against her clit.

"Are you going to come for me right now?" He thrust against her, teasing her.

"I might."

"I love how wet you get for me. Are you already wet? Are your panties soaked?"

"Yes."

"Are you going to come fast with my cock against your clit? Imagining my fingers teasing you, my dick inside you."

"Please, Zeke."

He kissed her hard, teeth clashing. He moved them, slamming her back against the wall and grinding against her hard. Everything was hard. His kisses were rough, his dick insistent, his hands demanding. He plucked one nipple and lifted the other leg, spreading her wide and rubbing himself against her.

Need welled up inside her, the orgasm rushing through her body. Everything ignited before all the sparks centered between her thighs and she came with a rush that made her dizzy. "Zeke," she breathed against his lips.

"Fuck, you're so beautiful when you come."

"I need you in my mouth," she said, pulling back and dropping to her knees. Before she could unbutton his jeans, a knock on the door had her swearing.

"He wanted to come for dinner," Zeke grunted. "Said he hasn't seen us lately."

Nina rose to her feet. "Is it horrible of me to have enjoyed that? Not because I didn't want to see my brother but because I was having fun with you."

Zeke kissed her hard, pulling back far too soon. "Same, angel. But he won't be here all night. I'm getting my tongue inside you later. And my dick."

"You're a tease."

"Nope, just making you a promise." Zeke moved to go around her, squeezing her gently on the backside. "Do you need to go clean up?"

Nina nodded, her heart clenching at his suggestion. He always made sure she felt clean after they had any kind of sex. She'd stopped feeling like it was all gross and loved laying in bed with him and smelling like sex, but she wasn't sure she should smell like an orgasm for dinner with her brother. "I'll be back in a minute."

"No rush, angel. We're not going anywhere."

Nina smiled and hurried up the stairs. She heard the two men's voices and smiled before she closed the bedroom door.

She'd made herself at home in Zeke's house. The clothes he bought her took up space in his dresser and closet. Her bathroom products lined his sink and shower. Everything he had, he let her use. And everything she had, he gave her.

Nina used the bathroom, then changed into clean panties that weren't soaked through. She hurried back downstairs and threw her arms around her brother. "Hey, Monty."

"Hey, sis. How are you?"

Nina shrugged. "Good, I think. Unless you have bad news."

"No news. Just wanted to see you."

"Good. I've missed too much time with you."

"I agree. What do you think about going somewhere with me tomorrow?"

"Where do you want to go?"

Monty shrugged. "Don't know yet. Just want to spend some time with you. Work has been busy the last month, but I took tomorrow off so I could see you. This one's been monopolizing you." He hooked his thumb toward Zeke.

Nina grinned, not allowing her gaze to go to the man who gave her an orgasm just a few minutes ago and was definitely worthy of the monopolization. "You know he'd do anything for either of us."

"I know." Monty pulled Nina in for a hug. "I just miss you. He's going to handle some things at the office for the day."

Nina nodded, trying not to miss Zeke before she was already away from him. She could handle one day. "Sounds good."

"Ready to eat?" Zeke asked from the kitchen.

Monty let Nina go first and followed her into the kitchen. They all grabbed food and sat on the couch. The men argued about the game they were watching, and Nina just listened, enjoying the sounds that she'd long ago forgotten. Them laughing and arguing and challenging each other. It was so good to be home.

"Are you done?" Zeke asked, drawing her attention back to the moment.

Both men had finished eating, and Monty was heading for the door. "Yeah. I'm good."

Zeke hesitated and narrowed his eyes at her.

She waved him off, smiling to let him know she really was okay, then followed Monty to the door. "Tomorrow?"

Monty nodded. "Tomorrow. I'll be here around eight."

"Can't wait."

He hugged her. "Me, too. We'll have fun."

Nina nodded and stepped back before Monty opened the door. The usual fear rushed in, but the door closed and she flipped the lock and she trusted that she was safe again.

"He sprung the idea on me when you were upstairs," Zeke said. "Are you good with it?"

Nina went to where he stood next to the kitchen counter. Gene rubbed his head against Zeke's hand, making sure Zeke got the right spot behind his ear.

"Of course. I know he'll protect me, too. One day, maybe I won't need you guys to put your lives on hold for me. I can leave the house and open the door and do all the things normal people do without worrying."

Zeke stared at the cat as he spoke. "My life was on hold before you came back. I feel like I'm living now."

"You know what I mean," she said, looking down at Franklin as he wound between her ankles.

Zeke looked up at her and nodded once.

"Are you okay with me going with Monty?" Nina asked.

"Of course. I'd never stand between you two. Or you and anything you want to do."

She smiled. "What if I want to do you?"

He chuckled. "That's a horrible pickup line."

"Do I need one?" She tapped her lip with her fingertip. "Let's see. I could say I'm still wet from the orgasm you gave me earlier. Or I could tell you I want more. Or I could say I put on those lace panties you bought me last week."

"Fuck me," he growled.

She threw her hands in the air. "That's what I'm saying."

Zeke breathed a laugh. "You are so fucking perfect, Nina."

"Can we focus on the fucking part?"

"Absolutely."

Zeke was on her in a second, his arm binding her to him in a bruising hold that made her even wetter than she was a second ago. His teeth nipped at her lips before she had a chance to open for him.

She gasped and held on to him, wrapping her legs around his waist when he started walking toward the stairs. His erection pressed against her body, and she shifted to ride it.

"You need to wait until we get upstairs or I might drop you."

"Hurry," she breathed into his ear.

Zeke growled and took the stairs two at a time, slapping his hands against the walls to keep them steady while she held on for the ride. He shoved the door closed and had his hands back on her in seconds. "Let me see those panties, angel."

He helped her down, holding her hips steady until her feet hit the floor. As soon as they did, he stepped back, his gaze blazing her through her clothes.

Nina's hands shook as she grabbed her shirt. She lifted it over her head, letting the fabric fall.

He sucked in a breath, one that drew all the air from the room. "Fucking hell, you're stunning. Keep going." He dropped his jeans, palming himself through his boxer briefs.

Her thighs shook as she watched him watching her. She hooked her thumbs in the waistband of her sweatpants and drew them down her legs. She stepped away from them, looking at him.

He licked his lips. One hand went to the back of his neck and yanked his tee off. The other slid beneath his boxer briefs and wrapped around his cock, his fist pulling the fabric from him before he shoved it to the floor.

Nina's core flooded, looking at him and the way he stared at her. Devoured her with his gaze.

"On the bed."

She reached back to unclasp her bra, but he shook his head.

"Just like that."

She trembled at the commanding tone of his voice. He hadn't used it with her before, but she loved it.

Over the last month, he'd taught her what pleasure meant, what a lover truly was. He'd delivered on every fantasy she'd had about vanilla sex. Most people wanted something that toed a line, but after all the things men wanted to do to her, Nina wanted a man who was more worried about her pleasure than his own. And she found that in Zeke.

She laid on the bed, but he shook his head again. "Feet over the edge. I need to taste you."

Nina repositioned herself, letting her feet dangle over the edge of his bed.

Zeke dropped to his knees next to the mattress and groaned. "You've already soaked through the lace."

Before she could say anything, his mouth was on her, the sensation of his tongue dulled by the fabric. "Zeke."

He pressed her thighs wider and slid a finger inside her.

"Oh, yes."

He added a second finger, curling them as he sucked her clit through the lace.

"Zeke!" She came instantly, her body pulsing around his fingers.

He tugged the lace, dragging the fabric over her clit, and she splintered. The rough tug of the fabric and the soft touch of his tongue the perfect combination of pleasure and pain.

"Fuck. Zeke. So good."

He withdrew his fingers and pressed his tongue inside her, swirling the tip around and licking her clean. He surged to his feet and kissed her hard, letting her taste herself on his tongue.

Nina groaned. He made her so hot. So crazy. A month with him was nowhere near enough. She wasn't sure any amount of time with him would be enough.

His fingers pushed into her again, immediately followed by his cock.

She broke their kiss on a gasp when he filled her completely. "You feel so fucking good."

"I'm sorry, angel, but this is going to be quick."

"Fuck me hard, Zeke. Don't hold back. Let me have all of you."

"You already do, angel." Zeke slammed into her.

Nina cried out. The angle he hit was perfect. So fucking perfect. He grabbed one hand and brought their joined hands to her breast, tugging her bra to the side. His other hand went between her legs, grasping the panties she still wore. He tugged, dragging the fabric over her clit again.

Her body bowed, the pleasure so fierce she couldn't see straight. "Zeke."

"Come for me, angel. Let me feel you. Come."

Nina's body answered his demand, coiling tight, then releasing an orgasm so powerful her throat hurt and her body felt like it was being torn apart at the seams. She thrashed on the bed and bucked against him and fucked him harder.

"God, fuck, Nina. Shit." He slammed into her, stilling

deep inside as he trembled with his own orgasm. His entire body shook with aftershocks, sending a shiver through her.

"Wow," she breathed after a minute.

"Always wow." Zeke leaned down to kiss her hard, sliding from her body when he did. He helped her to her feet and steadied her before following her to the bathroom. He threw away the condom and cleaned up, then brushed his teeth in the sink next to hers.

Nina wondered if they would have had the same chance to be together if she'd never disappeared. What would life had been like?

As she crawled into bed with Zeke's arms around her, she kept thinking about it. He told her he wanted her years ago, but what would have happened? Would he have stayed with her instead of following Monty to the military? Would he have protected her and cared for her the same way? Would they have children?

A part of her wanted answers, but she knew they would never come. Instead, she had Zeke for the moment. She was safe. And she was cared for.

It had been a long time since she felt that way. Since the early days with Gwendolyn. In the house on the eastern edge of the city. Where they were like sisters. Where Gwendolyn protected her. Where...

Could Gwendolyn be there?

No. Nina dismissed the idea even as she knew it was possible. It had been a decade since they were at that house. Gwendolyn said she sold it. Nina had forgotten about it, but was it possible?

21

Zeke stretched, his hand searching for Nina in the bed. In the cold bed. In the empty bed.

He sat up, looking around the room like he missed her, but she was gone.

Panic set in. Was it possible someone snuck into his house and took her while he slept?

No. He couldn't think that.

He grabbed shorts and a tee from the floor and dragged the shorts on as he rushed to the door, nearly tripping when his toe caught on one pant leg. He slapped his palm against the door and shoved his foot into the shorts.

He yanked the door open and raced down the stairs, sighing with relief when she was sitting on the couch.

"Are you okay?" she asked, looking at him like he was only half as crazy as he felt. She turned back to Franklin, the lucky cat purring loudly enough for Zeke to hear from ten feet away.

"You weren't in bed. I thought something happened." He went to the couch, leaning down to kiss her.

She turned her head, letting his lips land on her cheek. "Morning breath. I couldn't sleep."

"I don't care about morning breath. And you love sleeping in."

She nodded. "I know. I'm tired. I guess I'm excited to spend the day with Monty."

"I never tried to keep you from him. Did you think I was?"

"No. I just woke up early and decided to come downstairs instead of risking waking you up."

She didn't look at him. She stayed focused on the cat. Zeke knew the move. Hell, he was a pro at it. Avoid eye contact and admit nothing. Brush them off until they stop calling.

She was done with him.

"Okay." He tried not to let it hurt, but fuck, it felt like someone pried his chest open and yanked his heart out, setting it in her lap like his greedy cats. He pulled his tee on, as if that would keep all the loose parts inside instead of spilling everywhere.

She didn't say anything, so he went to the kitchen. Coffee was made. He filled a mug and took a sip. The bitter taste was horrible, but he needed things to suck for a while. He needed the reminder that there was something to look forward to. Even if it was as stupid as sugar in his damn coffee.

Because looking forward to Nina leaving him was going to fucking hurt.

"Do you want breakfast?"

Nina shook her head and eased Franklin to the cushion next to her. She stood and pointed to the stairs. "I'm going to go take a shower. Monty is going to be here in a little while to get me."

Zeke nodded. Monty was going to be there in an hour, but he wasn't going to argue with her or tell her she had plenty of time. If she wanted to get away from him, he was going to let her go.

Franklin and Gene sat at the bottom of the stairs and watched Nina race up them. They both meowed, then looked at Zeke like he fucked up.

"I don't know what I did, but thanks for having my back," he told the traitors.

The shower turned on upstairs, and Zeke gripped the edge of the counter. She was in his bathroom, naked and wet, for what could be the last time.

He should have insisted she stayed with Montgomery. If she had, he wouldn't have known what he was letting go of. He wouldn't have the memories of being inside her to keep him up at night, wondering about who she wanted more than him.

He closed his eyes and let himself have a pity party for one minute. Sixty seconds, then he had to get the fuck over it.

He breathed slowly, absorbing all the fear he felt over her leaving. At the end of his sixty seconds, he put it all aside and boxed up his love for her, the same way he did for the twelve years she was gone.

Zeke fixed breakfast while she was in the shower. He sent a text to Montgomery letting him know they were up and he was making breakfast if Mont wanted to join them.

The knock on the door and the key in the lock answered the text. "I was just trying to figure out what to eat. Where's Nina?"

"In the shower. Did you come up with a plan for today?" Zeke asked, hoping he sounded normal.

Montgomery nodded. "Yeah, I was thinking we could

walk around the city a little, go to the Falls, then get lunch and maybe talk her into a tattoo."

"Really?" Zeke asked.

Mont shrugged. "I figured I have one that matches my brother, it would be nice to match my sister, too. If you're okay with that."

Zeke nodded, choking back the emotion in his throat. Fuck, he'd been feeling too many of those lately. "I think she'll be open to that."

"Hey," Mont said. His voice was softer and closer, and when Zeke turned, Mont was only a few feet behind him. "I can't thank you enough for watching out for her this last month. I haven't handled all of this very well, and knowing you were here for Nina gave me the space to get my head in order."

"You okay?" Zeke asked.

Mont nodded. "Yeah, I'm getting there. I just... Knowing what she went through makes me feel like even more of an asshole. What if we'd been able to find her? What if I never left?"

"You can't think about that. She said she doesn't blame either of us."

"I know, but shit, she was right here in Niagara Falls. She was here."

"Yeah." Zeke thought about the same thing every night since Nina came back. He drove himself crazy with regret and guilt. Especially when he laughed and teased and loved her. He didn't deserve to be happy to have her back when she had so many painful memories.

"This is why we do what we do," Mont said. "Why we started Rose Protection Agency. No one else should go through what we did. But having my brother with me through all of this made it bearable."

"Same, Mont."

Montgomery grabbed Zeke's hand and jerked him in for a hug, slapping Zeke's back. Zeke returned the gesture, grateful he'd always have Montgomery in his life. Zeke's days of dreaming Mont would be more than just his brother by choice were gone, but they always had that.

"What's going on?" Nina asked from behind Mont.

Mont and Zeke pulled apart, both sniffing and wiping their eyes while pretending not to.

"Just thanking Zeke for being here for you the last month and for me my whole life. He's one of the good ones." Mont cupped Zeke's neck and squeezed.

"He is," Nina whispered. She met his gaze, and he saw a glimpse of what they shared in her eyes.

He turned back to the stove. "Food's about ready. You guys hungry?"

"Always," Mont said.

The rest of the morning was a combination of food and laughter and teasing, but Zeke stayed mostly quiet. He wasn't ready to say goodbye to her, so he said nothing at all. And when Mont and Nina left to go on their adventure, Zeke resisted the urge to punch a hole in his wall.

NINA LAUGHED at Monty when he made a funny face for their picture. He wanted to document their day, something about needing new pictures of her, and she was on board.

It was a good day. She felt uncomfortable being out in the open at first, but if Monty thought it was okay, Nina was not going to argue. She'd missed the fresh air and the wide open spaces around Niagara Falls.

Even though she'd never left the city, she hadn't seen the

iconic and masterful waterfall since she was a teenager. "It's still so beautiful."

Monty leaned against the metal railing between them and the rushing water and nodded. "It is. I don't come here often, but it's stunning."

"Why don't you come here?"

"Busy." Monty shrugged. "Mostly work, but I always thought of you when I would come here. It wasn't easy."

"I'm sorry I left."

He shook his head. "You don't need to apologize. Not to me. You did what you thought was best, and I appreciate you doing that. I hate the outcome for you, but I'm moving forward."

"Me, too."

Monty was quiet for several minutes, staring out at the water with Nina. When he turned to face her, she matched his pose. "What do you think you might want to do with your life?"

Nina shook her head. "I have no idea."

"Did you have any ideas before?"

Nina laughed. "I wanted to be a professional soccer player."

Monty grinned. "You would have been good. You were good."

"I know. But that was not reality, and obviously now, it's not something I'd do."

"What is?"

Nina shrugged. She hadn't given much thought to a future. When she was with Zeke, she wanted to imagine the possibility of one, but most of the time she couldn't think past Gwendolyn.

And where she might be.

Monty's phone rang before Nina could tell him any of

that. He answered it in a clipped tone, and Nina stared at the water again, trying not to think about Gwendolyn and the first house.

It was useless, though. The idea that she could still be in the area ran around in Nina's head all night. Nina dreamed of the early days with Gwendolyn and the house they lived in. She had a particularly vivid dream of Gwendolyn threatening to kill Nina.

She couldn't sleep after that, not even with Zeke wrapped around her.

A month was a long time to go without any word from Gwendolyn. She had to be gone. Nina was mostly sure of it.

"We have to go," Monty said, grabbing Nina's arm.

"What? Where are we going? What's wrong?"

"Zeke is going to meet us at his house, and I need to go to meet with the FBI."

"Why? What happened?"

Monty stopped next to his SUV and faced her. The pain on his face broke Nina's heart. "One of the people you identified as a known associate of Gwendolyn's is dead."

"What?"

"Get in the SUV."

Nina looked around and realized how exposed they were. She scrambled into the front seat, fighting the flood of fear pressing down on her.

Monty climbed in next to her and started up the SUV. He pulled away from the Falls and drove quickly through the city.

Nina wanted to ask questions. To know who it was. To know where the body was found and what happened. To know everything. But she couldn't bring herself to ask anything. She just sat there, silent, while Monty raced through the city and pulled into the driveway of the townhouse.

Zeke opened her door and shielded her while Monty blocked her from behind. Nina wanted to cry. She thought she was free. She thought she had a chance at being safe. But it would never happen. Not with Gwendolyn out there.

Nina was such a fool hoping Gwendolyn left the area. Maybe she did, but it didn't matter. Gwendolyn would kill without conscience. She would sell women into slavery and allow them to be drugged and raped without a care.

No one was safe with someone like Gwendolyn free in the world.

Nina wanted to scream and cry and hunt Gwendolyn down and kill her. She wanted to know the bitch was dead. She wanted to know Monty and Zeke and the other Curvy Vigilantes were safe.

But none of them were.

The front door closed and locked, and Nina turned to face Zeke. "I need to know what happened."

"I'm not sure that's a good idea," he said carefully.

"Please tell me."

"Why? What will it do?"

"Zeke, please," she cried.

He sighed, running a hand over his head. His eyes closed, holding back everything from her. If he was hesitating, it was bad.

How bad?

"The body was the only woman you identified."

"Joyce."

Zeke nodded.

"What happened to her?" Nina whispered. Joyce was always nasty, but that didn't mean she deserved to die. She was the woman tasked with taking care of the girls Gwendolyn kept in her house. She was the one who brought in the doctor when someone needed medical care and delivered the scraps Gwendolyn gave everyone for food. Joyce took care of them, in a way.

"Her body was at Olcott Beach, where we went right after you came back."

"Oh my God."

Zeke stopped talking.

"There's more. Tell me."

He sighed. "She was dressed in the same thing you were wearing the night I picked you up."

Nina closed her eyes. "She never dressed like that. She wore plain clothes."

Zeke didn't move from his spot near the door.

"What else?" Nina asked.

"She had a coffee cup from the shop where you and Frannie met Robert, and she had been assaulted."

"No one deserves that," Nina breathed. "I didn't like her, but I didn't want her to die like that."

Zeke didn't say anything, and he didn't reach for her.

Nina needed to feel his strength and comfort. She needed to know she was safe, and that he was there for her. "Can I... Will you let me hug you?"

Zeke swore and crossed the room to where Nina stood. He wrapped his arms tightly around her and held her body against his from shoulders to knees.

Nina sighed, feeling better with him close. It wasn't okay for her to take advantage of him like she was, but she needed him. "I hate her."

"We all do, angel. We'll find her and stop her."

Nina pulled back, needing a minute before she admitted the truth.

"We won't give up until she's in custody, Nina. I promise

you that. There are so many people looking for her. The drawings have been all over the news and people are calling in all the time. It's only a matter of time."

"I think I know where she is."

Zeke stopped, frozen in time, like his brain ceased and the rest of him had to catch up. "What do you mean you know where she is?"

"Well, I don't know for sure, but there was this house. It was where I first lived when I was with her. We haven't been back in years, and I thought it was sold, but I don't know."

"You didn't tell the FBI about it?"

Nina shook her head. "No. I didn't think about it. It had been so long, and Gwendolyn took me to all her houses, so I don't think... I don't know."

"So, what makes you think she might be there?"

"I don't..."

"Don't fucking lie to me, Nina. Although, it sounds like you have been. When did you figure this out?"

Nina thought about lying, but she couldn't do it. Not to Zeke. Of all people, he deserved the truth. "I've been trying to figure it out for a while. There were little things, and I felt like I was missing something. Robert said something, and Frannie made comments, and even some of the things Lorelei said. But—"

"When, Nina?"

"Last night."

"Last night." Zeke took a step back. "Before or after we slept together?"

"After," she whispered.

He nodded. "That's why you were up early this morning. You couldn't stay in bed with me when you knew you were lying to me."

"I was in bed with you and felt safe. I felt like you cared

about me and knew you were going to protect me. I was thinking it had been a long time since I felt that way, and I realized it was like that with Gwendolyn when I was seventeen. In the first house she had."

"Where she would brush your hair at night and you would have dinner together."

Nina nodded, swallowing to keep the pain inside. "Yes."

"You need to tell the FBI. They need to know she could be there. So they can capture her before the psycho kills someone else."

"I know. And I'm sorry. I thought maybe she was gone. It's been a month, and I hoped..."

"You hoped your fake sister was going to move to another city and kill people there instead of continuing to take her wrath out on you? Would that have been better, Nina?"

Nina shook her head. "No. But I hoped she changed. That maybe she would just leave town and not kill people. That maybe she was like I thought when we met."

"People don't change, Nina. Not people like her. She's evil. She's a murderer. And it doesn't matter if you have some twisted sense of loyalty to her, she doesn't feel the same. She will kill you, and anyone else who stands in her way."

"I know."

"You need to report this. And you need to do it now."

Nina nodded. "Okay."

22

———

Zeke couldn't bring himself to talk to her. He was furious. How could she protect the woman who ruined her life? Who kept her captive and sold her to anyone who wanted a piece of her?

Not only that, but she lied to him. It wasn't the part that should be most significant, but it hurt. She pulled back because she was lying, because she knew keeping the truth from him was bad, but she still did it.

Yeah, maybe Gwendolyn wasn't there. But maybe she was.

And someone died because Nina didn't share her suspicion right away.

Zeke texted Montgomery they were coming in and to get the FBI there, so Mont met them at the SUV and got Nina inside. Zeke hung back, needing space from Nina. He needed space from all of it. From loving her and protecting her and hoping she would want him.

He felt like a fool. And he needed space from that, too.

"You okay?" Samuel asked, sidling up to Zeke as he watched Nina and Lorelei talk in Mont's office.

Zeke shook his head. "No. What's going on around here?"

"Picked up a new case. Getting ready to head out and meet with the client."

"Need some help?"

Samuel's brows went high. He rocked back on his heels. "I thought you were protecting Nina."

Zeke shook his head. "I'm available."

"Everything good?"

"No."

"Need to talk about it?"

"No. When do we need to go?"

"Whenever you're ready."

Zeke pulled out his phone. "Let me tell Mont I'm going with you, then we can get out of here."

Samuel nodded and kept his mouth shut.

Zeke appreciated that last part.

He sent a quick text to Montgomery that he needed to talk. Zeke watched through the glass as Mont read the text and looked out to where Zeke was.

Mont nodded, then turned to Nina and Lorelei. A second later, he walked out of his office. "What's going on?"

"I'm going to tag along with Samuel to meet the new client."

"What about Nina?" Mont asked.

Zeke shook his head. "I think it's best if she stays with you."

Mont narrowed his eyes at Zeke.

Zeke didn't flinch. He expected an inquisition. He didn't expect an agreement.

"Okay. Done. Be careful out there."

Zeke nodded, then followed Samuel to the door, not looking back to see if Nina watched him leave.

"Are you okay?" Lorelei asked.

Nina dragged her gaze from Zeke's retreating back and shook her head. "No."

"Do you need a break?"

"No. Let's continue."

"Okay." Lorelei turned back to her notes. "This house you lived in, you moved out when you were eighteen?"

Nina nodded. "Nineteen. When I left home, I went to Club Curves where Beth worked, where I'd met Gwendolyn. I told the bartender I was looking for Gwendolyn, and someone called her for me. She came and got me and took me to that house."

"And she lived there with you?"

Nina nodded again. "Yeah. For almost two years."

Monty came back into his office, letting the door close behind him. He didn't say a word, just stood there like he was doing before.

"Where did Zeke go?" Nina asked.

"He's helping Samuel with another case," Monty said. He didn't meet Nina's gaze.

"Is he coming back?"

Monty shook his head slowly, as though he didn't want to answer the question.

"Why not? Where am I going to stay?"

"With me." Monty finally looked at her. His eyes held all his love. His pain and his hope, too. "I won't let anything happen to you."

Nina swallowed roughly. She never wanted to hurt her brother. When she called Zeke, she thought Monty was gone. When she learned he was there, she still wanted to stay with Zeke. She felt safe with Zeke. She knew Monty would protect her, but Zeke was different. She could crawl on his lap and not feel weird about it. And when he admitted how much he wanted her, she knew going to him was the best choice. She was able to heal in ways she never would have if it weren't for Zeke.

But he was leaving her.

"I think I have enough," Lorelei said, moving toward the door. "I'll keep you posted on what we find."

"When do you think you'll be able to check out the house?" Nina asked.

"We can't sit on this, so we'll do everything possible to get over there today."

Nina nodded.

"Thanks for coming so quickly," Monty said. He ushered Lorelei to the door and left with her, leaving Nina alone.

She curled up on the couch and tried not to cry. She didn't blame Zeke for being angry, but she thought he would be there. He promised to keep her safe.

And she promised not to lie to him.

Nina held her stomach and let the pain of losing him fill her. She'd been through it before. She would survive.

"Are you okay?" Monty asked when he walked back into the office.

"No."

Monty was quiet for a minute. "I need to take care of a few things. Frannie said you could stay with her while I'm unavailable."

Nina shook her head and sat up. "I hate being a burden."

Monty sat next to her. He took her hands and squeezed them. "You are not a burden. You never have been. I had some meetings lined up today and didn't realize Zeke would be unavailable. I don't want you alone. That doesn't mean you're a burden. I would feel the same about any client, too."

Nina nodded, trying to get past the hurt. If Monty didn't know Zeke was going to be unavailable, then he didn't send Zeke on whatever job he was on. Zeke chose to leave. He chose to leave her.

Monty led her out of the office and into his SUV. Nina stared out the window at the passing city, thinking how different things were just a few hours earlier. She went to see the Falls. She laughed with her brother. She didn't worry about someone trying to kill her.

And one dead body changed all of that.

Monty parked in front of Shelter in the Storm. Before he could walk around to Nina's side of the SUV, Frannie was walking out.

"Hello!" she said warmly, wrapping Nina in a hug. "I'm so happy you're going to spend the day here."

Nina made a noise she hoped Frannie took as agreement. She liked Frannie, but being there was not her first choice.

"I'll be back around dinner, if that's okay," Monty said.

Frannie nodded. "Of course. We'll see you then."

Nina hugged her brother and felt like the child in the middle of divorced parents, being passed between them like she couldn't take care of herself.

She supposed she couldn't. She didn't know how to defend herself. She didn't know how to stop Gwendolyn. She didn't know anything.

Frannie ushered Nina inside and led her to the living room.

Nina sat on the couch and grabbed a pillow, holding it over her stomach and hugging it tight.

"How is Zeke? I'm guessing he's busy chasing down something for you to need a place to stay for the day,"

Frannie said. Her smile was bright and happy, like she was sharing a secret.

"I don't know."

Frannie's smile faded. "What do you mean? You two have been attached at the hip since you came back. I thought you were together."

Nina shook her head. "It was a fling. Temporary. Casual, I guess. It's over now."

Frannie drew back in shock. "Wow, I never thought you'd turn him down. The way you two looked at each other, I thought you loved him as much as he loves you."

"He doesn't love me. He's the one that left."

Frannie laughed. "Oh, honey, you don't believe that, do you?"

"Um, yeah. He walked out. Didn't even tell me he was leaving."

"That's not what I'm talking about. He's in love with you. Hands down, head over heels, totally gone."

Nina shook her head. "No. No, he loves me, but it's not like that. I'm like his sister."

Frannie choked. "Sorry, but no brother should look at his sister the way that man looks at you."

"Not like a real sister. He just... He loves me because he's known me forever. But it's not romantic love. It's comfortable, familiar."

"Is that how you feel about him?"

Nina picked at her nail. "It doesn't matter how I feel about him."

"It might matter to him. Because you can tell yourself he doesn't love you, but you're wrong."

"You don't even know us."

Frannie laughed. "Nina, I've watched people come

through those doors for years. A lot of years. I've seen what love really looks like. I've seen a lot of the manipulation and danger that comes with control and possession, but I've seen love, too. I've watched Stacey and Wray find their way back to each other. I was there as Jessica and Braden admitted they weren't just friends. I saw Karli and Cade fall in love. Mackenzie and Holden knew each other long before I met them, but when she finally let him in, he was all in. Raina and Adam were the same, but she knew he was one of the good ones from day one. Edie and Pryce were the hardest ones because she had so much pain and he didn't trust very easily, but their love is solid. Dawn and Gage almost didn't survive, but their love held them together. And Lorelei and Vinnie? Those two went through the worst of it with her memory loss, but he was there every step of the way for her. All those couples know what love is. They know it's not sticking around for the good times, but being there for the bad ones, too."

"Then that proves I'm right because as soon as things went bad, Zeke took off."

Frannie shook her head. "I don't believe that. I think maybe he's hurting for some reason. He doesn't trust that you feel the same way he does, and he needs a break. To protect his heart after a month of loving you and thinking he's going to lose you."

"I thought of another place Gwendolyn could be, and I didn't tell him."

Frannie sucked in a sharp breath. "And the body..."

Nina nodded. "Joyce."

"So he feels betrayed."

"It wasn't about him."

"No, honey, it's about you. He's terrified of losing you for good. There's a threat out there, a very real one, and you didn't share information that could have stopped Gwennie. He might be mad, but I think it's more likely he's scared and doesn't know how to handle that. Men like him, men who are so capable and strong, they fall hard. And when they do, the woman they love is everything to them. Give him time. He'll come back to you soon. He won't be able to stay away, even if he knows it'll destroy him to be near you when you don't feel the same way he does."

Nina sucked in a breath. Tears dripped down her cheeks.

"Unless you do feel the same," Frannie said.

Nina nodded.

Frannie smiled. "I think maybe you should tell him. The next time you see him. Because he needs to know, and right now, he doesn't."

Nina inhaled a full breath, finding it impossible to not smile. Zeke loved her. And she loved him. Everything would be okay.

As the day wore on, Nina tried to convince herself everything would be over soon. Lorelei would find Gwendolyn, Zeke would come back, and Nina would be able to move on with her life.

But the longer all of that took, the less she believed it would happen. When Monty showed up just before dinner, the look on his face said none of it had happened yet.

"Any news from Lorelei?" Nina asked when Monty led her outside to his SUV.

Monty hung his head. "They can't get a team together to check out the house until tomorrow."

"I thought they were going to go there today."

Monty nodded. "That's what she said, but I guess plans changed when she got back to their office. They don't want to risk tipping Gwendolyn off if they drive by. She could run. So they decided to wait until they had time to plan a full scale operation."

"And they're just going to risk her getting away?"

"Unfortunately, yeah."

"No. They can't. What if she kills someone else?"

"It's on them if she does. You did what you needed to do and told them as soon as you remembered the house. None of this is on you."

"But I didn't," Nina admitted. "I thought about the house last night, and I didn't say anything. Even this morning, I didn't know if I wanted to tell them."

"What? Why would you do that? She held you against your will. She used you. She profited from the horrible things you went through."

"Yeah, and she was there for me at a time when I didn't feel like anyone else was," Nina confessed. "I'm not saying that to make you feel bad, Monty, I'm not, but I left because I knew I was stopping you from living your life. You wanted to go. You chose the military. If Dad moved back in with me, you wouldn't have left. You would have given up your spot and your career would have been over before it started. Gwendolyn was there for me when I knew I had to leave. She was good to me the first few months."

"And then she sold your body and took all the money and threatened to kill you if you left." Monty's growl was low and dangerous. His anger was a living thing in the SUV with them. "I will never forgive myself for not sticking around and finding you. For not seeing how scared you were and what you were willing to do before you left. But I'll be damned if I'm going to let that monster make you feel like you owe her something. You were her possession for twelve years. It might not have been as horrible that first year, but if she really cared, she would have let you call me. She would have given you the freedom to leave the house. She would have let you have a connection to me and promised to care for you when I was gone. She hid you. She lied, and she kept you from seeing anyone."

Shock had Nina sucking in a breath. She hadn't thought of her first year with Gwendolyn that way, but Monty was right. It could have been better. It could have been normal. But Gwendolyn didn't allow it. She told Nina to stay inside where no one could see her because it wasn't safe. She said Nina would be arrested or sent to a foster home if the police found her.

Nina believed all of it. She trusted what Gwendolyn said. She let it happen.

Monty pulled into his driveway and turned off the SUV. Nina realized she'd never been into his side of the town-house. Zeke's side was dark, his garage closed. She stared at it for a minute, wishing she could go back to Zeke.

"All my stuff is there," Nina said, pointing to Zeke's place.

"Uh, no. I met up with Zeke earlier. He packed every-thing for you and we put it in my house." Monty was uncomfortable with the admission.

"Oh." She swallowed through the pain. Frannie was wrong. Zeke didn't love her.

Nina followed Monty into the townhouse that was a mirror of Zeke's. Monty disarmed the alarm and turned on lights. He moved through the space, showing her where things were.

His home was comfortable but masculine. It felt like a

bachelor pad, whereas Zeke's felt like a home. Like her home.

She had to stop. It wasn't her home. It never was, and it never would be.

Monty made them a quick dinner, then settled on his black couch with the remote. His TV was massive, taking up the entire wall. His furniture was arranged differently from Zeke's, focusing everything on the TV.

Nina sat next to her brother and wondered what Zeke was doing. She hoped he was safe. She hoped Gwendolyn didn't find him.

Her breath caught with the fear that the next body would be Zeke's. Nina couldn't let it happen. She couldn't sit there and wait it out and hope Gwendolyn didn't find Zeke. Or Monty. Or anyone she cared about.

"I need to go see her," she breathed.

"See who?" Monty asked.

"Gwendolyn."

"No. No. Hell no. Why would you even think that?"

"Because this doesn't end until I do. I know she's there. I can feel it. But she won't be for long. She'll have an escape plan. If the FBI get there before I do, people will die."

"She'll kill you, Nina."

Nina surged to her feet. "I need to do it, anyway. I need to go."

"Then I'm going with you," Monty said, standing with her.

"No. I can't have her hurt you."

"I'm not going to sit here and watch TV while you go off and face her alone. I'm going. If you're going, I'm going."

Nina wanted to tell him no, but she knew there was no way he'd let her leave alone. If she was honest, it made her feel better to know he would be there with her. She would protect him. Trade herself for him if it came down to that.

"Are you sure about this?" she asked.

Monty shook his head. "No. But I'm doing it anyway. I'm not going to risk you sneaking out and going without me."

"Let's go."

Monty nodded and followed her to the door.

Zeke's house was still dark when they walked outside. A part of Nina wanted to see him before she left, but it wouldn't change anything.

Monty drove the city streets like he knew exactly where he was going. Nina assumed he did as they drew closer to the house she'd once called home.

Monty parked a block away, tucking his SUV among dozens of other vehicles where it wouldn't be noticed right away. He made a move to open his door, but she stopped him with a hand on his arm.

"I love you, big brother. I know I haven't shown it in the best way, but I do. I love you so much, and I need you to do one thing for me."

"Anything, as long as it's not staying put."

Nina breathed a laugh. "No, I know you won't do that."

"Okay, then what it is?"

"I need you to tell Zeke I love him."

"No. Don't do that. You're going to tell him yourself."

Nina shook her head. "I don't know if I'll have the chance to."

"You can't walk into that house thinking you'll never walk out, Nina."

"I know what she's capable of, Monty. I know how she operates. And I know my odds are not great. So, please, promise me you'll tell Zeke I love him. I'm in love with him.

I wish things could have been different, but I have to do this."

"Fuck, Nina."

"Please promise me you'll tell him."

Monty nodded and dragged her in for a hug. He held her tight for several moments, then kissed the top of her head. "Let's go stop this bitch so you can have that happy ending you deserve."

Nina smiled. "Let's do it."

23

GWENDOLYN SMILED AS SHE SIPPED HER DRINK. IT WAS A GOOD night for visitors. She had the house ready for them, knowing her bait was more compelling than theirs had been.

Gwendolyn would miss Joyce, but she was a sacrifice Gwendolyn was willing to make. Dead weight, so to speak. Without any girls around to take care of, Joyce's usefulness had run out. Gwendolyn made Joyce available for the men who wouldn't accept that the supply wasn't there and needed a woman's body, willing or not.

But Joyce was gone, and Gwendolyn would not offer herself up as the next available body. She needed to regain her favorite girl.

Sometimes it was just too easy.

"Two people are approaching," Fernando said. "Walking up but not as subtle as they think."

"It's Nina and her brother," Gwendolyn said, watching the camera she installed down the street. The entire house was surrounded by them, with many more in places no one knew about. Like the camera on Shelter in the Storm, and the one outside Zeke and Montgomery's house, the one at Rose Protection Agency, and the ones near the police station. Gwendolyn didn't take chances.

"Do you want me to kill them?" Fernando asked, his trigger-happy hand already reaching for the gun on his side.

"No. I want them to think they're smarter than me and get inside. Then I want you to tie up the brother. Nina and I have things to discuss."

Fernando nodded, then let himself out of the room silently.

Gwendolyn watched, and waited for her sister to come home to her.

It was easy to get inside. Too easy. Every step Nina took told her the only thing waiting for them was a trap.

But she couldn't turn back. She had to see it through. She had to stop Gwendolyn once and for all.

Nina fingered the knife in her pocket. Monty gave it to her on the ride. He had guns, but she refused. A knife wasn't better, but it felt less threatening. After everything, Nina knew she wouldn't be able to kill Gwendolyn.

She almost laughed. The night she left, she wanted to kill Gwendolyn, and probably would have if she'd had the chance. But a month with Zeke and Monty and the Curvy Vigilantes changed Nina. She saw the light in the world. She knew things could be different. She didn't want Gwendolyn free, but Nina agreed with Frannie that Gwendolyn needed to face the consequences of her actions.

Nina could convince her. She had to. Tell Gwendolyn to stop killing people and take her in. If the FBI found her,

Gwendolyn would not give up. But Nina could reason with her. She had to.

Nina's old room was upstairs, at the back of the house, but she knew that wasn't where Gwendolyn would be waiting for her. Gwendolyn didn't come into Nina's room often. When they were together, they were always in the family room. The cozy, sunken room was a converted old porch. It was cold in the winter, and hot in the summer, but Nina and Gwendolyn loved it. They spent all winter snuggling under blankets and watching movies about people falling in love and happy families and holidays neither of them had ever known.

It felt like a bonding experience back then. Not the manipulation it clearly was.

"Come in and sit, little sis," Gwendolyn said once Nina got to the door. Her voice drifted from the darkness. "Bring your brother in, too."

Nina took a step into the room, then heard an oof and a thud. She turned back and saw Monty on the floor. "Monty!"

"I wouldn't do that," Gwendolyn snarled.

Her threat was reinforced with a gun to Monty's head. "Go sit, Nina," Fernando growled.

Nina tore her gaze from Monty and walked into the room.

Gwendolyn lifted the blanket next to her for Nina to sit while Fernando dragged Monty into the room and propped him up in the armchair in the corner.

Nina stared at her brother and prayed he was just faking it. That he would jump up at any second and overpower Fernando and Gwendolyn and the whole thing would be over.

Zip-ties went around Monty's wrists and ankles. He didn't fight once, not even a groan.

"Is he dead?" Nina whispered. A trickle of blood ran down the side of Monty's face.

"No reason to tie him up if he's dead, sis. He'll be fine. Killer headache, though." Gwendolyn waved her fingers at Fernando.

He produced a small vial from his pocket.

Nina flinched and drew back. More drugs. No. She couldn't leave Monty, but she couldn't...

Fernando waved it under Monty's nose.

Monty inhaled and jerked, snapping back. His eyes opened, and he instantly fought the binds. "Leave her alone."

"You're not in a position to make demands right now," Gwendolyn said.

"Nina, get away from her," Monty growled.

Gwendolyn slapped a hand onto Nina's lap. Her nails dug into Nina's thigh, and she winced.

"She's not moving. We're all going to have a little chat."

"I have no interest in anything you have to say," Nina said.

"That's not very nice. After everything I've done for you." Gwendolyn shook her head. "It doesn't really matter what you say, though, because we're going to sit here and talk like we used to. Maybe watch a movie. Didn't you have a favorite?" Gwendolyn picked up the remote. "Maybe we can find it and watch it tonight. Then we're going to leave, and your brother is going to sit here until the house is demolished."

"What? Gwendolyn, no," Nina said.

Gwendolyn turned to her. "You don't get to tell me what to do."

Nina closed her mouth, the years of threats and having them carried out far too fresh in her mind to ignore.

"I've missed you, sis," Gwendolyn said, her voice soft. "I was so hurt when you left. And then you tried to trick me. I thought you cared about me."

"You held her hostage. Why would she care about you?" Monty hissed.

Gwendolyn flicked her wrist. Fernando stepped forward and punched Monty in the face.

"No!" Nina shouted, moving to get up. Gwendolyn's fingers tightened on Nina's thigh, making her cry out in pain.

"If you move, he does it again," Gwendolyn snarled. "If he keeps interrupting, Fernando will keep going. We're going to talk. He doesn't get to interrupt."

"Monty, please," Nina whispered.

Monty met her gaze and nodded once. He slid an angry look to Gwendolyn, but he kept his mouth shut.

"Good boy. You would have done well for me if I rented out my men. I never liked to do that, though. Too emotional. Women were much easier. I only had to kill one every few years to keep the rest in line."

"Why did you kill them? Any of them?"

Gwendolyn looked at Nina as though she was the biggest moron. "To make sure the rest of you listened. I couldn't have anyone trying to sneak out or fighting back. I had a few men that would take care of the women who were fighters, men who liked that kind of thing, but the rest of you just needed one dead body to remember what your duty was."

"There's no one left. No one to threaten. Why didn't you just leave? Why didn't you stop killing people and just leave?"

"You know the answer, sis. I needed you. Your brother doesn't care about you the same way I do. He stopped looking for you a week after you came to me. Forgot all about you. I've been watching you every day since you left me."

"You're a psycho," Monty growled.

Gwendolyn clucked her tongue at Monty, holding her hand up to stop Fernando from punching him again. "You think you're so good, but I know all about you, Montgomery Rose. I am not afraid to use deadly force when necessary, but you have your father's blood in your veins. There's a dark side to you, one you can't always control. Like the night your father left."

"What is she talking about?" Nina asked her brother.

Monty didn't answer.

Nina swung her gaze to Gwendolyn.

Gwendolyn looked surprised. A hand to her chest. "Me? Now you want to know what I have to say?"

Nina choked back a sob. "You're a liar."

"Then why would you ask me? Just ask your perfect brother. Ask him why your father finally left. Ask him how long he pounded on dear old daddy's face. Ask him if he broke poor dad's hand."

"Monty? She's lying. I know she's lying. Tell me she's lying."

Monty looked at Nina, the truth written all over him. "She's not lying. I... I beat him until he couldn't fight back. Until he was almost unconscious. Mom pulled me off of him."

"Monty, no."

"See, Nina? This is the monster I was saving you from. You thought he was so good, but he's no better than your father. The man you told me you were terrified of when you moved in with me. I took care of you. I made sure you were safe and strong. I made sure you had everything you needed. Come home, Nina. We can start over."

"She's lying," Monty growled.

"You would think so, Montgomery. You've lied your whole life. Not everyone is like you, though. Not everyone has to manipulate the truth to make others think they're decent."

"No." Nina shook her head. "No. You're wrong. My brother is a good man. He was protecting Mom and me. He didn't hurt our dad for sport. Not like what you do."

"It's not sport, Nina. It's business. If you don't like it, you can leave."

"I've seen what you do to people who try to leave!"

"And yet you left. And you talked to the FBI. My homes, my privacy, my legacy! You're the one who stole all of that from me. After everything I did for you, you stole it all."

"None of it was yours, Gwendolyn. You cheated and stole and lied and built everything on the lives of people you kidnapped."

"They all wanted a better life. Something new. Different. Flashier and more fun. Just like you," Gwendolyn growled.

"I didn't want to be raped when I was eighteen. Or drugged. I didn't want to be offered up to whatever man paid for me. I didn't choose any of that."

"You chose when you walked into Club Curves and asked someone to call me. When you handed your innocence and your life over to me. When you moved into this house and asked me to provide for you. Did you really think I was doing all of that for free? Did you think I was going to pay for you to live here out of the goodness of my heart?" Gwendolyn cackled like the crazy person she was. "God, Nina, you are so stupid. You want me to treat you like you matter, but you just don't see things the way they are. Like going to visit Star and Monica. You thought you could walk in and they would be all happy to see you? So stupid."

"What did you do to them?" Nina snarled.

Gwendolyn glared back. "What should I do to them? I left them alone for now, but if you don't behave, I will go get them. Are you willing to trade your life for theirs?"

"Nina, no," Monty demanded.

"Stay out of it, big brother," Gwendolyn taunted. "I have no problem gutting you and dragging her away while you bleed out on the floor."

"No," Nina shouted. "Leave him alone. Leave all of them alone. You can't. I'll go."

"Nina, no! You can't. She'll kill you," Monty yelled.

"I love you, Monty. So much. But I can't let her hurt you. Or anyone else. I have to go with her."

Monty struggled against his binds. Red marks screamed on his wrists, droplets of blood forming.

Nina wanted a proper goodbye with her brother. A chance to tell him how she felt. A real moment to hug him and forget about everything else.

But she didn't have that.

"Time to go," Gwendolyn said, her voice victorious and cheerful. She stood and reached for Nina's hand.

"I will hunt you down," Monty growled at Gwendolyn.

Gwendolyn grinned. "I look forward to the chase, Monty. It'll be fun watching you run around in circles and acting like you know where you're going, the whole time wondering if the next delivery you get will be a piece of your sister or if she's still alive somewhere."

"I'll kill you!"

"Oh, there's the monster I know and love. Threatening an unarmed woman. Wow. Such chivalry."

"Nina, don't go. Please, Nina."

"You'll be safe, Monty. Everyone will be safe."

"Let go of her," Zeke growled from the doorway.

"Zeke," Nina breathed.

Gwendolyn pulled Nina in front of her, using her as a shield. "Oh, the boyfriend is here. I was hoping I'd get to meet you. Obviously, my sister didn't share anything before, so I had to do some digging. But it's so much better to get to know you in person."

"Get the hell away from her." Zeke had a gun pointed at them.

Gwendolyn put a gun to Nina's head, the edge of the barrel pressing into her temple.

Nina yelped and tried to move away. She'd prayed for death a few times. Hoped the hell would end. But facing it, having a gun to her head and knowing she really was not going to have a future was so much worse than she'd feared.

"Don't fucking move," Gwendolyn growled, yanking Nina's hair.

"This isn't going to end well for you," Zeke said.

Gwendolyn snorted. "You clearly didn't take stock of the situation, boyfriend. We have big brother in here, and he's not going to be very helpful to you. So, you're outgunned."

"I'm willing to take that chance. You're not taking Nina. She's mine."

Nina shivered at the possessive tone of his voice, a smile lifting the edges of her lips.

Gwendolyn laughed. "Oh, this is rich. I love it. This is just like the movies we used to watch where the hero comes in and saves the day, acting all chivalrous and good. But you're not good. You're not even mediocre. Barely made it out of high school. Zero ambition or goals in life. You've been hanging on to big brother's coattails forever. Just waiting for the chance that you could be a part of their family. Why would Nina want you?"

Zeke blanched, drawing back for half a second.

"Don't listen to her," Nina said.

Gwendolyn yanked Nina's hair, keeping her in place as her shield. "Boyfriend and Big Brother are going to be good boys and they're going to listen right now. We are going to walk out of this house, Nina, me, and Fernando. And if you try any funny stuff, someone gets a bullet."

"We can't let them come after us," Fernando said.

"Hmm. You're right," Gwendolyn said. "Shoot him."

Nina screamed as a gunshot went off behind her. "Monty!" Nina shoved Gwendolyn, breaking free and sliding on her knees to her brother's side.

Monty laid on the floor, one hand free. Blood seeped from his arm onto the wood. Nina pressed her hand over the wound, hoping it was enough to stop the bleeding.

Another gunshot rang out, and a thud behind her said Fernando was down.

"NO!" Gwendolyn shouted.

"Hands up," Zeke growled.

Nina watched them over her shoulder.

Zeke's gun was on Gwendolyn. His eyes were hard, unyielding.

Gwendolyn snarled at him, but she raised her hands. The gun she'd stuck against Nina's head dangled from one finger.

"Put the gun down," Zeke commanded.

"I don't think I'm going to do that." Gwendolyn spun the gun into her hand and pointed it at Nina. "Are you willing to risk that you're faster than me?"

Gwendolyn didn't give Zeke a chance to answer before she pulled the trigger.

The spark at the end of the gun was bright. Brighter than Nina expected. She'd never stared into the end of a gun as it was fired. She drew back, as though that would help. As though it would save her.

She watched, waiting for the bullet to hit her, waiting for death to claim her.

Zeke shouted. His body flashed in front of Nina.

She flinched.

The sound of the bullet hitting Zeke was made worse by the way he collapsed to the ground in a heap, not bracing himself before he hit the floor.

"Zeke!"

"Come with me, Nina. We can call the police when we're gone. They might survive. But if you refuse, I'll kill you, too." Gwendolyn pointed her gun at Nina again.

"Don't go," Monty breathed. He pressed something against her hand.

Cold metal. With a trigger.

Nina didn't think or wonder or hesitate. She grabbed the gun and swung, pulling the trigger as many times as she could, bullets popping out like fireworks.

Gwendolyn jerked as a bullet hit her arm, then again when one hit her chest. Her gun slid across the floor away from her as she fell.

Nina drew a sharp breath. The silence was almost as deafening as the gunshots.

Laughter came from Gwendolyn, a wheezing sound breaking up the evil laugh. "I always knew you had it in you, Nina. That's why I took you in."

Nina went to Gwendolyn, standing over her as blood pumped out of her body. "What are you talking about?"

Gwendolyn grinned. Blood stained her clothes. Her teeth were red. Her blonde hair was copper. "That evil runs deep in you. You're a killer, just like me. Your brother and your father were your first examples, but they scared you. I made you strong. I made you what you are today. I raised you well, Nina."

"I'm nothing like you," Nina breathed.

"I'm so proud of you, sis. So proud." Gwendolyn exhaled and went still.

Nina stared at the woman. Tears streamed down Nina's face. Her gut clenched with fear, her hand on the gun that gave her the power to take a life. "I'm nothing like you."

24

———

THE CRACK OF WOOD SPLINTERING WAS IMMEDIATELY followed by the pounding of footsteps and shouts from a dozen people pointing flashlights and guns at Nina.

"Freeze! Hands up. Drop the gun!"

Nina took a step back and let the gun fall to the floor. Hands grabbed her, shoving her to the wall. A man pressed against her back, his hands sliding over her body.

Panic gripped her throat. Tears filled her gaze. She wanted to fight, to push back against the man feeling her up, but she couldn't. She was done. She might as well be the one with a bullet in her, dead on the floor.

"What the hell happened here?"

Nina knew that voice. "Lorelei?"

"Nina. What's going on? Let her go," Lorelei commanded.

"She's clean, ma'am," the man said, letting Nina up. "No more weapons."

Nina sagged with relief, falling to her knees.

"Nina, what happened? Why did you come here?"

"Monty said you couldn't come until tomorrow. I didn't want her to get away."

Lorelei's gaze landed on Gwendolyn and hung there.

Nina watched the other woman, knowing Lorelei would feel the same about Gwendolyn being dead. Relieved. At peace. Safe.

"Did you kill her?" Lorelei asked.

Nina nodded. "I did." Nina stood, using the wall for support. She walked to Lorelei with her hands together. "I know you have to arrest me."

Lorelei looked around the room, and Nina remembered the rest of the night.

"Monty. Zeke! They were shot. They need help." Nina tried to rush to them, but she was stopped. "No. Please. Let me see them!"

"I'm fine, Nina," Monty said. "Barely grazed me."

"You need to go to hospital," the woman with Monty said. "Stitches at least."

"I'm good."

"You're going to the hospital," Lorelei said. "No choice. How's Zeke?"

"In and out of consciousness, ma'am."

"Where's the ambulance?" Lorelei barked.

"Here!" Two men rushed in, one Nina recognized.

"Holden?"

Holden stopped and looked at Nina, then nodded to Lorelei and hurried to Zeke.

Lorelei stepped up next to Nina. "Was this self-defense?"

Nina nodded. "Monty and I came. I wanted to come. She knew we were here. Fernando knocked Monty out and tied him up. She... We talked. She wanted me to leave with her or she was going to kill Monty."

"Obviously, things changed."

Nina nodded and stared at Holden as he worked on Zeke. The rip of bandages seemed loud in the otherwise quiet house. The tinge of blood in the air was bigger than everything else.

"Zeke saved me. I don't know how he knew we were here, but he wouldn't let her take me. Fernando shot Monty, Zeke shot Fernando, then Gwendolyn tried to shoot me. Zeke jumped in front of her bullet, and I shot her."

"She still had a gun on you?"

"Yes."

Lorelei drew a breath as Zeke was lifted onto a stretcher. He groaned, then cursed when he was moved.

"Zeke!"

"Nina." Zeke swore again.

"I'm coming."

"You're under arrest," a man said.

"She can go," Lorelei said. "She's not going to go anywhere else. Montgomery will be in the next ambulance. Call the ME for the other two."

"But—"

"I'm in charge. She can go. You're welcome to follow in your car and stay with her, but Captain Patrick is aware of the situation and he will be there to meet the ambulance."

"Captain Patrick?" the officer asked.

"Yes."

"Oh. Okay." The officer backed off.

"Go ahead, Nina." Lorelei pointed for Nina to leave behind Zeke, and Nina didn't hesitate to follow.

"Thank you," she said as she raced out the door, calling to Holden to wait for her.

Holden rode in the back of the ambulance with her, working on Zeke the whole time.

A mask was over his face, giving him oxygen. Blood

oozed through the bandage on his side. His shirt was gone, cut off and left behind in the house. His skin had a red tint to it from all the blood that spilled when Gwendolyn shot him.

Nina sat still and tried not to cry.

Zeke reached for her hand.

"Can I touch him?" Nina asked.

"Yeah, just don't pull any wires or bandages off," Holden said.

Nina nodded and grabbed Zeke's hand. "What were you thinking?"

"I was thinking I couldn't let her kill you. When Mont texted me and said you were going to confront her, I couldn't let you go alone. I couldn't risk something happening to you and never seeing you again. And when she pulled that trigger, saving you was all that mattered."

"But you might die."

"I'd die a thousand times to save your life," Zeke said.

"Don't say things like that."

Zeke pulled the mask off his face and squeezed her hand. "I love you, Nina Rose. Not like a sister. Not like a friend. I'm in love with you. I want to spend the rest of my life with you. And if that doesn't last longer than this ambulance ride, I'm happy you're here. I love you, Nina."

"Zeke," she breathed. Tears poured down her cheeks. She smiled at him and kissed his hand. "I—"

The machine behind Zeke's head screeched. One thing beeped loudly, then another.

Nina stared at the machines for a second, then looked down at Zeke. "Zeke!"

His head fell back on the bed, mouth open. His eyes were closed, his hand limp in hers.

"Zeke!"

"Nina, sit back. Let go of his hand. I need to shock him." Holden pushed her out of the way, breaking her connection to him.

Nina put her hands over her face. She couldn't watch him die, but she couldn't hide herself from it.

Holden put the mask back over Zeke's face, then grabbed a package of something else from a cabinet next to him. He unwrapped it, letting the garbage fly. He stuck one pad to Zeke's upper chest, the other on his opposite side. Holden pressed a button on a machine and snapped cords onto the pads.

"Clear!" Holden called. He pushed a button, and Zeke's body jerked.

"What are you doing to him?" Nina screamed, trying to grab for Zeke.

"I'm saving him, Nina. This machine is going to start his heart again."

"His heart's not beating?"

Holden shook his head. "Clear." He checked that Nina wasn't touching Zeke, then pressed the button again.

The screeching noises stopped and a rhythmic beeping started up again.

"He's back. But I need to intubate him. I'm going to put a tube down his throat so he doesn't have to work so hard to breathe. The hospital knows we're coming. They're going to take him right back into surgery."

"Surgery?"

Holden nodded and positioned himself at Zeke's head. A few seconds later, a tube stuck out from Zeke's mouth. Holden attached a hose to it and squeezed the balloon on the other end.

The ambulance stopped, and the doors opened. People

asked questions, and Holden answered all of them, racing with the people in scrubs.

Nina followed behind them until she heard her name.

"Nina!"

Nina glanced back and saw Frannie chasing after her.

"Nina, wait!"

"They're taking him away," Nina called.

Frannie didn't stop, just hurried after Nina until someone stepped in Nina's way.

"We are taking him to the OR. As soon as we can, we will let you know how he's doing, but you can't come past here," a young man said, pointing to the red line on the floor.

Nina read HOSPITAL PERSONNEL ONLY on the floor and stopped.

"I'll be with her. We all will be, Doctor. Thank you," Frannie said, putting her arm around Nina and holding her up while the doors slid closed in front of her, and Zeke disappeared.

"He saved me," Nina breathed.

"And now they're going to save him. Let's go back to the waiting room, Nina. Come on."

Nina nodded and let Frannie guide her away from the door. Nina couldn't have found her way back if someone paid her, but Frannie didn't hesitate.

The waiting room was full. The crowd made Nina stop until she realized she recognized most of the faces.

"Lorelei called Marcus, and we all came," Frannie said.

"Everyone?" Nina asked.

Frannie nodded and moved Nina into the center of the room. Raina moved her handbag from the seat next to her and reached for Nina. Karli sat on Nina's other side. Stacey and Frannie sat across from her, with Jessica and Dawn next to them. Edie sat next to Raina.

The rest of the room pressed in around them. The men from Rose were all there. Kyra and Liam sat nearby with another group of men.

"Mackenzie is at work. She got the nine-one-one call and sent Holden to you. Lorelei called Marcus, and we started calling everyone else," Frannie said. "Everyone is here for you and Zeke."

Nina burst into tears, her fear and gratitude blending together. "Thank you."

"Montgomery should be here any second, but he's refusing treatment. Saying he's fine," Frannie said. "Lorelei is keeping me updated on everything. Including what she knows about what happened."

Nina sucked in a breath. She met Frannie's gaze. "I'm sorry."

"What in the world for?"

"I know you cared about her."

Frannie shook her head and dropped to her knees in front of Nina. "The woman I thought I knew was a fabrication. She didn't exist. My friend, Gwennie, wasn't the real person. Gwendolyn Lennox was cruel and evil and hurt so many people. I'm sorry you had to go through what you did. I'm sorry you had to pull that trigger."

"She said she was proud of me," Nina admitted.

"For what?" Frannie asked.

Nina looked into Frannie's eyes. "For shooting her. Said I'm just like my father and brother and her. That I'm a killer like she always knew I would be."

"Even in her last moments, she manipulated you. She lied to you and tried to control you. None of that is true," Frannie said.

"It is, though. I did kill her. I shot her. She's dead because of me."

"She's dead because of herself. Because she tried to kill all three of you tonight, and you were defending yourself. You didn't do anything anyone else wouldn't have done in the same situation."

All the women nodded in agreement.

"But—"

"I've done it," Raina said. "I would do it again."

"I wanted to," Stacey confessed. "I thought about it so many times."

"Me, too," Karli and Jessica said together.

"It's not easy to take a life. To feel responsible for ending someone's time on earth. But you didn't get to that point the same way Gwendolyn did. You didn't kill her for fun." Frannie squeezed Nina's hand.

"I wanted her dead. I thought about it for a long time. The night I left..." Nina rubbed her throat. "I would have killed her that night if I'd had the chance."

"But you didn't. Even if you had, she wasn't a good person. The things you've been through..." Stacey shook her head. "You are strong, Nina. So strong. For getting away, for building a life with Zeke, for facing Gwendolyn again. Don't let her take anything else from you."

"Zeke," Nina whispered. "She might have taken him."

"The doctors are going to do everything possible to make sure that doesn't happen." Raina rubbed Nina's back and hugged her side.

"He said he loved me," Nina confessed.

The women all smiled and congratulated her.

"Then he stopped breathing. I didn't have a chance to say it back. He just..."

"You will tell him as soon as he wakes up," Frannie said. "And he's going to wake up. We are sending him all the positive energy and prayers we have. Everyone is."

Nina looked around the room at all the people waiting for news about Zeke. Heads were bowed in prayer. Hands clasped together in groups. Soft voices spoke to each other.

Love filled her for all the people in the room. People she didn't know, but who showed up for the man she loved. People who were there for them, no matter what.

She looked at the women around her, and she knew they were the same. The Curvy Vigilantes had supported her since they met. They'd welcomed her in and gotten to know her and fought right along with her, even if they didn't all know each other the whole time.

Nina reached for Raina and Karli's hands. Both women held her hand tightly and reached to hold another woman's hand. They circled around Nina, giving her their strength.

For the first time since the gun went off, Nina believed Zeke would be okay. She believed everything would be okay. Because Gwendolyn was dead, and she would never hurt anyone else again. And Nina was not alone. She had her brother, and Zeke, and her new friends.

"Is it Zeke?" Monty asked, his voice low and scared.

"You're here," Nina said, jumping up and rushing to Monty.

"Is he dead?" Monty hugged her tight, wincing when she squeezed back.

"What? Why would you say that?" Nina asked.

"You're all sitting here and holding hands. You're crying. What am I supposed to think?"

"We haven't heard," Frannie answered, joining Nina and Monty. "Come sit. Did you get stitches?"

"I'm fine," Monty said, brushing off Frannie's concern. "I don't want to miss any updates on Zeke."

"I'll be right back," Dawn said, walking to the desk.

"We haven't heard anything," Frannie said. "They took him back to surgery as soon as we got here."

"Fuck," Monty breathed, rocking back on his heels and pinching the bridge of his nose. "He can't die. He fucking can't."

"The doctors are going to do everything possible," Stacey said.

Monty nodded, but he didn't take his hand away from his face.

Nina leaned her head on Monty's good shoulder.

"I'm going to check out your arm right here," Dawn said, joining the group again. "Since basically everyone here is for Zeke, I asked them to give me a stitch kit."

"Do you know what you're doing?" Monty asked.

"I'm a nurse. I worked in a nursing home, but I can stitch up a stubborn man's arm." Dawn pursed her lips at Monty and raised one eyebrow.

Monty breathed and nodded, moving to the side of the waiting room where Dawn directed him.

Nina hovered nearby, not willing to go far from her brother. They both loved Zeke, and losing him would destroy Monty as much as it would destroy Nina.

Dawn spoke softly to Monty while she worked. First an injection that made him wince, then a minute of waiting while she poked around and looked at the wound.

It wasn't bad, like he said, but Nina was happy he was letting Dawn take care of it. His face was already bruising, but bruises would heal.

Dawn stitched Monty's arm up quickly, giving him eight stitches before she gently pressed a bandage over the wound and said he was good.

Monty sat in a chair and rested his head against the wall. The Rose Protection Agency team surrounded Monty, keeping his spirits up and making him laugh with stories about Zeke.

Nina walked away, unable to think about all the time she missed and all the things they would never do if he didn't make it. She found herself in front of a vending machine, staring at the options without seeing any of them.

"Anything look good?" Frannie asked.

Nina jumped, smiling at Frannie and shaking her head. "I keep seeing her."

"Gwennie? Gwendolyn?"

Nina nodded. "She was so happy when I shot her. Am I like her?"

"No," Frannie turned Nina to face her, hands on both shoulders. "You are nothing like her. I know I don't know you well, but I know that. You are kind, Nina. You care about people. You were willing to sacrifice yourself for your brother and Zeke. Your first instinct when you heard some of the women were out was to go see them. She would never have done any of that."

"They were afraid of me. They said I was just like her, too."

"We do whatever we have to do to survive. Sometimes those things don't make sense to anyone else. Sometimes they don't even make sense to us. Everything that happened when you were with her was survival."

"I still killed her."

"And the fact that you're worried that you're a bad person tells me you're not. She never questioned it. She would kill without remorse. Good people do bad things and regret them. Bad people do bad things and then do more."

Nina inhaled a sharp breath and nodded.

"You have to forgive yourself for all of it, Nina. It's not easy, but the only one you have to forgive is yourself. I know you cared about her. I know what you went through today couldn't have been easy. But I also know you had no choice. Stacey can help with therapy, if you want, or we can help you find someone else, but you need to forgive yourself. And know you are nothing like her."

"Thank you, Frannie."

Frannie nodded. She slid two dollars into the machine and punched a few buttons, waiting as two candy bars dropped to the bottom. She offered one to Nina.

Nina smiled and took it, letting Frannie lead her back to the waiting room.

They sat and opened the candy just as the door opened from the operating room.

"Zeke Donovan's family?" the man asked.

Everyone in the room stood.

The doctor blanched. "All of you?"

"I'm his brother," Monty said, stepping forward. "All these people are loved ones here to find out how he is."

"We should speak in private," the doctor said.

Monty shook his head and reached for Nina's hand.

Nina looked up at the doctor. "I'm going to marry Zeke. And all these people care about him. Tell us how he is. Is he alive?"

25

———

"CAN YOU ZIP ME UP?" NINA ASKED, LIFTING HER HAIR OUT OF the way.

Zeke kissed the center of her spine, only wincing slightly. Unfortunately, she heard the breath he sucked in.

"Are you okay?" She turned, her hair falling over her back as she studied him carefully.

"I'm fine."

"No, you're not. I'll go ask Monty to help."

"The fuck you will. I can zip up your dress. And you better believe I'm going to be unzipping it later."

"You're still restricted."

"Fuck my restrictions, I need you."

She cupped his jaw and sighed. "I'm not going anywhere. I love you, Zeke."

"Yeah, yeah," he growled.

Nina chuckled, and he immediately felt like an asshole. "It's a good thing I know you're just mad about going to a Christmas party with a cane."

"Fucking cane," he snarled. "Fuck all this. I'm glad you killed that bitch."

Nina's inhale slammed his eyes closed.

"Sorry. Fuck. I'm not myself. I should just stay home tonight."

"Not a chance. We said we'd be there. So pull yourself together while I go have my brother zip up my dress."

"Bring your ass back here. Now, angel."

Nina hesitated at the door, then returned to his side.

"I hate that you've had to take care of me so much the last month and a half. I should be the one taking care of you."

"You do, Zeke. And I'm just happy you're alive."

He nodded and put his forehead against hers. The doctors said he lost a lot of blood and was in bad shape. If Lorelei and her team hadn't shown up when they did, Zeke wouldn't have survived. "I am, too."

"I love you," she whispered, her voice soft and broken.

"I love you, angel. I'm okay. We're both okay. And I'm sick of you acting like I can't make love to you. Tonight, you're going to scream my name."

"Zeke," she said with a laugh.

"Turn around, angel. Let me zip up this dress so I know how to take it off you later."

Nina breathed a laugh and spun. She lifted her hair and looked back at him over her shoulder.

Zeke kissed her softly and slid his hands inside the velvety fabric that encased her curvy body. He'd never get enough of her, and after tonight, she would have proof of his love every time she looked at her ring finger.

Nina shivered and pressed against him.

Zeke growled. "It's been too damn long, angel." He was hard and could barely see straight. The doctor who did his surgery said he couldn't do anything strenuous for six-to-eight weeks, and Nina refused to be the reason he wasn't recovering faster. She'd been generous with blowjobs, but she refused sex.

He was going to make love to his fiancée. The second she became his fiancée.

The sound of the zipper climbing her spine was almost as loud as her pants. She was just as ready for their hiatus to be over as he was.

"You two ready yet?" Montgomery called up the stairs.

Zeke growled. "We need to take his keys away."

Nina chuckled and spun in Zeke's arms. "You know you'd never do that."

"The first time he walks in when I'm making you scream, he's done."

"I think he'll agree to that one."

Zeke leaned forward and captured her lips. "Can we try now?"

Nina squirted away from him. "We have to go. We promised we'd be there. I'll make it up to you when we get home."

"I'm not sure I can wait that long."

"You're going to have to."

"Will you sit on my face?" Zeke breathed against her neck, wrapping his arms around her from behind.

"Anything you want."

"Anything?"

Nina breathed. "You have to behave at the party."

"What does that mean?"

"It means you are going to participate and talk to people and have a good night."

"Oh, I'll have a good night when I get you naked."

Nina chuckled. "Let's go."

Zeke let her go ahead of him, partly so he could watch her ass in the dress she wore and partly because he was slow as fuck on the damn stairs with his cane. Montgomery came into view once Nina was on the ground floor. Mont was holding Franklin, rubbing under the cat's chin.

"You need some help?" Mont asked.

"Fuck you."

"Sunny as always." Mont shook his head and grinned up at Zeke.

Zeke took the steps slowly, one at a time, and would never admit it, but he was thankful Mont was there in case he lost his balance.

The bullet ripped a hole through Zeke's abdomen and tried to dump his guts all over the fucking place. The way he landed kept things inside. That and the paramedics that saved his damn life.

And Nina. He dreamed about her when he was in surgery, and every night after. She never left his side in the hospital. The nurses wheeled in a pullout chair for her to sleep in at night and treated her like she was his wife.

Zeke was past ready to make that reality.

Montgomery drove the three of them, Zeke in the front and Nina in the back out of his reach. Zeke hated not having his hand on her, but he would again soon.

"I'm glad you two were ready to go. I didn't want to hear anything that would have made me want to burn my ears off," Mont teased.

"You walk in on that and your key privileges are gone."

"I walk in on that and I'll leave the key on my way out." Mont reached his fist out for Zeke, who bumped it with his.

"Did you two just fist-bump about sex with me?" Nina asked from the back.

"Aw, come on. Did you have to say it like that?" Mont cried.

"So worth it."

Mont chuckled and shook his head. "It's good to have you back, Nina. And I'm happy you two are together."

"Thanks, Mont," Zeke said. Of all the things Zeke and Mont had shared over the years, keeping how much he loved Nina from Mont had never sat right with Zeke. Mont came to the hospital one day and asked about it. Zeke didn't lie. He told Montgomery he'd been in love with Nina forever and intended to marry her.

Montgomery gave Zeke his blessing and said there was no one else who would take better care of his sister.

Zeke admitted he worried Montgomery would think Zeke wasn't good enough for Nina, but Montgomery told him he was crazy. With that conversation out of the way, Zeke wasn't willing to wait to marry Nina. And Mont helped put the first part of his plan into motion.

Tonight.

Mont pulled into the long driveway, and all three of them gasped.

"Wow. It's so beautiful," Nina said, her voice soft and dreamy.

"Yeah, it is," Mont agreed.

Zeke had never seen anything like it. The driveway was lined with brightly lit trees, leading the way to Dawn's mansion. The house glowed with lights strung from the gutters and outlining each of the windows. A pile of gifts glowed from the front porch, and more lit trees spotted the expansive yard.

"They went all out," Zeke said.

"It's impressive." Nina scrambled out of the SUV and opened Zeke's door, offering him his cane and wrapping her arm through his good arm once he closed his door.

The three of them walked up the front steps, slowly for

Zeke's sake, Mont carrying the bags of gifts they all chipped in for.

Cole, Dawn's caretaker, opened the door before they made it to the front and welcomed them in. "Good evening, everyone. Can I take your coats?" They'd all gotten to know Cole over the last few weeks. He was kind and dedicated to Dawn, just like he'd been to his previous boss.

"Thank you, Cole. How are you tonight?" Mont asked as he unbuttoned his coat.

"I'm well, thank you, sir. How are all of you?"

"Good," they said together.

"Excellent. The others are in the sunroom. Ms. Dawn has all the supplies in there." Cole gathered their coats and nodded to the hallway.

"Thank you, Cole," Mont said for them.

Mont led the way, the massive bag of gifts in his hand once more. Zeke felt guilty for not helping Mont carry anything. He should be helping. He should have been doing something.

Voices reached them before they made it to the room at the back of the house where Dawn liked to spend most of her time. She'd redecorated since she moved in, and Gage had put his touches on the home as well, from what Zeke could tell.

"Hey, you're here!" Pryce called out when he saw the three of them. "We were just getting started."

"We have gifts," Mont said, lifting the bag. "From all of us."

"Perfect. Thank you guys. I know these will help out so much," Dawn said. She hugged each of them, kissing cheeks, then showed Mont where the gifts could go.

"Can I get you anything?" Nina asked.

"A kiss?" Zeke replied.

Nina smiled and stepped into his arms, wrapping herself around him before she lifted her lips to his. "I love you," she whispered before she pressed her lips to his.

Zeke growled and licked his way into her mouth.

Nina pulled back and gave him a look. "You're supposed to behave."

"That list did not include not kissing you."

Nina breathed a laugh. "Should I revise it?"

"Nope. Too late."

"Okay, everyone, let's get started so we can enjoy the rest of the night. Thank you all for helping and for bringing stuff. I wasn't sure how I was going to pull all of this off, but it's so much more fun with all of you here to join us," Dawn said. She reached for Gage, who nodded as she spoke. "When I first thought of donating to the children's hospital, I knew there was only so much I could do, even with all this money that I don't deserve—"

"Yes, you do!" Edie called. "Every penny!"

"Thank you," Dawn said, her cheeks turning pink. "But none of this would be as much fun without people to share it with." She clapped her hands. "Okay, enough of me talking. We have wrapping paper and bows and ribbons and bags and all kinds of stuff, so we can get started, and then dinner will be ready in an hour. And the bar is fully stocked, so if you want a drink, help yourselves."

"Thank you, Dawn!" Raina said.

Zeke let Nina lead him to a table on the side of the room. She grabbed a few gifts from the massive pile and carried them to where Zeke sat. They all laughed and wrapped presents, the pile of gifts to take to the hospital growing as the unwrapped pile got smaller.

"There's one more left," Gage said. "It has a name on it. Nina?"

"What?" Nina asked.

"I think this is for you."

Gage was in on the whole thing, too. All the men were.

Gage walked over to Nina, the velvet box hidden in his hand. "It has your name on it. I think it's for you." Gage opened his hand and revealed the box.

Nina gasped, and all the other women in the room did the same.

She looked back at Zeke, but he was already on one knee.

"Nina Marie Rose, I've loved you most of my life. I lost too many years with you, wishing you were by my side, and I don't want to lose one more second. I want you as my wife. I want you as my partner. I want you as the best part of my day every single day. Will you marry me?"

"Are you kidding? Why would you think you have to ask?"

"Well, I could have demanded you marry me, but I was told that was not the right way to start a life together."

Everyone in the room chuckled. Zeke noticed the couples going to each other, the men hugging their women to their sides.

"I would love nothing more than to marry you, Zeke," Nina said, dropping to her knees with him. She kissed him on the lips, prying his lips apart.

"I thought I had to behave."

She smiled against his lips. "I never promised I would."

"Damn, I love you, angel."

"Think anyone will notice if we leave early?"

Zeke snorted. "Considering we rode with your brother, I think it'll be obvious."

"Damn."

"Come on, angel, let's celebrate that you said yes and we're going to be married soon."

"Soon?"

"Hell yes, very soon."

"Music to my ears."

Nina loved her new friends, but she loved the ring on her finger even more. She loved her future husband. And their cats. And their quiet townhouse, where she could scream as loud as she wanted when he made her orgasm.

"I think it's time for that dress to take a break," Zeke growled as soon as they walked in the door.

"Are you sure? I was thinking maybe I'll keep it on a little longer."

Zeke groaned. "I can crawl underneath it."

Nina chuckled. "Take me to bed, future husband."

Zeke groaned. "It would be my pleasure, future wife."

"How long until you're going to make an honest woman out of me?"

"How about tomorrow?" Zeke asked.

Nina laughed. "We can't get married that fast."

"Why not?"

"It takes longer to get a marriage license."

"Day after tomorrow?"

"Okay."

"Are you serious?" Zeke asked.

"Yeah. I don't want to wait. I don't need a big wedding. I just need you."

"Well, hell, that works for me."

"How about first you tell me what I need to do to thank you for going tonight?"

Zeke wrapped an arm around her waist and pulled her in one step at a time. "I had fun."

"Good."

"Thank you for saying yes."

Nina grinned. "Well, my other boyfriend was a psycho who would have killed me if I'd called him, so I guess it's good I called you that night."

"Yeah, I'm just going to keep you in bed until you can't breathe from all the orgasms you have."

"I can think of worse things."

"No more bad in your life, angel. All good things from here on out."

"I like the sound of that."

"I like the sound of you screaming my name."

"Zeke!" she cried when he pinched her nipple.

"Lift that dress for me, future wife. I need to taste you." He dropped to his knees and lifted her skirt.

"You're going to hurt yourself."

"Worth it. Let me lick you, Nina." He disappeared under her dress, his breath hot on her inner thighs.

She leaned back against the couch and spread her thighs, smiling when he reached her center and discovered she wasn't wearing panties.

"Fuck me," he growled. "I love you, soon-to-be wife."

"I love you, soon-to-be husband."

After that, no words were necessary. Or possible.

THANK YOU! My gratitude for you is so beyond words. Thank you for reading this series, for loving these books, for giving these characters your love and time. This series was one I loved before I started writing it. It was one I couldn't wait to write. And I am so grateful that you picked up these books and fell in love with these characters the same way I did. Thank you.

MORE IS COMING...

Curvy Vigilantes is over, but **Rose Protection Agency** is getting a series!

We hope to never meet, but if we do, we will do everything in our power to keep you safe.
Rose Protection Agency is the place to go when you have nowhere else to turn. When your life is in danger, and you don't know who to trust, they will be there. Always. No matter the time or the day, you can count on them.
Rose Protection Agency is a team of former military, special forces, and organizations you've never heard of. They are here to do what they were trained to do... Keep their country, and its citizens, safe.
No matter the cost.

The first two books in the series release in 2025. Check them out and preorder your copies today!

He shouldn't have survived. He doesn't know why he did, and he's not the only one who needs answers. She's too sweet, too innocent, and off-limits, but she's stuck with him, and danger is right outside the door. **Protecting His Curvy Girl** *releases March 25.*

Just when he starts to look forward to his nosy neighbor's visits, she stops coming over. But leaving wasn't her choice. **Searching For His Curvy Girl** *is available August 12.*

. . .

THE CURVY VIGILANTES **started with Frannie!** Have you read her story? It's only available to subscribers.

Everyone deserves justice. Even when they're no one.

Witnessing a murder was not on Frannie's bucket list. Marcus had to find out what the curvy dancer knew. They made a deal. She would help him, and he would find the murderers. No one would know she was involved. She hoped.

Frannie and Marcus's story is available only to subscribers.
Sign up at https://dl.bookfunnel.com/y9ms2k2dq8 to get FORSAKEN now.

ABOUT THE AUTHOR

USA TODAY Bestselling Author Mary E Thompson spent most of her childhood wishing she had a few less curves. She hid in the pages of books because her favorite characters never cared what size her clothes were. Now, neither does Mary, and she writes stories that celebrate women like her. Real women who have curves, chase dreams, and find love, because we should all be happy, no matter our dress size.

Mary spends her non-writing time with her husband and two kids, watching too much TV, cheering for her hometown football team (Go Bills!), and hiding chocolate from her family.

Visit https://MaryEThompson.com/ to sign up for Mary's newsletter, **Romancing the Curves**. Subscribers get free ebooks and other fun stuff, like exclusive, members only content and giveaways, plus are the first to know about new releases and sales!